THE SWORD OF
THE KING

BY
RONALD MACDONALD

NEW YORK
THE CENTURY CO.
1900

THE KNICKERBOCKER PRESS, NEW YORK

INTRODUCTION

IT is matter of no small difficulty and hesitation for a woman to tell a story—in especial, her own story — from the beginning of it even to the end, and to hold, as it were, a straight course throughout. The perplexities, I say, are many, and among them not the least is found in these same words, *beginning* and *end.* For where truly his story has its inception, and what will be its ultimate word, might well puzzle the wisest man of this age, or any other. It has been well said, indeed, that the history of a man is the history of his troubles — but that fashion of considering will bring us, by no devious road, to the latter days of the Garden of Eden and the Fall of Man. Now either I have somewhere read, or my own heart has privily told me, that the story of a woman is the story of her love. And this I take to be truth, and do therefore resolve that the first chapter of my story shall be the first of my heart.

But, lest my book itself should lack apology, I will first tell how it comes that I, the mere wife and daughter of country gentlemen, and of learning, as will be seen, wholly insufficient to the undertaking, should write a book at all.

I write, it is true, but for my own people—for the family that I pray may be long in the land. But in these days, fortunate indeed, yet full of swift and dubious change — these days when every second man, it would seem, must print a book—these days when all the presses in London are not enough to set before us the tithe of what is committed by ink to paper—in these days, I say, none can be assured that what he now pens shall not by some chance hit of fortune attain the resurrection of print. And if this thing befall my work of love, and if the book then prove, not the cere-cloth of the embalmer, but a second and perpetual life to the thoughts of a most happy daughter, wife, and mother long departed and forgotten, I would stand well with my reader.

If any stranger, then, do read, let him believe that I have no taint in me of that *scabies scribendi*, mentioned by Horace, and mightily inveighed against last Sunday in the pulpit of Royston Church by our good vicar. This itch must be spreading fast, I thought, if there be danger of it here, where scarce a full score of the good man's hearers can spell in a hornbook. And now, lo! I am in dread lest I be thought infected—I, a woman, with all good things that come to women, and one to whom the holding of the pen is soon a weariness.

There hangs yet (and long may it so hang!) in our
great hall at Drayton a sword—not in its sheath,
but naked, and broken some two parts of its length
from the hilt, but shining bright as on the day it
was first drawn by the great prince that once used
it.   Beneath it, also against the wall above the
hearth, is the scabbard.

It was on a fine morning of the fall of last year,
as I was tending Ned's new Dutch garden, that I
heard loud and childish altercation proceeding
through the open windows of the great hall above
me.   And there in a window arose the fair gilded
head of my seven-year Mary, my first and best gift
to Ned, and his best to me.

" Pray, madam, come up to the hall," she cried,
" for Will is ever doing things of naught, and he will
not be gainsaid by me."

" Nay, child," I replied, loath to lose the sweet
air of the morning and my labor below.   " Nay,
child, but you must take means and learn cunning
to control him."

" I cannot do so, madam," says poor Mary, well-
nigh in tears; " and he is even now about dismounting the broken sword from the wall.   But if you
will come, madam, I will hold his legs while I
may."

And with that I ascended in great haste, yet but
just in time to save the relic from desecration and

the heir of Royston and Drayton a backward fall of great peril. For the noise of my entrance caused his most unserene Highness to turn quick on his heel and to miss in part the footing, already precarious, that he had attained upon the mantel. In short, he fell into my arms and into tears with one and the same movement; tears shed for no danger run—such is not his habit—but of grief for the plaything that was but now within his grasp; for, though but rising five, Master William Maurice Royston would have the broken sword to fight battles with —against King Lewis, forsooth, and the wicked Frenchmen, in the garden.

"It is but a bwoken old sing, madam-muvver," he cried between his sobs, "and of a fit length for me, lacking the pointed end, which I did purpose leaving upon the wall." And so I must needs tell him how dearly I do prize that shattered weapon, thinking the while of the shame that was averted, in part by its means, from our houses — and of the honor, too, that came thereby.

Then Mistress Mary would have the tale of the sword, and Will, his grief forgot, and joyously bent on touzing my hair to the image of his own, made instant demand for the fullest narration — "Every word, madam-muvver — from *onceuponatime* to *happyeverafter*." Yet the attempt to bring my tale to the measure of childish apprehension did lead me

into quagmires of question and answer so vexing
to our diverse ignorance, that dinner and Colonel
Royston found us scarce advanced beyond Will's
onceuponatime. At meat the children demanded
and obtained permission to lay the matter before
their father—the promised history, and the obscur-
ity of word and idea found necessary by the historian
at the very commencement. At last Ned made as
if he would speak, when " Madam," cries Mary, as
one big with a great thought, " madam, will you
not write it all down, that we may read when we
have learned the long words ? "

" Wise maid ! " said her father. " And indeed,
Philippa, it is worth the doing. But, Mistress
Wisehead," he continued to the child, " when the
long words are spelt from thy mother's head upon
the paper, they will cry aloud to be spelt back into
thine, if you will have the tale."

Now these words did make my poor maid to blush
hotly, who had little love to her book. Yet she
answered well, saying: " I know, sir, that I have
been a poor scholar, but, if madam will write
the tale, I purpose to be diligent to the end that
I may read well and fitly against the time it is
written."

" 'T is plain, Phil," says Ned merrily, " that
here is your one hope to make a scholar of your
daughter. And, indeed, sweetheart," he went on,

with more of gravity, " 't is a book I should like well to read myself."

" And that, sir," said I, " is a compliment you pay to few. For, beyond M. Vauban's work on fortification, I vow I have not seen a book in your hand since we were wed."

So, what with a reluctant daughter to be tempted into the path of letters, and a husband to please,—as I knew by his face his heart was much set on this enterprise of little Mary's suggestion,—I found myself committed to the task. Yet, though I have thought much and uneasily of my promise, I know not indeed when I had begun the fulfilling it had not Mary this very afternoon brought ink and paper, while Will followed close with a new pen.

" Write now, madam," quoth the maid.

" Write now, madam-muvver," says Will in faithful echo.

" If I begin now," said I, hard driven for yet a new plea to postpone the first plunge, " William Maurice Royston will not be able to read the book when it is done."

" William Maurice Royston," said he, " does not purpose reading. Sis says reading is irksome. But, when the tale is wrote, madam-muvver is going to read it to him."

And so it is that I begin.

THE SWORD OF THE KING

CHAPTER I

I WAS a child of five years when I first saw my
lover, and a gallant sight I thought he made,
the more that he found me in sore trouble, and drew
me out of it, as is ever his way. Colonel Royston,
indeed, in these latter days, holds that what I call
my memory in this matter is but the light of his
after instruction thrown backward on the dark
screen of childish oblivion. Whether or no (though
I take much pride in the memory, and still will so
call it), between him and me the reader shall not
lose, but shall know that on that day my nurse,
weary and petulant with the great heat and our
long ramble afield, was leading me, Philippa Drayton, no less petulant and even more weary, by the
hand, or, rather, was hoisting me by the elbow, up
the great avenue of elms that leads to Drayton
Hall. And, fain as I was for home, her rough
speed was too great for my little legs, and her grip

pained my arm, so that I cried out.   And then I
heard the thud of hoofs upon the turf by the roadside, and I looked up to see the little horse pulled
well-nigh on his haunches by his rider, whom, from
his own mouth, I soon knew to be Master Edward
Royston, of Royston Chase.   As he pulled up,
Betty let go my arm, whereupon, for the greater
ease of my legs and the freer exercise of my voice
in weeping, I incontinently sat me down in the
road.

" For shame!" says Master Ned, looking down
from his galloway upon Betty, with a frown that
had sat well on thrice his years.

" Ay, shame indeed," says Betty, yet blushing
to the color of a well-boiled beet; for she well knew
it was at herself his words were aimed; " ·ay, 't is
shame indeed for a great maid like little mistress
here to sit in the road and weep."

Now Betty spoke in the broad fashion of our parts
—the Doric, as Mr. Telgrove calls it, that I have
heard is well-nigh a foreign language to many.   For
the not giving this outlandish speech to my readers
there are two reasons: the one, that, though I do
well understand it myself, as is but natural, and do
love the sound of it at times, and can even, at a
pinch, shape my own mouth to it as well as my ear,
I yet have by no means the skill to set it down,
knowing, indeed, no combination of letters able to

convey its sounds; and the second reason is, that could I make shift so to write, none could read what I had written—which perhaps, by the well-disposed at least, might be held a blemish in my book.

But Master Ned, brushing aside her endeavor to hand on her shame to me, at once declared himself my champion.

" You do not take me," he said, the dark cleft of his frown growing deeper between his brows, so that it was a marvel to see so much austerity on so smooth and young a face. " When little maids weep, my lass, 't is most times the blame of the great ones."

I know not indeed if Colonel Royston yet hold in this belief; but from that point did I love Master Ned, if, indeed, I had not begun to do so some seconds before. And I was glad that he sat upon his horse, that raised his head some few inches above Betty's cap, for she was indeed a great lass, and twice his age, and his reproof had in great measure lost its force had he stood dwarfed beside her great body.

From Betty he turned to me, as I sat in the road, and—" Thou art tired, little one," he cried, with a great tenderness in his young countenance, that to me seemed so old. " If you will ride before me, sweetheart," he said, patting the pommel of his saddle, which was new and fine, as all about his person, " I and Noll will take most gentle care of thee."

At which kind words I rose to my sore feet, stretching out my arms, and crying to him that I would go with him. And, while Betty stood aghast, yet with never a thought her timid and sickly nursling would venture such a deed, I had reached his down-reached hands, had scrambled or was pulled into the saddle before my knight-errant, the little horse had plunged beneath his double burden, and we were away. As I swayed and bounced on the pommel in the first strides of that gallop along the sward that lies between the elm trees and the road, where the air rushed by so cool and green in the shade, he seized me with his right arm, fetching me round against his body so that my chin lay on the arm above the elbow. As my eyes, close shut in the first shock of our flight, came wide in the great comfort of this security, I was gazing back over the way we had sped, and I laughed aloud to see the vain pursuit of Betty. For all but her great self seemed streaming behind her in the wind of her going — cap, hair, and petticoat, while the fatness of her trembled as she ran.

For all this, long as it has been in the telling, happened, as it were, in a single stroke of time, and we were yet little parted from the pursuer. And, as I laughed, Master Royston, between his chidings of his nag for so serving us, would know the reason of my mirth—so " Do but see," I cried, " how Betty runs, and you will laugh too." But he could not, till he had tamed and admonished little Noll to a better pace for my ease. And when it was time for him to laugh at the quaint figure Betty did cut, I had already begun to pity her. But Master Royston would none of it.

" She is very well served," he said, " for her rude manners to thee, little one. I have a mind to give her some more of it. She is weary, is she not ? "

" Ay, indeed, poor Bet ! " I answered, " else had she not so handled me."

Upon that he drew rein, saying we should wait till she drew near. After a while, as Noll did crop the grass at his feet, Master Royston asked me if I could sit astride. " It is no shame," he said, " thou art so small a maid." And when I was so set, grasping a double handful of the pony's mane, he said: " When she is close I shall run to the house. Hold thou fast, little love, for Betty must run as never before if she would catch us." And as I would have pleaded she drew near, all spent and blowing, and I felt his knee move, and little Noll did also feel it, and was gone.

Oh, that I had a pen to tell of that ride! This time I was not afraid. This time there was no starting aside, no uneasy casting of my poor small person from side to side in grievous oscillation. And, oh! I say again, for the pen of some poet (yet I cannot tell whose to wish) in order to describe this my first taste of the joy there is in a horse when he is between us and turf good and plenty! Many a mile and many a beast have I ridden since that summer afternoon, and I hope so to ride, by the goodness of God, many a year hence; and yet that long, clean, resilient flight through an air that seemed of liquid green, flecked with the gold of the sun dropping here and there through the elms; the soft, fresh thud of hoof meeting turf but to part anew with the impact — that meeting with the soil that gave so lively assurance that Mother Earth was yet kindly and strong beneath; the strong rushing of the wind cooling my face and lifting the tangled curls back over the close cap; the new-born trust, moreover, in the arm that held me—all these things are with me now, distilled into one golden drop of life's very elixir, being, indeed, one of those gems of memory whereof the sweetness can as little be set fast by words as the stamp of them can be erased from the mind so sweetly and strangely impressed.

So much for my memory rather of a frame of being than of an ordered consecution of events. The curtain of childish oblivion here descends, as it is wont to fall, swift and dark, on these pregnant spoils of recollection. I think my dear and honored father's arms were those that lifted me from the saddle. I have since heard that Betty was savèd by my new friend from the rating Sir Michael had ready for her, receiving privily from that youthful master of craft a mint-new crown in earnest of future subsidies, did she prove thenceforth tender to the little maid. And, indeed, I think she did deserve whatever wage of kindness the future may have brought her. For I have of her no further memory of harsh entreatment.

For Philippa Drayton there now began a new life of the happiest. I had found what all, at one time or another of life, will look for, yet find most often, I truly believe, when they seek him not—I mean a true friend. And there is none but his children and mine that can tell what a friendship it was my friend did give me. He was my playmate, yet of age and wit to control. He was at whiles my tutor, for I would learn of him when none else had the art to keep my eyes five minutes fast on the book. He was my master of equitation, and did teach me in such manner, not only to sit upon a horse's back, but also to understand what the animal would be at, that I learned in time to back many a beast that some could not mount with impunity. Before the five years of our early comradeship were past I

would ride the colts round the paddock, often with‚
out bridle or saddle, and seated astride, as in my
first ride with Ned, which I have described above.
And he would blame me for a madcap, and yet, if
none else were by to see, would laugh at the frolic,
and praise my sitting of the nag, and my tricks of
control. With his coming into my story, which
before was none at all, my old dread of animals,
along with the ill-health of my earlier days, had
vanished, to be replaced by a pure confidence in all
that breathed, which in itself, maybe, was to the
full as childish, but, without controversy, far safer
for the child. Anon, Ned was himself my steed, to
be guided by tuggings of the hair and ears often, I
doubt me, little merciful. And, if not the swiftest,
he was surely of all I have ridden the most willing.

It could not fail that, thus together, we should
quarrel often. I mean, it could not fail where such
a child as I made one of the pair. But Ned would
bear my poutings, my bickerings, and every way-
ward mood with a smile when he might, and without it when he must. But did some act of mine
wrong some other than himself, as when I would
cuff Betty, or strike dog or horse for the easing of
my own passion rather than the fit correction of the
animal, then would he show the sterner mettle that
was in him. Then he would not forgive till confession of wrong or pardon was asked. And, was I

stubborn, he would stay away, even days together, but I must submit. Once it was a week — seven days, most long and dark for erring Mistress Philippa. For he said: " You are my friend, little Phil, and some day I shall wed thee, and it is not for my honor that you do thus, or so."

Thus Master Edward Royston, aged some four-teen years. Yet was my Ned no untimely saint, fitted but for the fatal love of the gods. Passion and frolic were in him, laughter, and—no, not tears —only twice have I seen them in his eyes, heard them mar the government of his speech. Boyish escapades were plentiful enough with him to give his mother and my father some knowledge of the unbending nicety in the point of honor which was yet seen in his most boyish prank or his strongest passion of anger. For the power also of anger was in him, growing, indeed, in its outburst less frequent as he grew in stature, but gaining rather than losing force with its rarer manifestation. I touch on this note of his character designedly, inasmuch as it was the cause of the great change that was soon, I mean at the end of twelve years from our first meeting, to come into my life. But of that in its place.

Sir Michael Drayton, of Drayton Manor, in the southward part of the county of Somerset, was already well on in years when I, the second child of his second wife, was born. And that was in the

eighth year of the second Charles. For he, my
father, first saw the light in the year of grace 1609,
and thus, at the time of my meeting with Ned,
which was in the summer of the year 1673, and in
the sixth year of my little life, he had fulfilled
sixty-four years, of which number some five and
forty had brought him trouble sufficient, on moder-
ate computation, to furnish out a fair portion of
strife and affliction to six ordinary men.   For,
ardent and devoted Cavalier though he was, 't was
not the outburst of the great war of the Rebellion
that marked the worst point of his troubles.   Often
in his old age have I heard my dear father tell how,
after the tedious and ever embittering doubts and
hesitations of that civil strife that had endured in
England since the coming of the first Stuart, to
him as to many another the resort to arms came as
a clearing of the vexed mind and settlement of conscience perturbed.   Of the momentous action of the
Long Parliament, in the year 1642, I have heard
him say: " Then at length our duty was plain.   I,
for one, slept better o' nights thereafter than I had
done since the meeting of the Short Parliament."
For Sir Michael had been elected of the shire for
that hapless assembly, as subsequently for its suc-
cessor, the Long Parliament; of his seat in the latter
he was illegally deprived when he withdrew from
Westminster to join the King at Oxford, which he

did in the late spring of that same year (I mean
1642), in the excellent company of my Lord Falk-
land and the late Lord Chancellor Clarendon, then
Sir Edward Hyde. And thenceforth his life was
war, and raising of money in order to its prosecution;
in both which perilous and comfortless means of as-
sisting his sovereign and of hurting his foes Sir
Michael Drayton was ever forward, to the most
lamentable detriment of his own person and estate.
He raised on his own land, and maintained at his
own expense, a troop of horse that were ever with
him throughout the first period of that long and evil
war, I mean until the fight at Naseby in Yorkshire.
There he lost great part of his following upon the
field, and was himself grievously hurt. Yet with
that scent, as I may say, which led him in all those
years ever where the work was hottest, he was found
again in the Welsh rising three years later, whence,
escaping after the fall of Pembroke Castle, he joined
himself with his little remnant of troopers to the
Scots, in bare time to share their overthrow at War-
rington by the late Protector (although he had not
then that title).

Sore in mind, sick in body,—for he was never
wholly healed of his great wound in the right thigh
which he took at Naseby,—he reached home only
to hear of his King's terrible end. 'T is perhaps
strange to tell that this awful deed of murder and

sacrilege put a new heart in that much-buffeted and
enduring gentleman, my father.   That Martyrdom,
I think, went far to atone, in Sir Michael's mind
and heart, for certain wrongs and fickle veerings of
purpose, proceeding as much from the complexion
as the misfortunes of that pious Martyr and unhappy
King.   No word did he ever utter to asperse the
royal memory; yet once in the passage of these
more recent transactions of state, which have brought
into my life, as into that of the nation at large, so.
much of betterment, did I hear him murmur (though
but as for his own ear alone), " Ay, ay — he served
us best, when they served him worst."   Be that as
it may, from that hour until the happy restoration
of King Charles the Second, all that he had — the
remnant of health, much of his land, the lives of his
sons, the thoughts of his mind, and the prayer of his
heart, were given to forward that happy end, which
was achieved, as all men know and many remember, in the year 1660 — but, for the house of Drayton, at what a cost!

But my father's story I must not make overlong,
lest I never come at my own.   In brief, then, all
his money and much of the Drayton timber, with
here and there a fair slice of his land, were gone
while the head of the royal Martyr was yet where
God had set it.   From that fatal day, however, he
set himself to the husbanding what God and the

rebels had left to him. Here again was disaster in
wait for him; for when, by dint of living as a peas-
ant, and by help of his breeding of horses (for which
he was already famous in the west, and, in the early
years of the war, well known to the farriers of
Prince Rupert's Horse), he had begun to lay by the
means of one day aiding the cause to which his life
was given, he was, through the lust and malice of a
certain Puritan neighbor, denounced as a Malignant,
and most heavily fined by the despotic rule of the
late Lord Protector Cromwell. Through Mr. Nathaniel Royston (of whom more in good time), he
was warned of this instant spoliation, and was so
enabled privily to convey his store of gold into
France, and to lay it in the hands of his exiled
sovereign, to be spent, no doubt, in far other fashion than the earning of it. And though he proved
to the commissioners sent down upon that proditori-
ous information to be less worth the plucking than
had been supposed, yet his acts in the late troubles
being known, and somewhat, perhaps, of that sending of money into France leaking out, the blow fell
upon· him even as his psalm-singing but ungodly
neighbor had designed. So, the gold in France,
land must be sold. And sold it was, but not as
that *godly* brewer of Yeovil did intend—to wit, into
his own hand; for here again Mr. N. Royston did
us great service, buying of the land which adjoined

his own a small portion at so high a price that the
great fine was paid with the loss of a few fields.

Yet none the less was the work all to begin again.
So begun again it was, and that most stubbornly.
And it was well the land was fat, and the breed of
horses unmatched in the west country, for, when
our western discontent grew to a head in the year
1655, Rupert, his youngest son by his first lady, was
with Penruddock at Salisbury, whither he carried
and left, on his own undertaking, most of that painful saving. Some few of his following drifted back
to Drayton, but Rupert had spent the gold and
himself for his King, even as Sir Michael had now
spent all his family. For Henry and Maurice, the
elder sons, had fallen, the one at Worcester fight,
the other in duel with a Frenchman at The Hague,
whither he had followed his sovereign, his opponent,
it was said, being a spy of Cardinal Mazarin, and
suspected by my brother of some ill intent to his
exiled prince. Over and above all these troubles,
that same affair of Penruddock's, so foolish and ill-
devised, cost Sir Michael within the year the life of
his wife, after a union with her of six and twenty
years of that nature as to soften much the sting of
his many afflictions, though it could not keep her
own heart from bursting with the loss of the last
child of their love.

His thereafter speedy marriage with my own dear

mother, whom I do but faintly remember, had in it
no token, whatever the show may have been, of
disrespect to the former Lady Drayton. But here
again is a story to excel, perhaps, in the right telling
of it, the length of my own. Yet I do not purpose
a full relation of so much sorrow, holding that the
strong hand only of a master in letters should essay
the portraiture of such tragedy as was in those days
often enacted in the houses of many an old Royalist
family.

Mr. Denzil Holroyd's only surviving child, the
lady who afterwards became my mother, had passed
a jejune childhood in a house impoverished by her
father's loyalty to the Stuart cause, and persecuted
in the latter days, even to bitterness, for its stanch
adherence to the faith of Rome. She had been the
close and tender friend of the first Lady Drayton.
Following hard upon the death of that lady came
fresh ill-fortune upon the Holroyd family, of which
the death of Denzil, its head, was a part; and Mistress Alicia Holroyd, left without a natural protector, and stripped by cruel laws and wicked informers
of her last acres, flung herself late of a bitter winter's
night against my father's door, begging shelter from
the inclemency of Nature, and protection from the
baseness of her Puritan cousin, who, not content
with the filching her inheritance, would have added
her person to his plunder as the price of food and

lodging, hoping thus to make sure his title against
future turns of fate.   Silas Holroyd pursuing, found
her clinging as some frightened child to my father.
Silas soon returned the way he came, but after what
words with my father was never known, since he
dared tell no man what passed between them, and
none dared question Sir Michael.   Yet Alicia could
not dwell in the house where now was no mistress,
so out of this difficulty, as of so many another, my
father must needs find a way ; which indeed he
did, as the words he used in telling me of the matter shall now inform any that has read so far in my
narrative. " I told your good mother, little daughter
Phil," he said, " that I had little power or credit in
the land to help my friend. ' But,' said I, that
bitter night that she came to me, ' if you will wed
an old man and a broken, there is yet left in Drayton the strength to make some show of cover for the
mistress of his board and the partner of his bed.
'T is a poor thing to offer, but it will serve to make
a fool of that knave Silas, when he shall try, as well
I know he will, to recover the custody of your person by a process of law, charging me with your
abduction.   I will cherish you well, if you will have
me for husband.' "   And if the poor lady let gratitude usurp the place of love who shall blame her,
being in such straits ? Not I, her most happy
daughter.   Were it but for the father she gave me,

I will thank her next in order only to her God and mine till I die, and after, I do firmly trust.

And so out of hand they were married, nor do I think either found cause of regret. For the lady found peace, and license to practise, as far as might be, the duties of her faith, with now and again the comfort of its holiest offices at the hands of some wandering or hunted priest. For my father's old and loud-spoken hatred of Rome, now indeed much softened by the mellowing of his own temper and the fellow-feeling of a common persecution, was yet so well fixed in the memory of that countryside, that Mistress Alicia Holroyd was generally held to have abjured the errors of Rome in committing the error of becoming Lady Drayton. Certain it is, that none ever discovered the secret chapel so cunningly hid among the wine vaults, devised by Sir Michael, and painted and floored, dressed and furnished by no hands save his and those of Simon Emmet. I have heard that Simon would grumble as he worked, predicting ill to come of this idolatry. For his own soul, he would say, he cared not so greatly, in the pleasing of so sweet a lady —but, for Sir Michael's, his same sweet lady's, and their children's to come, he would the cursed job were not to do. But, if bidden then to lay down his tools, " Nay," he would say, " you cannot do alone in the business. And if it be sin, as I verily think it, I will not hand it on to another.''

From the few and petty memories of my infancy, antecedent to my first encounter with Ned, there stands out the vision of my mother's face, as she would ascend the stair that led, as I understood then, and for many a year thereafter, but from the cellars; the vision of a face shedding upon all a shining calm, so tender, and withal so glorious, as no cunning of the greatest painter's brush, I think, has ever coaxed into the nimbus of his saint. It is how I recall her face in my dreams, sleeping or waking. And when I learned at length the secret of the chapel I understood many things that each must find for himself.

Her first child was my brother Philip, born in the year 1658. Ten years later she gave my father his only girl and last child,—me, Philippa, to wit,—and died herself in the first days of the year 1673, some five months before my rescue from Betty at the hands of Master Royston, to which, in this opening chapter, as in my life, I will yet be referring all things, as it were an Hegira.

And all this time, though I am ever dinning this Master Royston, this Ned, this time-worn but, I hope, sempiternal lover, in your ears, as yet introduction of him into these pages does as much lack formal ceremony as did the beginning of our friendship.

Mr. Nathaniel Royston, of Cheapside, in the City of London, was of a well-known and highly respected west-country parentage. Apprenticed in London at an early age to a merchant of repute, he had soon displayed considerable sagacity, not only in the intricacies of the Turkey trade, but also in the more perilous and no less subtle labyrinth of matters political. As in the first, after winning his way to a large share in the undertakings of him who had been his master, he had devoted himself to the patient amassing of a large fortune, so in the second he had used his judgment and foresight to the one end of retaining intact what he had so laboriously gathered. I would not be understood to throw anything of blame on his conduct of his life. Ned hath often told me that to his father all governments were alike, for all, he would say, were equally at fault, and that it became a man of his temper and estate to make in each case the best of a bad business. The Turkey trade thriving, Mr. Royston continued to increase by this means of regarding affairs of state, in despite of King and Parliament, Army and Protector, Presbyterian and Independent. And this in so great measure that, in the year 1653, he acquired by honest purchase those lands of the family whose scion he was, which lay in the county of Somerset. So he came to live among us, but it was not until two years after the Restoration

that his son Edward was born, that being six
years after his marriage to the Lady Mary Harlowe.
He was wont to say that it was indeed strange that
the sole precarious venture in the life of a solid and
cautious merchant should prove his most profitable,
referring in this to his marriage with a lady whose
family had been proscribed for its affection to the
royal cause. In this circumstance, indeed, there
would appear to be some resemblance between the
fates of my mother and Ned's; with this difference,
however, that in Mr. Royston's case love impelled
to the single hazardous act of a lifetime, while in
my dear father's, duty and the very danger itself
brought about a union ultimately rewarded with
affection.

This Mr. Nathaniel Royston, after some twenty
years spent mostly at his estate of Royston Chase
in our neighborhood, during which time he had
much endeared himself to my father by many acts
of a thoughtful and temperate goodness, which his
wealth and general esteem well enabled him to per-
form, died quietly in his bed in the same winter as
my dear mother.

Of my own brother Philip, my early recollection
is most slender. His was, I believe, ever a studious
and contemplative complexion of mind, which had
led him at an early age to adopt, against the earnest
wish of his father, the erroneous opinions in the

matter of religion pressed on him, I am sure, far more earnestly by his mother's spiritual advisers than by herself. I have neither wish nor ability to expatiate on this subject, and will only say, in justice to both sides, that it was more on account of the sorrow I had seen deeply graved upon my father's face when Philip's adhesion to the Church of Rome was mentioned, than from any ecclesiastical predilection of my own, that I found means to resist certain assaults by Philip and others on my own acquiescence in the position and authority of the Church of England as by law established.

It fell shortly after the Restoration that the death of the childless Silas Holroyd much simplified the process at law whereby the attempt was making to recover my mother's property. The matter being brought to a successful issue, the revenues of our family became so vastly improved that in the year 1676, when I was eight years of age, and Philip eighteen, he was sent travelling on the continent of Europe with a governor. I heard my father murmur, as he returned to the house after bidding his son farewell: " Pray God it drive some of the folly out of him! "

This, in my father's view of it, was far from the result of that foreign tour. After a while he ceased to tell me of Philip and his letters, reading them ever in a clouded silence; till at length I was bidden not to speak of my brother, and I knew some bad thing had befallen, but what, for many years, I did not learn. Nor did I see him after that departure for a space of twelve years. And when at length I did see him—but that I will tell in its place.

I had thought clearly to lay, as it were, the groundwork of my narrative in far fewer words than these that stretch already behind me like a dusty and winding road at the traveller's back.

Now, when as a child I would read a tale or history (after that Ned had coaxed and driven both desire and skill of reading into my little head), I did use to pass over the early pages in scorn, and "to come to the part," I would tell the chiding Ned, "where things fall to happening." Since many in graver years do keep lively this desire of action and movement in what they read, I am now resolved to reach, as quickly as may be, the place "where things begin happening."

CHAPTER II

I HAVE said above of this early friendship between a lad of eleven and a maid not half that age, that it endured five years. For at the end of that period the comradeship indeed was broken, and a term was set to the habit of community in all things that was to me at least so comfortable. The day that took my companion to reside in the town of Sherborne, there to attend the King's School, brought on my small mind its first remembered sorrow; wherefore I wept greatly, and would not for many days be comforted. At the time I did not understand (as how should I, being but ten years of age ?) the reasons of this so sudden change in his mother's intention. But I have since learned that two causes, of which I myself, poor maid, was one, determined the Lady Mary Royston to take her son from the hands of the learned and pious governor who should have led him in the path of learning and conduct even up to the gates of the University of Oxford. Thus her late husband had intended, but, the tutor growing lazy and overeasy perhaps, while Ned would ever more frequently take the bit of control fast between the teeth of stubbornness, she was minded to subject him to sterner authority. She was moved, moreover, like many another parent of an only son, by some measure of jealousy, directed, in her case, toward " the wild little maid of Drayton," as she would call me; for, with all his duty to his mother, no words or wishes of hers could shake that notable and constant affection that Ned did then, as ever, spend upon me. Knowing, too, by her late husband, of the papistical bias (as she would say) of the Drayton family more than others of those parts had learned, she was ever in dread (pursuing Mr. Nathaniel Royston's policy of caution) lest our acquaintance should lead her or her son into some seeming of complicity with traitors. For we were then in the year 1678 and the full tide of the Popish Plot. But I have always believed that I was far more in this matter of sending Ned to Sherborne than Dr. Titus Oates or the whole College of Cardinals.

By this and by that, certain it is that go to Sherborne he did, and that my days had been from that hour very cheerless but for a notable addition to our family, bringing some measure of solace to a mighty sore little heart.

When he heard that Ned was gone, and that the tutor knew not where to turn himself for a living after his dismission by the Lady Mary, my good father mounted his horse and rode over to Royston, leaving me marvelling greatly at the courage and hardihood of a man that dared encounter a woman so formidable as I then held Ned's mother to be. For only twice had I been with him to Royston Chase, and the second time even happier to be gone than the first. So it was that I deemed my father a very St. George that could face cheerfully this dragon.

He had along with him a mounted servant, leading a quiet pad-nag, which returned after sundown sorely burdened with the great person of the Rev. Joshua Telgrove. I stood on the steps for my father's embrace (always my privilege on his return), and when the little party was dismounted with no small difficulty to Mr. Telgrove and the assistant groom, "Mistress Philippa," says Sir Michael, with something of ceremony in his manner of speech, "this is Mr. Telgrove, who hath taught your friend, Master Royston, these many years."

"That I know well, sir," I replied, trembling; for I feared the old man greatly, having seen him but thrice, and ascribing great austerity to him that had ruled a being so great as my friend and idol.

"And now," he continued, with a little grim smile that was yet not unkind, "Mr. Telgrove has a mind to teach my little half-broke filly" (for so the dear and tender gentleman was wont to pun upon my name), "and I have a mind he should at least make the endeavor."

At this I trembled yet more, and was abashed to a stubborn silence, resolving with a mighty vow in my heart that from none but Ned would I learn. And I finding in the days that followed that my tutor was the mildest of men, and in face of childish wilfulness the most indolent, it was like to have gone mighty hard with my advancement in learning had he not discovered a rod to rule me as by some charm of magic. For coming very soon, with the keen insight of childhood, to fear him not at all, I would in no manner give him rest nor ease, neither by learning my task nor by sitting mumchance, which at first, mayhap, had pleased him near as well, unless he would be talking of Ned. Now Mr. Telgrove had a great and tender affection to his late pupil, and perceiving that I even surpassed him in this, he came, I think, to some measure of love for his new one. With that rose in him the wish that I should do him credit, even as Ned had done; and he made an ordinance that the name, so dear alike to master and scholar, should not be breathed until the task of the day was not only conned but fairly committed and recited. To this rule he did so constantly, for a nature of his softness, adhere, that before six months were past I was much advanced in wisdom, and grown to love my lessons only next in

order to their reward—those long colloquies, to wit,
in which he would tell me every adventure, esca-
pade, and other act, good or bad, of Ned's childhood.
These stories, indeed, soon grew old, but to me and
my tutor never trite nor stale.   Then from time to
time he would read aloud to me, in part or at length,
the letters received from Sherborne.   But to me
Ned did not write.

Thus the months went by, and grew into years
less heavily than I had thought.   Mr. Telgrove was
well content, having found, as he would say, a refuge for his old age.   For the Act of Uniformity
and the Oath of Non-resistance being against his
conscience, had deprived him of his living, while
the Five-Mile Act had well-nigh forbidden him to
find another.   Mr. N. Royston, in the performance
of one of his politic acts of charity, his house of
Royston Chase being neither near Mr. Telgrove's
former incumbency, nor within the proscribed distance of a corporate town, had obtained a good
teacher for his son; but I think the good man's
power of struggling with a persecuting world was
exhausted in his one act of renunciation, and he was
left with little desire for aught but a peaceful abode
and the leisure to study the great writers of antiquity
in a cloud of smoke from his tobacco pipe.   His
opinions in matters theological and ecclesiastical
had, with the passage of time, so softened, that Sir

Michael would playfully attack him for a Latitudi-
narian, an Arminian, or what not, while I on winter
evenings would search among my tutor's books
that I might plague him with accusation of strange
heresies.

But this was after Mr. Telgrove had resided with
us some four years, and young Mr. Royston had
proceeded from Sherborne to Corpus Christi College, in the University of Oxford, having in the
meantime but once visited Royston — one happy
summer for me, in my fourteenth year, during two
months of which he would ride over to us, not
indeed with the frequency of the past, but often
twice, and sometimes even three times, in the seven
days. Yet, though I say I was happy, it was not
as it had been. Something of the distance that had
grown between him and me would force itself upon
the mind, now of one, now of the other. Pondering the matter from the watch-tower of my present
content, I hold that the child in Mistress Phil was
ever crying out for the older terms of alliance, with
their reckless mirth and unchecked license of jollity,
while the woman, unheeded, but waxing ever
stronger within, would as often clap stern hand
upon the clamorous lips of youth, and so produce
that outward show of petulance which is as baffling
to the youth in his twentieth as it is alluring to the
man in his thirtieth year. Then, too, it was that I

first gave thought to the manner of my appearance
in the eyes of others, and would ask my glass, I
knew not why, for evidence of grace and beauty in
person and countenance. And the mirror was a
stern arbiter, showing only gaunt length of limb
and sunbrowned uncouthness of feature, overhung
by heavy brows, and supported, when mirth would
display them, by a regiment of very white teeth.

"Dear Ned," I would say, "I would I were
fair!"

"Some day you will be so," he would answer.

"But you have grown to the stature of a man,
while I——"

"Be content, sweetheart," he would answer.
"You are like a yearling colt—nay, 't is filly I mean.
How dost spell that same word *filly* now, Mistress
Scholar? With the 'P' and the 'h' it should be,
in the Grecian manner. But indeed you will over-
take my growth soon enough. When I did first
know you, my age to yours was as two to one and
more. When I have done with Oxford, it will be
but as four to three, and thou older for a woman
than I for a man."

"Tell me, then," I said to him one day, after
some such talk, "when, last summer, you were at
the Court with madam your mother, and I saw you
not at all, did you not see many fine ladies and
women of great beauty?"

" Ay, many," quoth he, " but none such as you will be. Do but give the colt time."

And when he was gone I would marvel why I cared for the beauty I had not. And since I found no clear answer to the question in my own mind, and ventured to seek it from no other, it was well, maybe, that Ned's long absence at Oxford and in London with the Lady Mary, extending as it did over the better part of four years, put the matter in time clean out of my head. Indeed, even in our quiet corner, we had other matter to consider in those days than the vanity of a half-grown maid.

Now it is only in later times that I have come even to the most partial understanding of the many twists and turns in the fate of our perturbed island, that were then succeeding each other with so be-wildering rapidity. This is no public history, or my ignorance would make of it a worse book yet than it promises, and I shall but recall the memory of those unquiet events that affected at this time our quiet life.

That same year of Ned's coming again to Roy-ston, between his leaving Sherborne and going to Oxford, was the time of the late Duke of Mon-mouth's progress through England, wherein he did take upon himself so much of the state of his royal ancestry as to encourage greatly the fond belief of the common people, particularly in the west country, in that vain story of a certain Black Box, where should be found (did one credit these mystery-mongers) proof indisputable of the marriage of the Duke's mother, Mistress Lucy Walters, with his acknowledged father, King Charles II., then upon the throne. Of the merits of the matter I know nothing, but remember well how Sir Michael would say the wish was father to the thought in the minds of such as dreaded most the coming to the throne of the Papist Duke of York. He had no patience, he said, with those that went after these idle tales; yet he showed much in exhorting, threatening, and persuading those of his own people that seemed most in peril of misleading by these errors. In especial, I do recall something of a disputation between him and Simon Emmet, our steward. This good man was in a measure privileged in his intercourse with Sir Michael, being an old trooper of the first force my father had raised and led for King Charles the Martyr. He was, though Cavalier and Royalist to the marrow, a Protestant of an earnestness well-nigh fanatical.

Simon stood beneath the open window of my bedchamber, on the sward that there sweeps up right to the walls of the house from the park, so that I have often dropped bread to the deer grown bold in their feeding. My father leaned from the window beneath me, smoking a pipe of Virginia tobacco, while I sat gazing over the trees and busied, till my ear was caught by their words, with thought of Oxford and the Court at London. And this is what I heard:

Said Sir Michael Drayton: " Ill will come of this madness, Simon. To uphold the claim of a bastard to the throne you and I have fought for is not the work of a wise man nor a good."

" 'T is not so sure the Duke is that," answered Emmet. " I, for one, hold him as well born as the other Duke " (meaning the Duke of York), " and, at any rate, my lord of Monmouth is no Papist."

" I had not voted for the Exclusion Bill had I been at Westminster," said my father, yet as if he had a doubt in the matter; " for I do think a Catholic may be no bad king—if he will but uphold the law."

" If—ay, if! I do not say a Papist must needs be a bad man nor a bad king. Not but what they all are so—for the most part," said Simon as in fear of overmuch concession. " But this is a Papist for sure, and as surely a bad man. 'T is pretty work he has had the doing of in Scotland, sir; and that not for his own superstition, but for a faith he doth not hold. Give him power and the time to use it, and what will he not attempt for the Scarlet Woman? Moreover, if the Duke of Monmouth be the King's son, born in lawful wedlock, as this same story of the Black Box would show—— "

"No more, Simon," interrupted my father angrily. "Say not another word of that. It is rank blasphemy and treason, and I, being a faithful subject of His Majesty, and on his commission of the peace, and holding command in the train-bands, may not hear repeated what His Majesty has denied. And most of all, Simon," he continued more kindly, "I do fear this sort of wild talk will get thee into trouble. Leave it to Republicans and Fifth Monarchy Men, old friend. I fear you have been running after sectaries in your old age, Simon." He knew it well, for the old steward, like the poor land that had asked and taken many years and much blood of his youth, had passed through many contrarious fits of thought and sentiment. In religion his politic fear of Rome had well-nigh driven him out of the back door of the Church into the arms of the Puritans. As he hovered between respect of his ancient captain and present master, and the enticements of controversy, "Go, Simon!" cried Sir Michael; "bid Parson Greenlow pray with you, and read you a lecture on Passive Obedience and the Duty of Non-resistance."

"Humph!" muttered the old malcontent, as he walked toward the stable; "the parsons will be mighty ready to eat their sermons when the Duke's Scottish boot is on their leg. They'll resist then, Sir Michael, even as we resisted Old Noll."

And so three further years went by, and Ned came not, but did spend such time as he was not in Oxford with Madam Royston in his father's noble house in Basinghall Street in the City of London. Twice did he send me a letter in those days, with no word, indeed, of love in them, but so breathing the constancy of our old terms of alliance, and bringing me so much joy, that I cannot endure they should run the risk of the cold monument of print, and so will not here set down their words.

And I grew in length and thickness, and, I hope, in other things beside, and had almost forgot my mirror but for the kinder and more pleasing glance it would now and again, toward the latter part of my seventeenth year, begin to throw back upon me, as I would pin a collar, or struggle to twist into some show of order the stubborn and difficult blackness of my hair.

CHAPTER III

A ND then, one Sunday morning of late winter,
we heard from the pulpit of Drayton Parish
Church how the King was dead, when was read to
the congregation there assembled the speech to his
Council of the new King, James, in which he did
fairly promise to uphold the laws, and in especial to
respect the rights of the Church of which he was
the head, though no member. And my father was
cheered, and Emmet was sombrely downcast, and
the country people murmured of King Monmouth
under the breath. Later came the news of the late
King's apostasy in the very article of death. If
these things were true of Charles, whom in some
sort they had contrived to love, what should be
looked for, said Emmet and those of his kidney,
from him who, as Duke of York, was but lately
the most hated and hateful of all in the three
kingdoms ?

And then came the rumors of the late King's
doing to death by his brother now on the throne.
The truth, grave as it was, would not content our
more turbulent and hot-headed spirits of the west,

but they must even mix falsehood, none being too scandalous, to overseason a dish already too heavy for stomachs unused to high fare. And so there followed an indigestion—I mean the mad and wicked insurrection of the Duke of Monmouth. To this day I cannot think, and much less write, of the summer and autumn that followed the death of King Charles II. without some return upon my spirits of the horror and gloom that the doings of those days engendered. So I will pass over our share in these things as quickly as may be.

When we heard of the Duke's landing at Lyme Regis, in the county of Dorset, and not more than twenty good miles from our little village of Drayton, it was already late on the eleventh day of June; yet that very night did my father set himself to the task of getting at once under arms his small company of the yellow-coated Somerset train-bands. Receiving the next morning instructions from Sir William Portman, the colonel of that force and a near friend of his own, he was enabled to despatch them out of hand on their road to join with the red-coated militia of Dorset at Bridport, saying that thus the poor hinds might at least die cleanly, if die they must; while staying at home they had, like enough, taken the rebel infection and ended on a gallows. His old wound and other infirmities, to my great joy, kept him with me at Drayton. But,

not content with what was already done, he made
during the week that followed a visitation of the
neighborhood, exhorting all and sundry to loyalty,
and with so good result that our Drayton folk suffered less in the cruel days so near at hand than any
other village for forty miles round.

And these cruel days came upon us but too
quickly. In the latter end of June Simon Emmet
did one day make off, and we had great fear that
he was gone to join the rebel mob that of its friends
was flattered with the name of army. On the
seventh day of July came the news of the battle
fought at Sedgemoor, near the town of Bridge-
water ; and then of the great slaughter on that
field, to be followed day by day with yet more
grisly tales of the cruelty of the royal troops, in
especial those of wicked Colonel Kirke and his
regiment of soldiers from Tangier, as wicked and
ruthless as himself. This bad man, whose later
service in a nobler cause I can never hold as aton-
ing for his acts at this time among us, began, after
some days of butchery in the town of Taunton, to
send out small bodies of soldiers to spread his hor-
rid work in the smaller towns and villages in the
southern parts of the county. And then there
came in a party of the militiamen on their way
home, having passed through Taunton, with word
that some of Kirke's Lambs would next day visit

Drayton, having with them a batch of prisoners be-
longing to our part, in order to hanging them, with
all customary foulness of detail, on their own village-
green, the better to encourage the loyalty of those on
whom no faintest breath of suspicion could be raised.

It is said that when Will Blundell, the young
gentleman that had in my father's stead taken our
company of the militia to Bridport, had begged
Colonel Kirke to give our village at least, as un-
tainted in its loyalty, the go-by, that coarse and
evil-minded man had replied, with many foul words
and blasphemous oaths: " Are we then so loyal in
Drayton ? God's blood! I will keep them so, if a
few bleeding heads and mouldering quarters may in
Somerset do so hard a thing. And if my lads hang
a few beyond the number they take with them,
why," he said, " 't will but physic the land to a
better habit."

Now Simon Emmet had in the village a son,
Peter, who was by trade a blacksmith, and by custom a prudent fellow that kept to his anvil and
never vexed his head in these ill times to fever heat
by opening too wide his mouth. And this Peter
had a daughter, Prudence, the prettiest maid of the
village, and afterward, as you are to hear, my handmaid, and, indeed, my very dear friend. These
two (for her mother was dead) had all that day a
sore time of it, fearing that Simon was one of those

who should be brought and put to death. Well, the party of soldiers came in that night with their three prisoners, but too late of a clouded evening, as the ensign in command did say, with a most vile levity, "for the good and loyal folk of Drayton fitly to enjoy the sight of six traitor legs performing a saraband upon nothing."

And so they quartered themselves upon the village, and their victims in a barn, "until," said this same worthy follower of Kirke, "on the morrow they should be quartered for good and all." Moreover, with a more exquisite touch of that cruelty in which they were so skilled, they had concealed the faces of these three poor fellows from the public gaze, in the hope that anxiety for the morrow should be the more widely spread over the sleepless pillows of the village.

Now during that night, when few slept, but terror reigned more silent than sleep, a strange thing happened. For many a year after, the matter was known in full to few but myself, and to me not till little Prudence Emmet had come to trust and confide in her new mistress. So much narrative I have of my own to unwind, that I will waste little space upon hers, telling but in brief that the third of these men, taken in arms and condemned without judge or jury, was indeed her grandfather; that she and her father had come to know it; that in the dead of night she had contrived with liquor and flattery, and mayhap by implicit proffer of kindness she purposed never to grant, to keep the sentry busy, and even a little to draw him off, while her father, after forced and secret entry at the hinder part of the barn, had privily withdrawn that old hothead Simon (now like to pay so dear for his besotted enthusiasm) from his prison, and had carried him upon his great shoulders, an inglorious Anchises concealed in a sack, five miles across country, and there fairly buried him alive in a secret cave or hole in the hillside by well-nigh walling up the mouth thereof, and bodily transplanting a young tree to conceal all signs of his labors. Yet was he back in his cottage before the ensign and his men had slept off the fumes of their wine.

Thus it was not till near upon noon that they discovered their loss, whereat the greatness of the ensign's fury passes any power of description that is in my pen. He said the two remaining should hang twice or thrice ere they died, to make of the spectacle as good entertainment as he had promised to the folk of that most loyal village of Drayton; but, proceeding to the execution of this cruelty, and having, to the enhancement of his wrath, but a small band of spectators, the most part keeping their houses in fear and sorrow, before he had ordered the hapless men, already in the agony of death, to be

cut down the first time, his evil work was interrupted
by the coming of that soldier who had on the previous evening been so cunningly cajoled by Mistress
Prue and her cozening flatteries. This man had
been threatened with the anger of Colonel Kirke
and the most terrible military punishments unless
he succeeded in discovering his escaped prisoner.
Failing in this, he had, on encountering Prudence
in a back passage leading to her father's forge,
thought at least to display his zeal in hauling her
by the hair before his officer, there to denounce her
as his seducer from duty. In so doing he gave
those two poor rebels a quick and easy death of
their first hanging, while Prue shortly found, to
the great altering of my after-life, a champion with
a strong hand—no other, indeed, than him of whom
is my book and my thought while I live.

Two days before this time Mr. Edward Royston
was about leaving Oxford to visit Lady Mary at her
house in London, when he was apprised of the suf-
ferings of our western folk subsequent to the battle
of Sedgemoor. Being now of a man's estate (for
his entrance at the College of Corpus Christi was at
an age much beyond the common) and of a nature
graver than his years, he was impelled by his love
for his people of Royston, and his pity of the dangers their misleading might bring upon them, without delay to set out for his home in Somerset,

resolved to do what he might to order things fitly
Warning his mother by letter of his purpose, he
took the road by Reading and Salisbury, in which
city, arrived late at night, he heard what did but
increase his desire to be at Royston, so that with
moonrise he was again in the saddle, riding all that
night alone; for his servant's horse had reached
Salisbury clean foundered, and, nags being mighty
scarce from the needs of two armies lately in the
field at no great distance, he was forced to leave
the man behind until he could be mounted. Thus
it was that he came riding through Drayton village
just in the last struggles of those two poor rebels,
and amid the lamentable cries of Prudence in the
rough grasp of her outwitted redcoat.

Of what here immediately followed I have received
no account of that fulness which would enable me
to give a narrative in detail. For Prudence was so
mortally in fear, she says, that she remembers little
but a quarrel and the noise of a great blow, from
the moment of her seizure until she found herself
coming again to her wits from a fit of fainting, in
her father's arms and cottage. And Ned, when at
length the occasion for talking of the matter could
be had, did show a reluctance so great to speak of
that which he has called the most painful spot in
his memory, that even for the purpose of this book
I forbear to question him with any particularity.

But this much is sure, that in the winking of an eye
Mr. Royston was off his horse, the frightened and
brutal musketeer was stretched in the dust, and
Prudence freed from his clutch only to be seized,
with a coarse jest, into a lewd embrace by the
officer of the party.   There is little reason to doubt
that he would shortly, in his anger and with his
power at the moment so unbridled, have brought
my life's joy to an end by the shooting or hanging
of the gallant lad for his resistance to the military
authority.   But poor Ned's passion, so terrible, as
I have said, in certain moments of just anger, was
in a moment out of the cage where it had slumbered, and, before the vile words were well cooled
upon the wicked lips, the handle of a heavy riding-
whip had cut short the sentence with the life of the
speaker.   It must indeed have been a blow of fear-
ful force (for in those days Ned's strength was growing great even beyond his own knowledge of it),
and, falling as it did on the right temple, no other
was needed.   It was more than an hour before they
had sure knowledge that the man was dead, and in
the meantime all was confusion; for Ned, seeing
Prudence borne off in the arms of her father, leapt
upon his horse, and clattered down the village
street.   Three harmless musket-shots were dis-
charged after him, of which indeed we heard the
report up at the house, and then followed a babel

of questions and oaths. Some demanded horses, others the name of the miscreant and rebel that had stricken their officer. Now " young master of Royston," as they did use to call him, was as well loved as known in Drayton village; yet on this day there was found, of those that saw his deed, no man, woman, or child that could put a name to him. Nay, I am wrong, for two indeed there were did name him, but so diversely both from each other and from the truth that little was gained, even when, for the better convincing the sergeant, they came to blows over the difference. And on this matter of the death of that poor young ensign, hot, as it were, from his sins, I will say at once that you should have searched our west country for ten years and never found a man to blame his slayer. I am no Papist, nor do I know if this be sound in any theology, but certain it is that in our eyes to this day the blood of one of Kirke's Lambs upon his hands was held fit to wash many a sin from a man's soul.

Now, knowing his life not worth a hoof's paring if he fell into their hands, and unwilling to lead those men of blood to Royston, Ned did lie all that day in some deep woodland near Crewkerne, trusting his knowledge of the roads should give him by night the greater advantage over his pursuers, and hoping to obtain privily a fresh horse, when the sun was well set, for his journey to the coast.

CHAPTER IV

NOW all this day I had been keeping the house, at my father's strict command, he being most solicitous that for their safety none of his household should meet with the gang of cutthroats he knew to be then in the village. Being thus cut off from news, we had no knowledge of what was toward, conjecturing, however, some wickedness from the sound of those three musket-shots that I have mentioned.

About nine o'clock of the evening, then, I went to my chamber, sad, indeed, and anxious for the fate of the Drayton folk, and with many a shudder of horror as the things I had heard tell of that regiment, called at one time of Tangier, at another, Queen Catharine's, came unwelcome to my mind. And I remember that, as I put off my clothes, I marvelled how a woman high and gently born as that lady of Portugal could take pleasure to have such men bear her name. But, with all my perturbation, my mood was mild and peaceful to what it had been had I known at whom those same shots had been fired. Yet was there on my spirit a sense

of unrest, and (as it seems to me now, perhaps in
the light of after knowledge) of foreboded evil that
would in no manner let me sleep.   So it was that,
about half an hour after I had bidden good-night to
my father and Mr. Telgrove, I extinguished my one
candle, and, it being a warm but clouded night, sat
at the open window in my night-robe, trying idly to
bring my eyes to pierce the darkness, and as idly
considering when I was like again to see Ned.   Here
I sat, but for how long a period of time I know not.
Yet I do remember that I heard all those sounds
that indicate the closing in of night and sleep over
a great house.   And last came the drawing of bolts
and setting of bars below, and the slow and halting
step of my father's ascent of the stairs, and, with
the closing of his chamber door, a stillness as of the
grave was over all things.   I thought it was such a
stillness as I had never known; and then there grew
upon my spirit (or, at least, it now seems to me that
it was so) a foreknowledge that something, I knew
not what, but something — something — something
was coming out from this silence to break it.   And
with a slowly growing horror I did then fall to
speculating upon the nature of this so certain inter-
ruption; would it be some ghastly vision of another
world, or a cry of wrath, or some more horrible
scream of terror ?   As one grown suddenly cold I
arose from my seat by the window, with a shudder

at the creatures of my imagination, gently drew to
the casement, and got into my bed, as I should have
done an hour, perhaps, before.   But I found there
no refuge from the silence that should be broke, but
was not.   And this sense of loneliness brought me
in mind of the forgotten duty of prayer, so that I
was quickly again out of my bed and on my knees
by its side, hoping, childlike, great solace to my
oppression of spirit.   And then it came,—not
the solace, but the breaking of the silence.   And,
though it was not such as I had looked for, being
but the slight click of a pebble upon the glass of my
window, yet did it send, as they say, my heart into
my throat, and my whole body was a-tremble, as it
had been a harpstring overstrained.   It is a thing
for which I can never to the day of my death sufficiently thank the goodness of God, that my terror
took from me the voice in which I would have cried
aloud upon the house.   And so I gasped for breath,
and clutched the clothes of the bed in a fear quite
out of reason; and had I been upon my feet instead
of my knees, 't is sure I could not have kept them.
And then I heard the jingle of a bridle and the
thud of an impatient hoof falling soft upon the sod,
so that even in my passion of fear I knew it was
under my window, or I had not heard it, for the
grass was soft with the rain that fell at sunset.
Upon that strange thoughts of our bugbear Kirke

and of those devils that he ruled crept in my mind;
but surely, I thought, my father's good affections
to the throne should protect us; and, some movement of curiosity stirring in my breast to combat its
army of terrors, I made shift to creep with knees
and hands to the window, whence, with caution
raising myself and peering through the lower panes,
I espied dimly the shape of a man standing beside
his horse. Thereupon, perchance having seen the
whiteness of face, hand, or sleeve at the window,
though the light was almost none, the man below
uttered that whimsical little whistle of three notes
that was a signal and warning of childhood to me,
and I knew it was Ned. And my joy was so great
that I forgot the hour, the place, the strangeness in
him to come to my chamber window, and the un-
seemliness of my attire. Indeed I thought but of
him as I gently flung back the casement, and cried,
but softly: " Ned, dear Ned, is it indeed thou ? "

Whereupon he replied, in a voice, as I thought,
strangely altered from that I had known (but indeed
it was but the day's anxiety and alarms that had so
changed its sound): " I indeed it is, dear Mistress
Phil. But, I pray you, speak low and secretly, for
I do think they will be even now upon me."

" And who are 'they' ? " I asked, lightly enough,
having as yet no fear that any would harm such as
he.

"Kirke's mercenaries, that, because they bear
upon their flag the Lamb that doth signify our
blessed Redeemer, and because they do never use
to show mercy," he said bitterly, "they do call
Lambs. 'T is not likely they will show me the
mercy of sword-thrust or musket-ball if there be
a rope handy where we meet. And hanging is a
death I have little love to, Phil."

"But, Ned, O Ned!" I cried, leaning from the
window the better to speak low, "what hast done,
dear, to be out with these men? Surely you did
not fight with the Duke."

"Nay, mistress," says he, "but I have this day
struck down, and maybe worse, one that did fight
against that same poor foolish man. He was their
officer, and I doubt he is not yet risen, for I struck
him as I never struck man before. All this day
have I lain hid, and should now be on my way to
Bridport if my life be worth the saving. But I
thought, even now as I was starting on my way,
sink or swim, live or swing, I would see Phil once
again — I would say, Mistress Philippa. So I rode
hither five miles from Crewkerne woods to bid you
good-by. And now I am sorry that I did so, for,
as I leapt the hedge down there from the lane into
the hollow, I saw one on a horse that made for the
village, and I doubt he was some picket set to watch
after me. 'T is certain they have gotten horses

4

enough by this, and I do fear my rashness may bring them hot foot about this house.''

He now mounted his horse, pushed him close to the wall, and went on speaking: '' I wish I could come at you,'' he said. '' Would you give a kiss to take over the sea with me, Mistress Phil, an I could reach your lips ? I have not felt their touch of velvet since I was a lad.''

Now we were indeed very foolish there, with danger so instant upon us, to pause for such a matter. But I, remembering how I had wept because he had not taken, when last we met, what I was ashamed to offer unasked, and being filled with joy at his words, did answer, bold as brass: '' That indeed would I, dear Ned, if you were three feet taller than your six.'' And with that he must again urge his nag close in to the wall, steady him with voice and rein, and then climb to his feet upon the cantel of his saddle; and there, resting one hand upon the ledge of the window, he did take what he had asked and I was not minded to refuse. And whether there were more kisses than one, or whether one did last much longer than the wonted time of such, concerns but two persons in the world.

But, on a sudden, passing athwart my new joy, a newer fear entered my heart; for I heard the sound of many hoofs coming breakneck up the avenue to the house. For the passing of one brief heart-beat

that yet seemed the time of an age I felt cold and
sick of an awful dread, when there sprang a picture
on my brain of import so appalling, that I was flung
by recoil from that depth of despair into as excellent a degree of courage.   For as in a flash of light
I saw a gallows, and thought of a rope clinging yet
closer where my arms now clung.   And as the courage thus sprang to life in me, and I whispered,
" They shall not have thee, Ned," the beat of hoofs
drew near with that pulse in the stroke of them that
tells of the sharpness of the rider's spur and the
wrath in his heart.   And that which next followed
was a plain effect of Ned's rashness, and of the folly
of us both at such a conjuncture to play with the
moments that should have been used to his escape.
For the horse, on which he precariously stood to
reach me, hearing the quick and stirring approach
of his kind, did incontinently fling his heels in the
air, and, with a shrill nickering, started away across
the park at a good round pace, leaving his master
hanging by his hands, and partly to a great stem of
the ivy that on this side covers the most part of the
stonework of the house.   After a little struggle he
did contrive some sort of footing among the lower
branching knots of the ivy, and with a whispered
adieu would have made his descent, very hazardous
for a man of weight, had I not clutched him hard.
For I heard the voices of some that were coming

round the house, drawn, doubtless, by the neighing
of the faithless nag.

" Come in, Ned, an you love me," I said.   " If
they see thee here all is done."   Now I can give no
good account of how it was achieved, remembering
but confusedly that I did get my hands beneath his
arms, and thereby pulled at him with a strength
raised, I do think, for some few moments of time,
by the mercy of God and my great fear, much
above what by nature was in me; and he, as he was
able, helping me, I did, in spite of the greatness of
his shoulders, and the narrowness of the casement,
with great silence and speed haul his long person
head foremost into my chamber; and that was done
but just as three of his pursuers, mounted on the
horses they had pressed for the service, did gallop
round the corner upon the grass.   And I thanked
God that I was burning no light within, else had
they spied the soles of his great riding-boots, which
yet rested upon the sill, while his head was on the
floor, and I crouched beside him to hide the whiteness of my bedgown.   To this day there is the mark
of his spur upon the sill of that casement—a sort of
dotted line, made as he did twist himself over on
the floor the better to drag the long legs of him to
the same level.   Of the three that rode by beneath,
it was afterwards supposed that they did further
scatter the deer that Ned's horse had roused from

sleep, each pursuing in the darkness a quarry of his
own, which he took for the nag that was now well
on his riderless way to Royston.

Now my first motion was to laugh loud and long,
which with some wisdom I did check. Then I
would have wept, but that desire too was speedily
overcome, as for the first time since the pebble
struck my window I remembered how I was clad,
and again thanked God there was not even a rush-
light in the chamber to show me so unmaidenly.
But we were not quit of Kirke's men for the three
that were so vainly and unseasonably chasing our
deer; for, as I turned to a closet to take down a
long cloak to throw over me, there arose a clamor
of knocking and shouting at the great door below.
For all that has been told since first we heard their
horses was the happening of seconds fewer than the
minutes spent in reading it.

"Where are you, mistress?" said Ned, now risen
to his feet, and so standing between me and the
window that I could make out the blackness of his
shape against the thinner darkness without.

"You must not speak, dear Ned," I answered,
laying my hand on his arm to show him where I
stood.

"I cannot see you even yet," said he, as he felt
my hand. "But now you were all white."

With which I was speedily all red with shame,

and whispered: "Hush, Ned, hush! Even now you are in great peril."

" 'T is no matter for that," he said. " The peril is for you, mistress. I did wrong to enter here, and must go, one way or the other."

And with that he looked warily from the window, but speedily drew back, having seen in that brief moment, by a faint gleaming of the moon through a thinness of the clouds, a sentry that moved to and fro beneath, musket on shoulder. And when he had told me in the lowest whisper what he had seen, he said: " So it must needs be by the door." And as he spoke we heard the clatter of bar and chain below, telling that the enemy was admitted among us. So he would have leapt from the window to take his chance with the sentry, rather than he should be so found closeted with me. But I would not, and ran between him and the window, saying low and quick that I would call aloud if he persisted. And since he knew me and the manner of voice I used to threat the thing I would surely do (for my crying out in such case had made things no worse for him, but only full of shame for me that called), he yielded, asking me, What, then, should we do? Which before I could answer, I heard them striking upon a door in the same gallery where stood the room we were in, and the slumberous expostulation of Mr. Telgrove, who there inhabited. There

was but one room between, and I felt our turn was
near and that the bitterness of death must soon
take hold on me unless I could think of a thing.
And truly I think that never before, and but once
since, did my mind think so many thoughts in so
short a space and to so much purpose.

Press, closet, and chimney — nay, even the space
beneath the bed — were swiftly tried in my mind,
and discarded as harborage too little secure to shelter what in all the world I did best love.   But at
last the thought came, and with it I was no longer
a maid shaking at approach of danger, but a general
with a device of strategy that should repel the
invader.

" Ned," I said, low and sharp, " will you do what
I bid ? "

" Ay, sweetheart—mistress, I would say," he replied, and in all my passion of fear and purpose of
action I marvelled, as I had done since he came
under my window, why he would ever style me
mistress.

Now, while we spoke beneath our breath, I had
tied my handkerchief over his head, and knotted it
under his chin.   Then I pushed him to the side of
the bed that was farther from the door, guiding
him with my hands, and bidding him lie down while
I should pull the covers over him.   But, " Nay,
that will I not," he said, with a perilous raising of

the voice. " Had rather swing than save my neck
by these means." And I, in despair, did clap my
hand over his mouth, and said with great fury of
passion I scarce knew what, and beat him with my
fists, till he was sorry to see me so moved, and suffered me, of his old gentle kindness, to force him
down, and, trembling, to drag blanket and quilt
over him, which in the dark did so fall foul of
sword-hilt and spur, that I had laughed had I not
been heart-sick with the fear of his life. When he
was covered I sat me upon his chest, and, as best I
might in the dark, twisted his long curls, which, in
the fashion of his father's youth, he would still wear
in place of peruke (and I think there is not a beau
in London that has a wig from Paris so fair as what
grew on his dear head), into some sort of womanish
knot to thrust up beneath the handkerchief that
must serve for night-cap. The sitting on him was
to keep him there till they began to knock at the
door, when I knew the desire to shield my fame
would keep him quiet to the end.

Heavy steps now drawing near, I spoke my last
word to him: " When they come lie thus, with thy
face from the door, and, prithee, Ned, breathe hard
and heavily, as you were Betty after a great supper."

" Nay," said he, " I will not stay to play the fool
like a mummer in a play-house."

" If you but so much as stir a finger," said I,

" you will put me to open shame before the servants of the house and those wicked soldiers.   I
think you will not so use your old playmate, Ned."

And then, to set my heart beating yet more horribly, so that it seemed I should never be able to
speak when the need came, the searchers reached our
door and knocked upon it, yet, from something more
of gentleness that was in this knocking than was used
upon the door of my tutor, I gathered a little hope.
At once I threw off my cloak and held my breath
in eagerness of hearing all that passed without.

" I say my daughter lies in that chamber," said
my father's voice, growing more clear as he limped
painfully up the gallery after his unwelcome visitors.
" She is sleeping, and it will serve no purpose to
arouse her."

" That 's my business," said a harsh voice in
surly reply.   " I will rouse whom I please, since I
am master here."

Sir Michael's voice rose somewhat higher, while
his utterance became slower and more severe, as he
answered this fellow.

" You mistake," said he, " for none is master
here save I alone.   And I will tell you, Master
Sergeant, that, though I have admitted you to my
house in the hope to do His Majesty the King a
service, I do not purpose to endure in this house
any show of ill manners such as your regiment is

commonly noised to show toward helpless yokels and misguided rebels."

The sergeant's voice was still surly, but had in it a degree more of respect, as he replied that Sir Michael talked a deal of doing His Majesty a service, but when they came hot on the track of a rebel who had slain one that held His Majesty's commission, and was not yet well cold, he fell at once to putting obstacles in the way; that he was informed by his scouts that the man was seen not half an hour back making for this house; that he did but wish to make thorough search for the young murderer, with all fit observance of respect for His Majesty's loyal subjects, and search every room in that house he would before he left it. And inside the chamber, when he heard that the man was indeed dead, poor Ned shuddered beneath the bedclothes, and I, sitting on the other side, did lay my hand upon him for comfort. At that time, when I knew nothing but the man was dead, I thought no ill of my friend for the killing. If Ned Royston should slay a man, why, to me, the man was better dead. Later, hearing the whole tale, I was like to have been jealous of little Prudence Emmet, for whom the man was killed. Yet I wondered not that he shuddered, for I had heard my father say that it does take an old soldier long years to forget the first shedding of blood.

I heard one tearless and hard kind of sob from the dear lad, while my heart was sore that I could not speak in consolation, and then gave ear to my father's answer to the sergeant, which was very calmly delivered: " That we shall see, Master Sergeant. I have held no mean rank in the armies of his late Majesty, King Charles I., from wounds received in whose cause I shall not be recovered this side the grave, from which you are to understand what manner of bearing I am wont to receive from inferiors in rank. Moreover, I am greatly at fault if I have not still some credit at Whitehall—enough, at least, Master Sergeant, to make me a safer friend than enemy. I shall thank you for a sight of your search-warrant."

To which the sergeant: " Indeed, Sir Michael, I have none. In these ill times, with so much treason abroad, we do not think much of a warrant. But I am under a great necessity in what I do. Our colonel is no man to take soft words as atonement for the death of an officer after his own heart. I must report in the town of Taunton at noon tomorrow, and I dare not take thither this story of murder without the murderer. You talk well of warrants, sir, but there is none of us but fears Colonel Kirke worse than the law."

And on the other side of the door I did most heartily agree with this sergeant of Queen Catharine's

Regiment of Foot. But my father continued:
" I perceive, sergeant, that you are a man of some
parts and education. Let us meet each other thus
—I to summon my daughter, and, after a space,
you and I alone of all these to enter the chamber."
At which words my heart did sink to the place
where the shoes had been but for my resolve, at
any cost to nicer feeling, of showing unprepared.

And, the sergeant heartily consenting, Sir Michael
himself rapped upon the door, and I still keeping
silence (knowing I must open, yet not thinking it
to be wise too soon to hear him, when I had been
deaf to the sergeant), he next tried the latch, and,
finding the door fast, knocked louder, and very
gently called my name. Whereat I groaned,
sighed, and cried, as one waking from sleep,
" What is to do ? Who is it, and what is
wanted?"

And my father answered, " It is I, your father.
Cloak yourself, Philippa, and open to me."

Whereupon I made my first mistake; for, to the
end they might think I had heard nothing but my
father's summons, I left my cloak lying upon the
bed, and ran in my white gown, and barefoot, to the
door, and suddenly flung it wide, when the glare of
the lights that several did carry gave me the appearance of blinking with sleep the most naturally in the
world. Then, putting a hand before my eyes to

keep off the suddenness of the light, I said, with a
little sharpness: " Well, sir, why am I roused ?
Does the house burn, or are Kirke and his Lambs
at the door ? "

And my father replied, with the first note of
trepidation in his voice that I had ever heard,
" Hush, child! All is well. There is no fire."

But I, resolved to show no dread, and now well
launched in my comedy of deceit (for which, indeed, I was little fit, being reared in the utmost
strictness of truth-telling), made answer I had rather
the fire than Kirke, who would be the harder to
sate. Then, taking my hand from my eyes, and
feigning now first to perceive the soldiers and other
company, cried out as one mightily abashed to be
so looked upon, and swiftly part-closed the door,
and, in a voice whose shaking was easy to compass,
asked who were all these with him. And he told
me that I need not fear; that they were but some
of the King's soldiers in search of a murderer, and
that none should enter my chamber but himself and
the sergeant of the party. So I left the door, seeing
that they must enter, and ran to the bed and lifted
my cloak, flung it over my shoulders, and turned
again to face them; when I perceived that the
sergeant, on my leaving the door, had thrust it
wide to watch my movements. So I bade him and
my father come in, begging at the same time that

they would have a care not to arouse Betty, who was that night sharing my bed.

" And why," asked Sir Michael, " is Betty here ? You do use to lie alone."

Nor were the words out of his mouth before I saw that he regretted them, and that he knew, whether from my face, or from the unwonted presence of Betty in my chamber, or from another cause that I did not then understand, that all was not well. He sat him down heavily upon the little settle at the bed's foot, with a countenance full of perplexity and astonishment. But the mischief was done, and I must find a reason for the presence in my bed of her who was safely snoring in her own above our heads. So I told him that I had been loath to sleep alone this night for the fear I had of the things that were afoot in Drayton village, and had begged Betty to keep me company. And with that the sergeant, who had, while we spoke, been peering about the dark corners of the room, turned and sharply enquired of me why this Betty that lay there in the bed must not be aroused. " Because," said I, taking refuge in the unreason of a woman's anger (for indeed I knew not what to say, and all seemed to go awry from what I had intended), " because I will not have it done. Is it become a custom with officers of the King to invade by force, and at dead of night, the sleeping chambers of ladies ? "

" Madam," he answered, somewhat abashed as I thought, " I am only a poor sergeant that would do his duty to his officer. If you will answer my questions, I will the sooner be gone."

In this gentle manner of taking it I saw some hope, and answered him thus: " Poor Betty was my nurse, sergeant, and I love her dearly; and she hath all day been afflicted with a most violent toothache, and 't is but a little while since I gave her a great draught of a most sovereign remedy— an electuary of poppy-seed — by which she is eased of her pain and now fallen asleep." And in the manner the most imploring I could compass I did here raise pitiful eyes to his face. " I do perceive, sir," I continued, " I had no need to be angry, but oh! I do pray you will not waken the poor woman; for a sudden waking from a slumber procured by that drug is very harmful. Search all the place— the closets, presses, and beneath the bed; though, in good sooth, I do not know how you should think to find here any murderer."

The sergeant smiled with a certain grimness, and asked was it not strange I should seek comfort for my fears in the company of one that was sick of a toothache; whereon I replied that Betty sick was better than many another whole.

" And were you sleeping, madam, when we first called upon you to open ? " says the sergeant.

" ' T was my father's voice aroused me," I answered, wondering whither he would lead me with his questioning.

" And had you then slept long ? " asked he.

" Since ten o'clock, I do suppose," I replied.

" Yet your cloak, that you now wear, lay, until we were about entering, there upon the bed," said he, with a meaning glance of which the significance was wholly hidden from me.

" Well, what if it did ? " said I.

" It lay, madam," he replied, " above the turned-down bedcover."

I now was near at an end of my strategy, but my dear father came at once to the rescue, saying that the sergeant was a clever fellow, but what in the devil's name did he argue from that ?

" That young Mistress Drayton has lately risen from her bed and covered herself with that same cloak she now wears, but wore not when she did now open to you, Sir Michael," said the man, with some acuteness, indeed, but not before I had my answer ready for him, and something over and above a mere answer.

" Why, indeed, you speak truth, sergeant," I said; and I had hope so great in what was next to come that I was enabled to laugh with much naturalness as I spoke; " you are a witch for certain, sir; for though I did forget the thing for a moment, having since slept, and being with sleep yet not a little confused, it is true that I did rise once before from my bed, when I fetched this cloak from the closet there, and did look from the window——"

" To what end did you do that, madam," said the sergeant, interrupting me, " on so dark a night ? "

" That I cannot say," I answered, " for I was half in sleep when I rose. But I think, sergeant, that I can tell you something of the man you seek. For as I looked forth there came a man from the way of the deer park, and in a little gleam of the moon that did then shine out for a moment I saw him, and that he was mounted on a dapple-gray horse. And as he came he stopped as if he heard a sound that he feared. And then he turned his nag in such haste, and made off the way he had come with such speed, that I had no time to mark his face; but I saw that he did lose his hat in turning, nor stayed to recover it. And not long after him came from the front of the house three men, mounted, who followed after him. But as they passed the moon was again clouded, and I can tell nothing of them nor their horses. And after this I got to bed again, and I must suppose," I said, looking doubtfully at the bed, " that I slept again, the night being so warm, without drawing over me the covers whereon I had laid the cloak."

5

" Truly, 't is warm," said the sergeant. " But I ask your pardon, madam, for thus discussing private matters. Your story is a plain one, and may help to the fellow's capture." And then he took some steps towards the door, and I thought the danger was over, and I had much ado to keep my countenance from showing the sudden lightening of my heart. But even as he was going some devil of raillery, or cruelty, prompted him to turn and say that in his company he was counted an excellent tooth-drawer, and that he would just have a look at poor Betty's mouth. For a moment I could not speak, but turned to the bed as if to protect my old nurse, perceiving, as I turned, a movement as of a hand beneath the quilt ; and I knew that Ned was feeling for his sword-hilt, and waiting to be discovered. At that I laid my hand upon his shoulder, and, finding again my voice, " Be still, dear Betty," I cried, " there is no need of rising yet. And I do pray you, Master Sergeant, that you will go now, when I have so fully told you everything. Her poor tooth will again be raging if she be disturbed." And this I said so pleadingly that the man was quite subdued, saying, with more of kindness than he had yet used: " Indeed, madam, I spoke but in jest, for which I ask your pardon."

And so he left the room, closing the door behind

him, and I turned to regard my father.   But before
I could reach him to tell in his ear the reason of it
all, and who it was indeed that there lay in the bed,
he rose from the seat he had not left since his entering, and I at once knew why he had sat so close.
For he lifted from the settle, crushed out of all
shape by his sitting upon it, Ned's hat, which, not
finding to be on the floor, I had thought to be
fallen upon the grass below.

Then did we look hard and long in each other's
eyes, and my father thrust out his thumb towards
the bed with a gesture of questioning, and I answered him with one word, so softly breathed that
his eyes must needs take the office of his ears.
Then he raised the hat.

" He must find it below," he said, and, stealing
to the window, of which the casement still stood
open, he leaned out, and, seeing the sentry at the
far end of his beat, flung out the hat softly with a
skimming motion, so that it fell upon the grass at
some distance from the house, and almost without
sound.   And returning from the window he found
Ned standing upright, freed from the kerchief I
had bound on his head, bearing in his countenance
the flush of a strong indignation; for he felt, as he
has explained to me, that the shame of that igno-
minious concealment would never leave him.   But
the flush died speedily away on my father's holding

out his hand, in silence, indeed, but with his old frank and kindly smile. They grasped each the other's with a great clasp, and then Sir Michael whispered: "We must get him out of this," and went out at the door.

And as he closed it we knew, by the voices without, that he had encountered the sergeant in the gallery.

CHAPTER V

SIR MICHAEL carried with him the one candle he had brought into my chamber, so we stood in the dark as if turned to stone by the sound of the sergeant's voice without, most horribly dreading that he would again enter, and all our work be undone. How long this lasted I do not know, but at last we heard him and my father walk together down the gallery to the stairhead, conversing in subdued tones. Sir Michael told him, as I did afterwards learn, that I had been mightily frightened and disturbed, and was now at his desire composing myself again to sleep. And the man replied that, as far as my chamber was concerned, he was satisfied, since he had discovered complete warranty of the tale I had told in the hat he then held in his hand, having found it where I had said it should lie. He added that he well knew the stigma of cruelty lying upon his regiment, yet he, for one, was vastly sorry that matters had so fallen as to discompose a young gentlewoman that was, he believed, the most beautiful and kind-hearted in the kingdom. And I have often thought of it as a thing passing strange

that the first tribute I received in my life to the
charms of my person did proceed from a man to
whom I had most shamelessly lied, he being one of
a company famed in all the world for wickedness
and cruelty.   And I have prayed to God that what
good there was in this man might not be utterly
cast away.

So, while we two, Ned and I, sat almost silent
above-stairs in the dark, striving to smother the
sound of the passion of tears that had seized upon
me, my father descended the stair with the sergeant,
thinking soon to be rid of him and his men; but was
speedily disappointed in finding that the man had
no intention to abandon his search, although he
showed his altered temper in putting himself at my
father's orders, whether to continue at once his
visitation of the house from garret to cellar, or to
set strict guard upon all its approaches till morning,
then to complete his survey in the better light.

" For," said he, throwing poor Ned's damaged
hat upon the table of the great hall where they
stood, " though we do know the rascal was without, and that your worship does not willingly harbor him, we have no testimony that he did not get
in after he had lost his hat.   Some soft-hearted
kitchen-maid might well—— "

" 'T is enough said, sergeant," interrupted Sir
Michael, resolving to put a good face upon his

choice of the lesser evil; "I commend the acuteness of your judgment. It is indeed as much for
my honor as yours that suspicion of harboring this
fellow should be removed from my house as well
as from myself and my daughter. Do you set at
once a sufficient guard without to watch every door
and window, and while you call into the hall here
all that are not needed for that duty, I will rouse
some of the fellows that sleep above, and see that
you have good food and drink in place of the sleep
you must lose. And I doubt not," he added, turning at the door, " such of you as remember Tangier
will find my old Burgundy, that has been much
praised by good judges, a better substitute for the
wines of Spain and Portugal than our west-country
ale."

Whereupon the sergeant, pleased with prospect of
good cheer, went out to make disposition of his
men, while my father again mounted the stairs,
turning swiftly in his mind the subterfuge by which
he purposed getting Ned Royston safely from the
house. And indeed I think he did devise a scheme
as cunning as any of those happy strokes of adroit-
ness and dexterity for which in the old wars he was
justly famous.

The soldiers being now below, and the few servants first roused sent to fetch food for the sergeant
and his men, my father found the stairs and galleries

deserted. Pausing at my door, he gently opened it, and hearing the sound of my half-stifled weeping he bid me not check it, saying that it fell well with his scheme.

" Do but as I bid you, my children," said he, " and in less than an hour the poor lad shall be on the road to Bridport; and with Skewbald Meg between his legs 't is pity of the horse and man that would catch him. I can give you no light, for the sentry that is below the window, but you, my little Phil, must make shift to cut away from him those unfashionable curls; and it is little matter for the dark, since the more raggedly you play the barber the better for him; also pull off his great boots, with the gay coat and the waistcoat, and when I return with the real Betty to take his place in the bed, where, I vow, I think she will sleep better than he, I will so clothe him and so raddle his face that his mother would not know him again; and if you must speak in the doing all this, let it be little and in the veriest of whispers." And at this my dear and most wise old father left us, saying aloud, as he shut the door, and with intent to be heard if any were spying upon him: " Get thee to sleep, child. There is no further cause of fear. None shall harm thee."

Silent as mice midway between cat and cheese we fell to doing all that he had bidden us. I was bitterly

sorry for the curls, and for the cruel fashion in
which my small shears did lop them, but said no
word till all was done.   And then we sat waiting in
the dark, and Ned found my hand and held it, and
whispered after a while that he had not yet seen my
face; that he doubted it was greatly altered, even
as he perceived my body was increased in stature.
And he asked me had I grown beautiful as he was
used to predict, and I could only answer that I did
not think I was fully so foul to look upon as I had
been.   And he was about getting hot in reply, and
even raising his voice a little to vow that I was never
that, nor thought he meant I was, and he had for
the moment quite forgot to *mistress* me, as hitherto
since I had dragged him headlong through my
window, when the door again opened to admit my
father, dragging by the arm poor sleep-dazed,
blanket-wrapped Betty, who was, I do suppose,
from the brief glimpse I caught of her figure as my
father did set his candle on the floor without the
door, a strange and admirable spectacle.   In the
darkened room she was mightily amazed, and we
must needs thrust her into the bed almost by force,
and had well-nigh to gag her mouth before we
might check the wheezy thunder that she honored
with the delicate title of whispering.   Indeed, all
this part of our night's adventure had been vastly
comical and mirth-provoking had not a life, tenderly

dear alike to father and daughter, hung upon
our secrecy and despatch. Now Sir Michael had
brought with him along with Betty the cast-off
clothes of one of the grooms that slept in the
garret. And there, still in darkness, we contrived
among us to habit Ned in them — foul old broken
shoes, a mile too large, which I stuffed with such
rags as would keep him from walking out of them;
rough woollen stockings, none too clean; his own
leathern breeches, which he said were much worn
and covered with the dust of all his ride from Oxford, my father did let pass; but the fine long-cloth
shirt he would in no manner concede, making him
take in its place a filthy clout it was well we could
not see as we pulled it over his shorn head. "For,"
said my father, "there is nothing will so play the
traitor to a gentleman disguised as his own linen.
The very fabric will still tell tales when the fairness
of it has disappeared under the dirt of long use."
And then all was done; Ned did take me for a little
moment in his arms, when Sir Michael bade him to
thrust a hand up the chimney to befoul it with soot,
with which, he said, he would have him bedaub face
and neck when they had again such light that it
might be done in measure and fitness.

"Good-by, Mistress Phil," said he, and "Good-
by, dear Ned," said I. My father here slipping
quietly out to spy up and down the gallery, and

holding the door to behind him, in that last moment
I seized Ned's hand, not knowing it was the sooty
one, and whispered in his ear: " Why will you be
ever throwing *mistress* at me, dear ? Am I not
your old friend Phil ?" And he: " I did but think,
Phil, that so unceremoniously visiting your chamber
at night-time, which you know is a thing I never
purposed, did call for terms of address more formal
than our usage of childhood." Which before I
could answer, Sir Michael, satisfied that he was not
observed, had him swiftly out in the gallery, my
door was closed for the last time that night, and I
fell weeping on the bed as if the sun should never
shine again.

I slept none of that night, and much of it I wept.
But, rising in the sheer idleness of fatigue, when
the dawn was well advanced, and chancing to see
my face in the mirror, I perceived that I had most
plentifully streaked and smeared a tear-wet countenance with the blackness of the soot that had passed
in our last moment together from Ned's fingers to
mine. Now my eyes and cheeks presented doubtless a spectacle that had moved another to laughter.
But from the eyes that alone beheld the figure of
ridicule that I was, the thought of how I became so
besmirched brought fresh tears, plentiful enough, in
all conscience, to have washed it clean of all the
grime that face ever carried. But I washed hands

and face, and so back to bed, where, worn out, and
by this tolerably secure of Ned's evasion, I fell
asleep, nor awoke until I was roused somewhat past
eight o'clock of the morning

Meantime to the tale of that same evasion which
was, as I supposed, well accomplished. To tell it
briefly, my father bade him play the clown as best
he could, and, after his face had been cunningly
smeared with that same soot, had led him by the
back stair to the kitchen; whence, after Sir Michael
had joined the soldiers eating and drinking in the
great hall, he was sent by the cook, who was in the
secret, to bear a dish of some dainty to the company. This, as before arranged, he let fall with a
great clatter, bringing Sir Michael down upon him
in pretence of anger; who did there, with many a
curse on his clumsiness, so cuff him about head and
ears, that it set all the redcoats laughing. "Silly
varlet!" quoth Sir Michael, "is the cook under-
handed that such as you must be fetched from
garden and stable to spoil our meat? I warrant
men are hanged for less in these days."

To this the seeming yokel blubbered in reply that
he did but wish a sight of the soldier gentlemen at
meat, which he said in that broad and slurring
speech of our country that he could ever from his
childhood put on with exact faithfulness to nature.
And just here one of the strangers' horses, neighing

wearily without, where he was tied to a tree, " Get
out," said my father, " and see to those horses.
Put them in the stable, and, if there be not room
for all, turn some of your own cattle to graze in the
park." And as he was going out slowly dragging
one loose shoe after the other, one of the soldiers
flung a bone at him, and threatened to flog the coat
off his back, and the skin to follow it, if he did
not rub down and well feed and water each of their
borrowed nags.

So to this task he went, with a hundred pounds
in gold of my father's in his one pocket that was
sound. And five horses he did groom and feed and
lodge in that stable, turning three of Sir Michael's
out of their places into the park. But one of these,
that is, Skewbald Meg, a mare of great hardness of
limb and lasting power of wind, though a mean and
ewe-necked thing to the eye, he tied, when out of
hearing of the sentry on that side of the house, to
a tree that stood handy for the direction he must
take. He then returned to the stable, and there
contrived an appearance of business about the nags,
while he concealed upon him a bridle, with which
about his waist he at last, having left his lantern
burning within, loitered down to Meg in the hollow,
where in a trice she was bridled and mounted by as
good a horseman and as ill-looking as ever bestrid
her lean and mottled ribs. And how he fared in

that ride of near upon twenty-five miles to Lyme, and how he was taken safely out of the country by sea, you shall hear when I am come to the letter that came to me out of Holland.

And here this episode of my life may be counted at an end. For my father, having pressed upon his guests both bottle and tankard, until each man made a pillow where his head did strike in falling, and having sent out copious flagons until the sentries lacked little of being in the same case, did in the leisure thus obtained so drill and instruct every waking soul in the house that it was a sure matter that all, in case of need, would have the same story to tell: as, that Sir Michael had no horses but what might now be seen upon the place; that any who thought he had a skewbald mare was vastly mistook; that the scullion that was so roundly cuffed and rated was a half-witted thing from the stable that had now run off in terror of the beating promised him the night before by one of the sergeant's men; and so forth. All that night, as I have said, my father came not near me, thinking there had been enough and to spare already done in that part of the house, and not wishing to arouse any suspicion that might, in the sergeant's muddled head, survive the fumes of the wine. But between eight and nine of the clock Sir Michael knocked loudly at my door, asking, so that all might hear if they

would, how I did, had I slept, and so forth. Then
in a little voice he bade me tell Betty to keep
her bed, to remember she was yet very sick,
and that I should hide Ned's boots, sword, and
clothes betwixt the mattresses, where Betty's huge
person should keep them safe. All this, said he,
merely as safeguard against another visit to my
room.

And very shortly thereafter arose a great cursing
below, and a swearing of many horrible oaths by
the sergeant, with low grumbling accompaniment of
his men, as they rose from many a twisted posture
of swinish slumber. When with sousing, brushing,
and breakfasting they were again brought to some
semblance of men, the futile search after him that
was by this well out of their reach was begun. Nor
did it cease till close on noon. Now, as the sergeant
and his file of men passed along the gallery, when
there was left no further corner into which they
might thrust nose, eyes, or sword-point seeking for
hidden softness of human flesh, some spirit of bra-
vado did seize upon me, and I flung open the door of
my chamber, where all morning I had kept pretence
of nursing poor Betty, sick only of an ill temper to
be kept a lie-a-bed against her will; and I called to
the sergeant that he had not searched here by daylight, and that all was at his service, even poor
Betty, being now awake; and he came to the door,

and stood upon the threshold, looking in upon us
while Betty sat up in the bed and glared upon him,
fear and anger struggling for mastery in her broad
countenance, and rendering it grotesquely terrible.
Now I was clothed this time in fit manner, with
gown and hair fresh and neat, and, spite of my sorrow at losing Ned and the terrors of the night just
passed, I had a sense of triumph in my growing
certainty of his escape that I think I scarce tried to
keep from appearing in my countenance. For a
moment he regarded me doubtfully, and then there
sprang into his eye a light as of days when he had
been other than he now seemed, and I thought he
would have spoken gaily and kindly. But, my
father coming to the door, the sergeant checked his
words, and, his eye lighting upon Betty, a dark
cloud of suspicion passed over his face. This was
succeeded by a look of resignation truly humorous
and comical, as he thanked me for the help I had
already given him, which was indeed, he said, more
than he had deserved, apologized for the disturb-
ance he had caused, and so bowed himself out. He
straightway marched his detachment into Drayton,
and, having failed by violent means to avenge the
death of his ensign, he now had recourse to the law,
summoning to him the coroner, and insisting upon
a speedy inquest, in hope to discover—the few wit-
nesses of the deed being put upon oath — the name

of whom, if taken *flagrante delicto*, he would have
hanged before it could be told.

To a wiser head than mine I must leave to be decided the point in casuistry, whether it was to the
honor or rather to the shame of our village folk
that among them could not be found two to give a
similar account of Ned's appearance, nor one that
knew his name or had ever set eyes upon him before; and this in spite of their oaths and their long
and kindly knowledge of him.   It may be they did
all grievously sin in thus shielding him; for me, I
can only say that, having myself done much the
same the night before, in intent at least, I am glad
they did what they did; and that I have always
held those three men and two women in a most
tender regard who did esteem the danger to his
dear body of more account than the risk to their
own souls.   While this inquest was holding, and
before its verdict of manslaughter by a person unknown had been delivered, there rode into the
village with a small body of dragoons no less a
person than Colonel Kirke himself, to whom our
sergeant had sent a messenger immediately upon
the death of his officer.   He came roaring and
ruffling into the room at the little inn where the
coroner sat, and 't is a hard thing to say what
might not have happened to many innocent persons
had he not there met with my father.   Sir Michael's

6

knowledge of men, and, perhaps, some secret information of Kirke's character, taught him the true
manner in which this hero, more deadly with the
rope than with the sword, must be handled.   I
need here say no more of the matter, but that Colonel Kirke did that afternoon march to Taunton,
with all his Lambs and dragoons, the body of the
dead ensign, and a sum of two hundred pounds of
my dear father's savings as ransom for the village.

Of Colonel Percy Kirke it was truly said that only
one thing did he love better than blood.

CHAPTER VI

A LITTLE sidelong eddy, it seemed, from the great tide of public events had washed up into our quiet backwater or creek of country life, setting us all agog with the tragic issues of death and dishonor. But the flutter and swirl of it had now drifted back into the main stream, leaving us, not indeed the same as we had been, but by contrast quieter than before. During some three years, for us at Drayton it might be said, with a measure of truth, that nothing happened. Yet of those things which I have recounted there were several consequences, so notable in effect upon our hearts and minds, that it were perhaps more true to say, in that same metaphor, that, after the first commotion, the tide maintained a steady though hourly imperceptible rise.

When I knew that Kirke and all his men were safely on their way for Taunton, I lost no time in riding across country in a bee-line to Royston Chase, which I found shut up in charge of three old servants. From these I learned that Ned's gray had that morning been discovered cropping a breakfast from the grass about his own stable door, and, while assuring them of their young master's safety, beyond, perhaps, what I truly felt myself, I bade them keep quiet tongues both about the horse and his master, who lay for safety, I said, in these perilous times, at the city of Oxford. Nor did I in truth lie to these good people, who from my manner of speaking did well perceive this was but the tale they must tell, I knowing what it were best they should not. Of the chief among them I had the promise that on the expected arrival of the Lady Mary my father should at once be advertised of it. And thence home, a little lighter in spirit to know that his horse was safe, and found my father musing heavily in his great chair in the hall, where the night before he had so feasted our enemies. At first it was a hard matter to bring him to talk, but at last, under stress of coaxing and such tricks of blandishment as I have practised from a child to win him from this heaviness of spirit, he broke silence.

" The times are hard when a Drayton must in his old age take to lying, little daughter Phil," he said.

"And his daughter in the days of her youth," I answered merrily. " But in truth 't is little I trouble myself for the falsehood. Whose, sir, upon the Day of Judgment, will be the blame of those untruths that were told to save from a death

both cruel and contrary to law so kind and Christian
a gentleman as my Ned ? "

Sir Michael smiled and rallied me on that word of
possession.

" Ho, ho ! " said he ; " ' my Ned,' indeed ! He is
by this in Holland, little lass, and already, it is like
enough, hath seen much that may put an unbroke
filly out of his mind." Then, growing grave,
" ' There is something rotten,' " he said, quoting
from Mr. Shakespeare's tragedy of *Hamlet* (for this
play, and others of that writer, were his chief reading), " ' There is something rotten in the state of
Denmark,' when honest youths must needs kill soldiers of their sovereign, and old men and young
maids must trump up a pack of lying tales to save a
good lad from rope without jury. I would I had
died when the late King did come again to his
own."

" And what, then, of poor Philippa ? " I piteously
asked.

" Why, then," said my father, smiling on me
with a countenance of great benignity, " poor Philippa had not been, and poor Michael had missed his
best gift of God. So let us leave it to Him, dear
maid, both for what is to be and for how much thy
father shall see of it." And it was long thereafter
before he would again talk to me of public matters;
but I knew by his face, which to me was ever print

of an open character, that he thought much, and that a strife was in his soul, waged between his life-long loyalty to the house of Stuart and the new thoughts born of his pity for the land that he loved as they had never loved but themselves.

If my father had hated in his life any man, it was Oliver, the late Protector.   Yet thrice within the year that followed, when some neighbor would speak of the low opinion into which we were come upon the continent of Europe, or when the news-letter would drop some covert hint of the subser-vience of St. James to Versailles, he said: " It had not been thus, or so, if Old Noll were alive."   And once to Mr. Greenlow: " Say what you will, Parson, Cromwell was an Englishman, and a brave one.   I would he had been born of a queen."

And if the circumstances of Ned's evasion brought some change to Sir Michael's way of thinking, they caused no less an alteration in the value set upon his daughter by one whose good opinion I had much desired and was now at last to obtain.

Three days after that vain inquest upon the body of the dead ensign word came from Royston that my Lady Mary was arrived, and, thinking there to have found her son, and finding neither him nor his news, was fallen into great distress of mind.   Sir Michael, being now somewhat better of his indis-position, made shift to ride back with the servant,

and straightway gave her, I think, full account of
all that had been done by her son and for him.
But, his tale ceasing with Ned's departure upon
Skewbald Meg, it can scarce be imagined he brought
much of comfort to that proud lady and doting
mother.

He returned the same afternoon, telling me in
words less of his converse with Lady Mary than
his face had already betrayed ere his feet were out
of the stirrups.

Now, about the hour of ten the next morning, I
was idling on the south terrace, feeding our doves
and playing with the dogs, when my eye was caught
by a strange fellow most uncouthly dressed that led
a horse up the avenue.   Nor did it take long gazing to see from the large maculation of its sides that
the horse was Skewbald Meg; the man proving, on
closer observation and his own rough introduction,
to be a petticoated seaman of Bridport.   But to our
enquiries after him who had lately ridden the mare
he would answer nothing.   He knew, he said,
naught but that one who was no longer this side the
water had told him the horse was owned at Drayton, in Somerset, and he would get twenty shillings
for the bringing it home; that he had done his best
to con the craft from the poop, but found she would
ever move *starn* foremost when he went on deck,
and so had taken her in tow; and he hoped the

lady would, an the patchwork quilt of a beast were indeed hers, not forget that he had walked all the way but two miles, which two were indeed the sorest of the road; had forgot (on further question) what town he was from, had forgot how far it was, but thought he could find his road again; had forgot the gentleman's name that sent him, and even, he thought, his own.   And Sir Michael laughed at the cunning of the fellow's folly, paid him well, and bade him go home and find his memory.   So, having drunk his ale, he trudged off with a sea bow and a twinkle in his eye more knowing than his words, but paused to twist his face over his shoulder and his thumb significantly toward the mare, saying he thought her mane in sore need of a good combing; and so off, leaving me sick at heart for news, that, pulling through the knots of Meg's matted neck-hair, I did speedily encounter in form of a letter securely tied beneath the tangled mass.   And, the string cut, seal broken, and paper unfolded, this is what we read within:

" *To my very dear Friends and Saviors both,* SIR MICHAEL DRAYTON *and* MISTRESS PHILIPPA, *his most sweet Daughter.*

"I write within thirty hours of leaving you, having already found a ship to set me beyond reach of harm.

"Good Meg did carry me well, and is, I hope, little worse of the twenty mile she ran in her never-changing

stride, with never a false step and scarce one sweat drop ;
and I do truly think she hath eyes of a cat. 'T is not
her fault if her back be first cousin to a handsaw, nor
mine that saddles grow not in the hedgerows hereabout.

"It was two of the morning when I roused from his
sleep old Jeremiah Soames, that I have known since
Lady Mary did bring me, a sickly child, to Bridport for
the sea-bathing. His boat is now about sailing for the
fishing, and in the meantime Meg has been well hid in
his curing-shed, and I in his little upper chamber. He
would not, for caution, advance his hour to drop out of
harbor, but once he has a fair offing will make a course
for the French coast, or, if the wind serve, up Channel
through the Straits for a Dutch port—Flushing perhaps,
or Rotterdam. I have yet no clear purpose for the future, but already some thought to obtain a commission
to serve under the great John Sobiesky against the Turk.
It were some pleasure, in these days when Christians will
be ever cutting each the other's throat for cause of heresy,
to rise a little above the policy of dog-eating dogs, and
to stand with men of all opinions for Christ against the
Infidel.

"To my mother I must not now run the danger of
writing, for since I know not surely where she is, whether
in London or at Royston, the letter might well fall into
other hands. So I will ask you, my two friends (the two
best I do suppose that ever man had), by some means to
advise her of all that has happened, and to convey to her
my great love and duty. To her at Royston I will write
so soon as I shall be landed, and in certainty of what is
best to be done.

"To you, Philippa, my old comrade, the letter all for
your private perusal that is in my mind must remain un-
written. 'T is not fit I should now ask more of you than

the life I have received at your hands in the moment when my own were stained with blood. For, though I do piously trust it is rather the stain that a soldier must bear than the murderer's, sinking through till the soul itself is spotted, yet will I now say no word but what your kind father's eyes may read in the same moment with your own. Yet, even with a price, 't is very like, set on my head, let me be in thought your old comrade, that do in exile most bitterly regret I saw not your face of late, guessing from the mellow notes of your voice how fair it has become.

"To you, Sir Michael, I would say, knowing not what report has run of the deed I did, that I truly believe yourself had done no less, placed as I was placed. I meant not indeed to kill the man, but, when I remember, can scarce find it in my heart to be sorry that he died.

"To both of you I am grateful beyond any proof of words. If the chance come you will know I speak truth, and am indeed the true servant of you both till death and after.

"E. ROYSTON."

At another time the approach of a thing so rare among us as a coach had taken my mind off the most ingenious tale or history ever printed. But the tale is not written, nor like to be, that could for me vie in interest with this simple letter. Being then in my second reading of it, while Sir Michael, content with one perusal over my shoulder, had in kindness walked away along the terrace to the steps of the great door, leaving me to squeeze a second cup of sweetness, as it were, for my sole drinking, out of that letter, I neither knew that a coach had come, nor that my father was leading from it in my direction the Lady Mary Royston.   And I, looking up in great joy of the letter, encountered with my eyes, in which I doubt not the light of my happiness was plain, her noble and austere countenance frowning upon me in manifest displeasure.   But I was not dashed in my spirits, as perhaps she intended, by the gloom of her regard, partly because in serious things my father had long ceased to use me as a child, and partly because I guessed that, with his habit of kindness that was ever mindful of the small matters that do please women, he had left to me the pleasant task to tell of the letter.   So I dropped my lady the finest courtesy I was mistress of, very freely thereafter smiling in her face, the letter whipt behind my back.

"Mistress Drayton seems but little cast down with all these terrible doings, Sir Michael," said her ladyship.

My father smiled grimly, but left reply to me, who answered: "Nay, dear madam, for we have but now received this news of Mr. Royston, which I believe as much intended for your ladyship as for my father and me."   And, seeing by his face my father was willing, I handed her the letter.

With little courtesy she seized, and with great

greediness perused, the letter, and her face was the
face of a woman that tears at food after a great
fasting; yet midway, at that passage, as I suppose,
wherein I was peculiarly addressed, she looked from
the letter to me in a manner to call to my mind
those words which, in my eagerness to give ease to
the mother's anxiety, I had forgotten the son to
have used. With that memory, and under her gaze,
the blood came hotly to my face, and I was glad
when her eyes speedily fell again to the letter,
which when she had finished, the heart of the
woman within broke down the iron gates of pride
and jealousy that had shut in the mother, even as
they had so long shut out the friends of her son;
for she now opened her arms to me, taking me to
her bosom, and weeping over me tears of joy, while
she blessed us, father and daughter, for the saving
of her boy's life, declaring herself to be a jealous
and wicked old woman, but, now she knew him
safe, a very happy one, if her friends and Ned's
would but forgive her.

When after a while she was soothed to a calmer
temper of mind, Lady Mary turned her regard to
my person and countenance, saying to Sir Michael
that I had grown out of all knowledge, which I
thought little wonderful, since it was some eight
years since she had set eyes upon me.

" So this young madam," she said, patting me on

the shoulder kindly enough, yet still with the grand air of the Court dame to a rustic damsel, "this is the child I have all these years envied and feared! I do trust, my dear, we shall be fast friends." Then after a little pause she added, as if in fear she had said too much: "But I would not have you think too gravely, Mistress Philippa, of what is said in that letter."

"That, madam, I could not do," I replied, leaving her in some doubt, it seemed, of my meaning. For, after a moment's musing:

"I will be plain with you, my child," she said. "I mean, although I am much your debtor, and do desire your love, I would not have you look to marry my son. He is yet but a lad, and I have a different purpose for him."

"Indeed, madam," I said with a little courtesy, "that must be, I think, as he wills."

"But you, my dear, who risked your good name of late to save his life, must be, I believe, of the mettle to deny your own happiness, were such denial plainly for his good," said her ladyship; and I was glad that the last week had taught me in some measure to conceal my thought.

"Nay, dear madam," I answered, holding my anger close within my heart, "I cannot believe that you think any woman will deny your son."

Whereat my dear father laughed softly, and my

lady looked upon me searchingly, as wondering
what animal this might be that looked so tender,
and yet was not wholly innocent of claws. Her
good humor, however, was speedily recovered, although it was long before she spoke again on that
delicate subject.

But she kept her purpose of friendship, giving me
constant and kindly welcome when I would ride
over to Royston, and coming herself once or more
in a month to us at Drayton. And in the two or
three years that followed her son's departure it was
to her kind instruction and wholesome advice that
I owed what advance I made in manner, bearing,
and knowledge of a greater world than I had seen;
she was, in short, just such a friend as my father's
daughter had need of; for there be many things
women learn only from each other; and, knowing
by some intuition of nature the need I was·in, I
was glad indeed, for all her intermittent asperities,
that it was Ned's mother that did take up the task
of leading me from the way of the hoyden into
something of the grace of womanhood.

As a pupil, indeed, she found in me little food of
complaint, but would be out with me for weeks at a
time if Sir Michael received a letter from Ned out
of his turn, as she counted, or one that covered
more paper than her last. But I fearing her not at
all, and she being a lady of high courage and loving

fearlessness in another, by degrees she came to love
me, and to forego much of her privilege of unrea-
soning displeasure.

The manners in which she was bred were more
akin to the severer model of the reign of the first
Charles than proper to this lighter age; but she had
never been wholly cut off from the great world, and,
knowing well what was doing and what changes
making, she professed inculcating a judicious modi-
fication of old and new, that should leave a young
woman open neither to the ridiculous charge of
aping her grandmother nor to the censure of shaping herself upon the frail and beautiful women of a
dissolute Court.   My wardrobe, too, at my father's
desire, she took in hand.   And I confess that this
was my favorite branch of study with my new
teacher; and when I remember the gowns that were
made in Taunton and the two that were fetched all
the way from London, and the changing, turning,
fitting, shaping, and trying done at Royston by my
lady, her woman, and myself, I am free to admit
that this matter of gowns was perhaps for more in
bringing about our lasting friendship than any other
thing that passed between us.   For here my lady
was not, as in the more serious domain of manners,
under a desire of reverting to the days of her own
upbringing, displaying rather the perennial youth
that, behind the deepening wrinkles of age, lurks

ever fresh in the feminine heart. She was in the
choice of my attire all for the newest mode, holding,
she would say, each fashion as it arose right and
seemly, if set out upon the person of one that had
the wit and discretion to fit new forms to her own
needs and the counsels of modesty. I wish I may
have done a little to lighten for Lady Mary the
tedium of those days while Ned was from home,
since I am deeply her debtor, as a maid must be to
her who takes up, in how slight soever a manner,
the office of the mother she has lost.

During the months of September and October of
that same year we lived in great horror and dread
of my Lord Chief Justice Jeffreys, whose terrible
circuit, I thank God, it does not fall to me even in
part to describe. For this storm passed us in Drayton and Royston safely by, though we both saw
and heard, as it were, the flash of its lightning and
roll of its thunder. The doings, however, of that
wicked and shameless man, so terribly disgracing
his high office and that of him from whom he de-
rived it, seemed to hold a ghastly and irresistible
attraction for my father. Every report, printed,
written, or spoken, that he could come at he de-
voured. The concern he showed in all this cruel
travesty of justice began with the report that reached
him in September of the trial and execution in Win-
chester of the Lady Alice Lisle — a case too well

known to need my telling, except in so far as it
affected Sir Michael.

John Lisle, a man high in the military service of
the Protector Cromwell, had once done great kindness to my father, who had come to know both him
and his wife, and to regard them with an affection
saddened only by the part the husband had adopted
in the affairs of the nation. The news of what he
called her murder moved him profoundly, and he
pursued the Chief Justice in his mind, as it were,
throughout his Bloody Assize, as one who waits to
see a bolt fall from Heaven on a malefactor beyond the reach of justice merely human. Of that
martyred lady I heard him one day speak in accents
of deep sorrow to Madam Royston, who, though
going with him heartily in abhorrence of the crime
done in the name of justice, took quick exception
to the title commonly bestowed on Mistress Lisle.

" For I do marvel, dear Sir Michael," she said,
" that you, being of such principles as you are,
should make use of a title bestowed by Cromwell in
blasphemous parody of that ennobling power which
on earth is granted to the Lord's Anointed alone."

" If God ever sent a lady on this sinful earth,"
said the old man, with a kind of holy exaltation in
his countenance, " Alice Lisle was she. And by
this, Lady Mary, she bears higher title and brighter
crown than the highest of her murderers. And I

7

pray that the fate of Gomorrah may not fall on
the land where such things are done.'' And Lady
Mary, perceiving well who was intended by that
word *murderer*, dared not reply, but marvelled much
afterwards, as I knew by words she would from time
to time let fall, whither my father's musings were
leading him. Which was, indeed, but to the same
goal to which the tide of events was leading us all.

Now ever since the hanging of those two men in
Drayton village, although Peter Emmet had continued to heat and hammer iron in the usual way,
nothing had been heard of Simon, his father, nor of
Prudence, his daughter. But one fine morning in
mid-October, when my Lord Chief Justice was well
back in London, receiving much honor and reward
for the evil he had wrought and the grief he had left
among us, but no thanks from any man for the only
good thing he ever did by us in the west (I mean
the leaving us), as I was going to the kitchen, my
father being not yet out of his chamber, I passed by
that little dark room we did use to call the steward's. But whether it were butler's pantry, museum
of weapons out of all date and fashion, or the place
where a steward should hold his audits, pay his
wages, and keep his books, a stranger had been hard
put to it to tell. I marked that the door stood
partly open, a thing unusual since we had none to
use it, and, peering within, perceived old Simon

poring over a book of accounts the most naturally
in the world.   Indeed, had it not been for some
trembling of the hand that held the pen, and the
great emaciation of his countenance, I might almost
have forgotten he had been absent at all, so fit and
proper was his presence there.   And the thought
of this put in my head, I think, the best and kindest
manner of welcoming his return; for I just nodded
my head to him, and said: " Ah, Simon, 't is a
fair morning, is it not ?   I trust the old Naseby
wound and the rheumatism are better."   And the
old man turned to me a face full of gratitude, that
'showed a fresh-healed scar upon the forehead and a
shaking smile about the lips.

" I am well recovered, pretty mistress, " he said;
then perceiving, perhaps, that in both dress and
manner I was grown deserving of a more formal address, he added, " Madam Philippa, I would say."

And so I left him in haste to persuade my father
to accept this aged prodigal's return even as I had
done.   And thus it came about that Simon Emmet
slipped back into his old place among us without
question asked; and I at least should never certainly have known he had been with Monmouth,
nor that he was the man that did escape that night
from the barn, if I had not, no long time after his
return, taken his granddaughter Prudence into the
house to be my handmaid, and in some sort, as it

proved, my companion. For she came to me, having returned to her father's house on the same day as Simon to us, and begged me, in pretty rustic manner, and with tears in her pretty eyes, that I would take her into my service, being determined, she said, to serve, if she might, her who had saved the brave gentleman that had so nearly given his life for her protection. And she proved indeed a good servant, a merry companion, and afterwards, upon a great occasion, as will be seen, a friend not to be despised.

In the month of November there came to Sir Michael a long letter from Mr. Edward Royston. It was dated from The Hague, and contained matter of much interest to us all. I see that I have here written his name in style more formal than I have hitherto generally used. And I let it so stand, to serve as a sign of the reserve to which I had by degrees found myself obliged, at least in speaking of him. For to Lady Mary, as was but natural after those words of hers which I have already given, I never mentioned him if it could in any way be avoided, while of Prue I was too proud to seek sympathy, although I loved best her prattle when it was of Ned.

And I knew that Sir Michael had been hurt more than a little in his pride by that same speech of Lady Mary, and sought to make me forego all thought of her son by speaking of him only in the rare and painful manner that some use of the dead. Yet when he saw my face, eager, I doubt not, against my will, as he looked up from the last words of this letter, he rose and left the room, the letter lying there before me on the table, muttering reluctantly some words to the effect that I should read it if I pleased, an the subject had interest for me. So read it I very speedily and hungrily did, learning that after his safe arrival in Holland (of which we had a month before been advised through a letter to his mother) he had made his way to The Hague; that there he had sought out a good old merchant that had been a correspondent in business of the late Mr. Nathaniel Royston, and remembered him, as did many another, with much kindness, on account as much of his great sobriety of judgment and honesty of dealing as of the many successful ventures they had together undertaken.

Now this Mynheer van Bierstenhagen belonged, in that country where party spirit runs so high, to the faction that was the more patriotically opposed to the influence and aggressions of His Majesty King Lewis of France—to that party, I mean, which followed after the Stadtholder, who was that Prince of Orange that had married, when I was child of nine years, the Princess Mary, the eldest child of our reigning King James. "And when it is remembered," wrote Mr. Royston, " that the Prince is himself the grandson of King Charles I., 't is little wonder that all the talk here among the exiled and malcontent English and Scotch is of the Princess Mary and her husband, she being next in succession to the throne and he so nearly allied." And the letter went on to tell how he had secured, through the influence of Mynheer van Bierstenhagen, a favorable introduction to the Prince, had told him his story, and received from him a commission in one of his regiments of horse. For this fat old Dutch merchant was held at the Court of The Hague in high esteem for his wealth, his zeal for the public good, and chiefly, no doubt, added Mr. Royston, for the reason that a wealthy burgher on the Prince's side in politics was not to be slighted, when most of his class were of French leanings, the Stadtholder's chief support being among the common people.

But in all this not one word, beyond a civil message of regard, for poor Philippa, who spent some tears and much thought to come at an answer to the question, whether her old comrade began to forget what she must ever remember, or was but obstinately adhering to his resolve to say no word of those feelings which he held forbidden by the cause of his flight out of England. No answer could I get to this for all my vexing of my mind

with questions, till one day Prue did find me in
tears, and contrived, my pride being a little weakened with a consciousness of swollen and blubbered
cheeks, to get some part of my woes from me.
Whereupon she nodded sagely her little head, and
asked if he was one wont to change.

" For sure, Mistress Phil," she said, " you have
by all accounts known him long enough to tell."

In some indignation I answered he was not.

" I thought he was not, indeed," says Prue;
" and you may take my word for it, madam, he but
waits to become a great captain in this army of the
Dutch to come riding home and claim you, as great
as a lord."

At this I was at first much pleased, perceiving
how likely a thing it was that Ned should so act;
and next I was angry with Prudence for her wisdom.
But when I petulantly would know how she came to
read him more justly than I, she said a little sadly
that it was not her own case she was judging, and
saw the clearer for being but an onlooker. For
which I kissed her, and so an end.

There is no need for me to tell ill what others
have told well; the history, I mean, of the three
years before the coming of His Highness of Orange.
I suppose I had taken little note of the affairs of
the country had I not heard much talk of them between my dear father and Mr. Telgrove. And as

time went on it was curious to note how both would
make me a party to their discussion of public matters, the reason being at first, I think, that their
differences required an arbiter, and an ignorant
girl was better than none, having indeed this advantage when fulfilling the office of judge, that
there was no need to abide by her decision; and
later, when they had begun to approach, if not
an agreement, at least a temporary alliance, they
would still be drawing me in because it had become
a thing of custom.   I learned then in this manner
more of the state of the nation than if I had read
every word of the London *Gazette* as it appeared in
the capital; and when, in the spring of the year
1687, the country was deeply perturbed by the
publication of the Declaration of Indulgence, which
my father and Mr. Telgrove abhorred in common,
I was able to bring the two old men at last to a
position of sympathy — representing to my tutor
that my father could never wish him to forego such
liberties as the Indulgence offered; to my father
that, in his heart, Mr. Telgrove scarce grudged the
same to those of my dear mother's faith; and to
both, that they were united to refuse a boon thus
illegally offered, lest a door should so be opened to
greater evils than the Indulgence pretended to cure.
They said I was a little stateswoman, kissed the
one my face, and the other my hand, and joined

their own in the closest grip of friendship. Yet all
this time my father neither let drop nor allowed
one word of changing the head that wore the crown,
while Mr. Telgrove was, I think, too wise to press
him in that direction.

And so, from London and all parts of the country,
we heard week after week that things went from bad
to worse; while at home I was riding new horses,
prinking myself out in new dresses, and reading new
books when I could get them, and the old when I
must; till I began at last to fancy, I suppose, that
I was grown a woman, and a person of no little
importance and consideration.

CHAPTER VII

CHRISTOPHER KIDD was a tenant farmer upon the Drayton land. Moreover, he was a suitor, earnest as bashful, for the hand of my little abigail, Prudence Emmet. While, therefore, matter of business might bring him four times in the year to the Manor House to speak with Sir Michael, love was used to fetch him thrice in a week dangling about the place for the chance of being well snubbed, mightily put upon, and most truculently railed at by little Prue. And she, for all her cruelty, was not to be thought altogether indifferent to this stalwart yeoman (for he was of that stock, though himself but a tenant). I at least could never think her intention to him unkindly after being witness of her distress when Mr. Kidd rode southwards on my father's behalf to seek news of the Prince of Orange more certain than the bare rumor that had reached us of his landing at Brixham. For no sooner was he departed than Prudence, although saucy with him even in her last words, became much cast down in spirit, fearing he would not return, and I know not what beside.

Now all the world knows that it was upon the fifth day of November, in the year 1688, that His Highness set foot on shore. And I remember well that the fifth fell that year upon a Monday. For ever since he had received by an unknown hand a printed copy of the Prince's Declaration, in which was set forth not only His Highness's purpose to come to the rescue of the liberties of England, but also at great length the reasons of this design, my father had resolved to throw in his lot with him; and, this resolve once made, he greatly desired to be among the very first to offer support, saying a Drayton should never be in the number of those that must wait to see how the cat would jump. And so he was, through the last days of October and the first week of November, in a great excitement of waiting ever for news that did not come. And, the first rumor of His Highness's coming reaching us on the morning after that landing in Torbay, Sir Michael came to the still-room, hobbling with his stick (for his wound was again troubling him) to find me, being in great hope that the news would prove true that the Prince had made choice of our coast, and not, as had been expected, that of Yorkshire. Now I was busied with the brewing of our gooseberry wine, while Prudence and two of the maids were mending the house-linen under my eyes for the greater despatch and fineness of their work. And it was of a Tuesday that this mending was always done, for Sir Michael had instilled much of the old soldier's order and system into my manner of housekeeping. But this day I do think the gooseberry wine had little thought or care, for to me the coming of the Prince meant the coming of Mr. Royston, that I had not encountered since I was a woman grown; it being indeed three years and over since he went out of the country, and near upon twice that space of time since we had so met that we might fairly perceive, the one what manner of man, the other what manner of woman, we were. And I laughed softly in myself to think at what advantage I held him. For him I should surely know among a thousand, while he—well, it would be as it should fall. For, knowing as I knew him, I was sure that if at all he remembered me, he had doubtless all those years been holding still in his inner eye the picture of a little, ugly, and ill-kempt hoyden. And I laughed again, and wondered why I laughed, finding my mind something of a puzzle to itself. For, while I knew I was no longer ill to look upon, I found my face grow hot at the thought of Ned's eyes on me, which before I had never done.

It was then upon the Tuesday that we heard the great news; upon the Wednesday that Mr. Kidd, at the instance of Sir Michael, rode off Exeter way to

hear more.   And so, in suspense little relieved by
further and growing rumor, we waited until the
Saturday, when about five in the afternoon Prudence, ever on the watch, was the first to spy her
lover as he rode up the avenue.   His horse was
caked over with mud to the very girths, for the
roads were foul with long and heavy rains.   Nor
had the mud spared the rider; but the soil borne by
the two was as nothing to the weight of mystery and
the burden of importance that I marked in Farmer
Kidd's bearing as he flung himself from the saddle,
and, brushing by little Prue with the briefest of
nods, strode big with news to the little parlor beyond the hall, where Sir Michael did use to sit of
an evening.   And then, as I looked from the window of the hall where I sat, I knew from her face
that Prudence would surely wed him some day,
but first would make the rude fellow most bitterly
repent that slight of counting her next to politics
and warfare.

For my part, since I was not Prue, I soon forgave
the man, in return for the great story he had to tell
of.the Prince's entry into the city of Exeter.   For
he had beheld that great pageant, with news of
which all the west was soon to be ringing, and, indeed, in no great space, the whole country.   And,
if it gained as much in many mouths as I have since
reason to suppose it gained in Farmer Kidd's, 't is

little wonder it was soon believed an army of giants
and magicians had crossed the sea in aid of the
Protestant religion. The Earl of Macclesfield, who
had come out of Holland with the Prince, leading a
band of English gentlemen, two hundred strong,
was with his following an object of wondrous ad-
miration to Mr. Kidd, who would never tire, I
thought, in telling of their great Flanders horses,
their glittering armor, and their negro slaves, one
to each man, in white and feathered turbans. And
then it was the bridge of boats laid across the Exe
in the twinkling of an eye to give passage to the
wagons; the twenty pieces of ordnance—great brass
cannon, only to be moved by teams of sixteen horses
to each; the stature of the men; the new sort of
muskets; the order of the discipline, so that none
would so much as steal a hen from a cottage garden,
but all things were as willingly paid for as supplied.
Then Kidd must draw comparisons between these
military manners and those of Kirke's and Trelaw-
ney's Regiments of Foot, as seen in the troubles of
three years ago; and all this time poor I waiting on
his words but half interested, and satisfied not at
all, until I could lead him, too full of his own great
importance to perceive the guidance, to some description of the Prince's Swedish Regiment of
Horse. For it was to this body that Mr. Royston
had, it was now some months, been transferred,

receiving at the same time promotion to the rank
of captain.

So as long as our messenger, between the draughts
of his ale fetched him by Prudence with hands as
willing as the pouting mouth would fain have shown
her reluctant, would descant of the black chargers,
the black armor, the great broadswords, and the
furred cloaks of this same Swedish cavalry, I listened
as eagerly as my father had done to it all.   And as
the man dwelt on the gallant show they did make
I was plotting to bring him to some mention of
what I doubted not was among them the gallantest
figure of all, but was prevented by my father asking
if Mr. Kidd would ride the same road again, and
carry a letter to His Highness of Orange.   " With
the best meal we can make you on short notice, Mr.
Kidd, to comfort you within, and the best nag in
Drayton stables between your knees ? " said Sir
Michael, in conclusion of his request.

Christopher Kidd was ready enough not only to
oblige Sir Michael, but also, I believe, to return to
the great sights and doings of which his mouth was
so full; so, he being despatched in care of Prudence
to be fed, I was left with my father.   And when I
had given him his writing things he opened his mind
a little to me.

"'I had gathered from Kidd, before you entered,"
he said, " that the common people are ready to do

all and risk all for the Prince, but that since he
landed no man of substance and gentry has joined
his army." And here for a moment he did bite the
feather of his pen, and looked in my face, so that I
knew that the mind that was now long made up still
felt pain to tell its resolve. Then he went on thus:
" You that know me so well, little daughter Phil,
have guessed, I do not doubt, this many a day how
my mind was going in these matters. And seeing
that it was decided, contrary to the use and belief
of my life, in favor of His Highness before ever he
came, I cannot now in honor hang back. It cannot
be recruits for rank and file, raw soldiers at the
best, that he needs, with such an army at his back;
but I believe it is rather the countenance and support of the solid men of the country he asks, to take
from his presence the odious seeming of invasion.
And I am in great fear it may all miscarry, even as
Monmouth's wicked business, on account of the
behavior of those who, willing to bring, yet fear
to welcome His Highness. You have, I do think,
partly seen what it has cost your old Cavalier father
to adopt a part against his old master's son. But
it would cost me more if my hand were not as good
as my thought. Yet, if I so make it, I risk all that
is yours who but enter upon life,— little for myself
whose sands are at the last falling grains. Sedgemoor, Kirke, Jeffreys, were summer-evening ripples

on a mill-pond to the storm that is coming, if His
Highness meet defeat in the field or abandon his
undertaking, which last I take it he is like enough
to do, if forced to the appearance of a foreign
enemy.   I did purpose now writing a letter to His
Highness.   The act will be mine, but the danger,
my daughter, will be yours.   How shall it be ? ''

I pushed the inkhorn to him over the table.

'' Write, dear sir,'' I said.   '' Your hand shall
not fail your thought for me.   And I would mine,''
I added, putting a hand in his, '' were as strong for
the cause my heart holds the better as yours has
ever been.''

He looked in my face as he took it, and the
old gleam flashed a moment in his age-saddened
eyes.

'' My lass,'' he said, '' there 's Drayton in you
for two men,'' and began to write forthwith; but
soon paused, saying: '' Wilt run, child, to the
stable, and choose for Mr. Kidd ?   We have here
no better head for horseflesh, and my old piece cannot keep these new nags well distinguished.''   And
as I reached the door he called after me that I
should not give him Skewbald Meg, whose appearance would do little honor to his errand or His
Highness of Orange.   And I cried back that poor
Meg would break her heart with the weight of the
man, and so to the stable.   For, since her midnight

8

ride to Lyme, I was never pleased that any but I should mount the mare.

And when I returned to my father the letter was written, which he would have me read. As I remember, it ran in this way:

" YOUR HIGHNESS,—I have within this hour in which I write received the certain news of Your Highness's coming into England. Without delay, then, I do myself the honor to inform Your Highness that I have attached myself and my household to his party and interest. The reasons that have led me to this are for the most part set out in that noble declaration published by Your Highness before his coming among us. Yet it is not without great pain that I, an old servant and soldier of Your Highness's grandfather of blessed memory, King Charles I., find myself inditing an epistle that sets me in a manner at war with his son. It is written with a hand that now finds the pen heavier than the sword was wont to be. I am too old and too infirm to pay to Your Highness in person the respect I feel. And I am too old a soldier to embarrass Your Highness's encampment with even my small body of men; it is possible they are not needed. Yet Your Highness is to know that they are to the number of a dozen, at his command, living mean-time at free quarters, and getting such drill and practice in arms and evolutions, both men and beasts, as two old-fashioned soldiers can give. May God use Your Highness as you shall use this unhappy land. Your Highness's most respectful and obedient servant,

" M. DRAYTON."

And this letter, somewhat proud in its tones, as I thought (but not one word of it would Sir Michael change), reached the hand of the Prince by that of Christopher Kidd early upon the following morning, which was Sunday. It seems, from what I afterwards heard, that being deep in affairs His Highness did not break the seal until after the great and solemn service in the cathedral that was that morning held.

Now the bishop had fled to London before the gates of Exeter were opened to the Prince. The dean had followed him, and from this service the canons of the chapter carefully abstained themselves. Even the prebendaries and the singers of the choir fled from their stalls on the first words of Dr. Burnet's reading from the pulpit the Prince's famous Declaration. So, for all the pomp and the noble sermon of that great divine, it was in no mild or pleasant humor that His Highness returned to his lodging at the Deanery. Here chancing to open my father's letter, he took great pleasure in it, remarking to Mr. Bentinck that there was, after all, hope that he had not come in vain, when so stanch and famous a Cavalier as Sir Michael Drayton, of whom he had often heard, did so address him. He sent at once for Christopher Kidd, and very graciously bade him thank Sir Michael for his promptitude, which, he said, had done much to console him in a grievous hour; adding that he would send in good time for his little band, and hoped himself to pass, within some days, so near to Drayton that he might thank him in person. And with this message Christopher returned.

I have been thus particular because I would have it known that my father was the first of that great and distinguished number of gentlemen and noble-men that soon began to flock to the Prince's stand-ard. I know it has been said that Mr. Burrington, of Crediton, was the first that came in, bringing with him a good company of followers. Now it is well known that Mr. Burrington did not arrive in Exeter till the Monday. But Sir Michael Drayton's adhesion to the cause being conveyed by letter, and his men kept a-drilling at his cost until they should be required, has put my dear father's name out of the histories, where it should stand as that of the man who first held out a hand to comfort a great Prince oppressed to despondency of mind by a backwardness that seemed ingratitude.

CHAPTER VIII

A T an early hour on Monday there were gathered
on the level turf that stretched beneath my
chamber window some five and twenty men, with
as many horses, from whom Sir Michael, with old
Emmet to help him, was now to select that twelve
he had promised to hold at the service of the
Prince. And I thought it a clear mark of my
father's nature that he did prefer furnishing a small
number, but serviceable, when, had he measured
his own importance by the rule that many gentlemen at that time did use, he might have sent a
hungry and unruly band three times as great.

From my window the humors of the scene were
strange and various, and at first not a little laugh-
able. Simon bustled to and fro, urging and direct-
ing stable lads sweating under load after load of
armor, and weapons from the hall, the armory, and
the steward's room. At last, all being in some
manner armed and mounted, they were gotten into
a semblance of order, and their instruction and
weeding out began. At first, I say, I laughed
much at one man's hopeless perplexity in handling

together sword and reins, or at another, being
undersized and of even less strength than skill, to
see him strive in vain to control a fat and lusty
charger, fresh from the plough, and grown wanton
to feel so little weight upon his back and none at his
tail.   But, as one after another these were discarded
and went their ways, some in evident dudgeon
and others in as plain relief of mind, and as the
dwindling number grew even more martial in mount,
bearing, and accoutrement, the sight did begin to
make some corresponding emotion in my heart;
and I almost found myself wishing that I had been
born a man, the more that my dear father had that
same morning lamented there was none of Drayton
blood to lead the little band.   He had let drop, too,
some words, as bitter as few, of my brother Philip,
and had told me then, for the first time, how my
mother's two children did come to bear one name.

" Your mother bore her first child, little Phil,"
he said, " in the early days of the horse-breeding
that has brought us so much wealth.   And I loved
the beasts, spending once my last guineas and the
price of a farm besides to bring to my stud the Barbary sire you remember.   So when I knew it was a
man child I called him Philip, saying he should love
horses as his father, and do great things for the
breed, and his name be famous in England.   And
as he grew 't was harder to get him inside a stable

than to keep most lads without it. To this day I
know not if he would distinguish your ugly Meg
from the noblest charger of His Highness of Orange.
When ten years were gone, and there was again
hope for us, I said, if it prove a girl, we 'll e'en try
the name on her. And give it you I did, with a
little tag or handle to mark you woman. Poor
child," he added kindly, yet sorrowfully, " 't is not
thy fault thou hast the wrong sex, and, Gad 's
my life! you have been a better son to me than
Philip."

" And I love horses, sir," I answered, " and, indeed, many other things that my Lady Mary will
ever say are not women's matters." Whereupon
we laughed at Lady Mary a little, and the matter
dropped, as he went to the muster. But I knew he
felt in great need of a son that day, or he had never
come so near throwing reproach on me that he loved
so well for a fault that at another time he would not
have had me change for a man's best virtue. Yet,
as I gazed from the window at this threshing and
winnowing of men, to make of them soldiers, the
memory of that reproach rankled a little in me, and
a small plot began to take form.

At the time when I commenced housewife at
home I had in a disused chamber above found a
closet filled with clothes once worn by my half-
brothers of the elder family that I had come into

the world too late to know. These were the only
relics, I believe, of three good and honest gentlemen
that, in the strange and ghostly manner of a child
as I then was, I reverenced much, and even contrived to love a little; I had therefore rescued many
of these garments from the moth, and, deciding in
my mind by the varying fashions and much guess-
work to which brother the different pieces had belonged, bestowed them in three ordered piles in a
wide shelf of my great oak press. " So these," I
would say, as I brushed and folded them once a
month, " were Henry's; these Maurice used to
wear." And I always held that the morion and
the back- and breast-pieces, which were all the
armor found with the clothes, had belonged to
Rupert. For they were wondrous small for a man,
and I knew he had been the least of them all in
stature, and had scarce attained his full growth
when he fell at Salisbury.

Now, in my excitement with the martial sounds
without, and a good part, I doubt not, in mischief
that meant going no further than gently avenging
his slight of my sex upon my father, I suddenly
thought of this wardrobe so little proper to a young
maid's chamber; and at once began with trembling
hands to choose from my store such garments as I
thought would best become the son my father
wished me, giving, I doubt not, an undue value to

color and to that size which nearest approached my
own, and little to coherence of fashion.

The troop were now reduced to eleven, for Christopher Kidd, making the twelfth, and having leave
of absence after his services to my father in riding
to Exeter, was expected to return from his farm but
for the afternoon's drill; lacking whom, the rest
had been dismissed for dinner at noon, which was
the hour when I began so unmaidenly to dress myself out in my dead brothers' clothes. It was a
business that occupied me longer than I had
thought for, and when it came to the boots and
the armor I wished I had Prue's nimble fingers to
help me. But she, I knew, though she would
never have confessed so much, was somewhere
watching for the return of Christopher. At last,
however, I made shift to fasten together about me
the back- and breast-pieces; for the boots, I stuffed
the toes of each with an handkerchief, and so made
them sit passably well, the practising which device
called to my mind how in the dark I had done the
same for Ned to the filthy brogues he wore in
leaving us. So, being dressed at all points to my
satisfaction, the next thing was to contrive reaching
the stables unobserved. For this my reasons were
two: I knew the men would soon reassemble, and
wished, in my folly, to take part in their evolutions
in such manner that none could forbid without

openly chiding me before the yokels; which I knew neither my father nor Emmet would do, whatever their censures might be in private.   But far stronger was the other reason for privacy.   Being now ready, I began to feel shame of what I was doing, and, being too petulant and obstinate to give it up, I felt that a horse beneath me and the necessity of handling him in unwonted movements would do near as much to cover my shyness as the skirt I lacked.

Whether this be clear to a masculine reader or no, confident I was of a lessened sense of bareness, and so of greater boldness in the saddle.   Hearing, then, the bugle blown without, and seeing the men canter up by ones and twos from the stable, the few old soldiers among them roundly cursing the lag-gards, I opened my chamber door, peeped up and down the gallery, and made a bold run for the head of the great stair.   That it was before I reached it my sword, catching between my legs, did fling me prone, I must ever thank Providence.   Had it hap-pened in my descent with the same force, I had broken my neck at the foot of the stair.   For, though I could handle the small-sword, and even the heavier weapon of a soldier, " passably well for a maid," as Mr. Royston did use to say in the days when he taught me something of fence, yet never before, even in our games, had I worn one hung from my side.   I picked myself up more shamefaced

than hurt, and made my way sneakingly and gingerly, holding my sword in my left hand, down the
stair and into the great hall, making for its further
door which leads to the kitchens. I was already
half-way toward it, walking most cat-like in that
shyness so little fitted to my garb and action, when
I heard the heaving of a great sigh. Turning my
head, I saw, at the further end of the hall, standing
with his back to me, and gazing from a window, a
man dressed in sad-colored clothes. More quickly,
I suppose, than the stranger could turn to observe
me, I was through the door and in the flagged gallery that leads to the kitchens and pantries. Cutting across this gallery is a shorter one leading to a
side door of entrance to the house, and as I drew
near this I heard voices at the outer door. At once
I knew the speakers for Prue and Christopher Kidd,
and now more than ever did I feel that the salvation
of my plan was to get me astride of a good horse; I
would not, even to save changing my mind, a thing
always hateful to me, be seen walking thus dressed.
So, coming silently to a stand in hope that they
would move away, I was for some minutes an involuntary eavesdropper. The stables were opposite
this same door, with a paved yard between, and I
could tell by the sound of hoof on stone that Mr.
Kidd was mounted and on his way to the muster on
the other side of the house. But I believe that he

had learned since his first return from Exeter that it was ill policy to hide fresh news, good or bad, from little Prudence. Yet did he make some show of resistance. The first words that I clearly heard were his:

" But where is Sir Michael ? I have news."

" News good or ill, Mr. Kidd ? " says Prue.

" That is for him to say," replied Kidd. " Are they at the exercises, mistress ? "

" Nay, but Mr. Kidd — Christopher," said the little rogue, in tones most winning and persuasive, " will you not dismount and stay a while to pleasure me ? Shall I fetch you a horn of ale ? " Then there was silence for a little space, and I could fancy her little red and pouting mouth turned up to the man in such wise that it could scarce be three heart-beats ere his spurs would ring on the flags. Nor was it. And then she continued: " And the news, Mr. Kidd ? Perhaps it would not taint it if my lips should sip it first." And so a pause, and a little soft sound of kissing, with a small scream of formal hypocrisy.

Then Christopher: " Faith, mistress, a kiss from you would win all things from a man, even to his soul's health, let alone a trifle of news."

" I gave you no kiss," says Prue, saucily enough; " you did but take it."

" Then take my news," quoth Kidd, with a

stride, I thought, towards his horse. And then, I think, she did buy his news, and pay in advance. For although I cannot say that this time I heard the ring of the coin, yet Christopher's next words showed him proceeding to delivery of the goods. " You know, mistress, that Sir Michael would have me lead these men to the Prince when he shall call on them. So I have been to the farm to settle things for a long absence. I thought my nag here well recovered of his last week's ride to Exeter and beyond, but find there is little spirit left in him, and was ambling gently down the old road by the water-mill about an hour back, and cursing both luck and horse to be late for the work a-doing here, when there comes by a great coach, with much foul speech and cracking of whips. And whose face dost think I saw looking from the window, all drawn and wan ? "

" Oh, I know not," said Prue, in anger of impatience; " tell me, and quickly."

" Well, 't was Madam Royston," says Christopher.

" Lady Mary!" says Prue, with a little gasp. " What did she there ? "

" 'T is the very thing I would know, dear lass," replied Kidd. " The fellows round her were ill-looking, and she was about calling to me when she was dragged back within the coach."

" Well, you are a man," cried Prue, raising her voice in excitement.   " What did you do ? "

" Little to purpose, sweetheart," answered Kidd; and, though I was as eager now as little Prue to hear more, I could have laughed to note how the man took advantage of her emotion to edge in these lover's terms unchecked; " I spurred after them, but a fellow on a sorrel nag turned and drew a great pistol and let fly at me.   Do but see the hole his ball made in my coat."   And here I heard a very genuine cry of fear from Prudence.   And Kidd went on, with a slight note of exultation in his voice, the result, I do not doubt, of her perturbation.   " It did me no hurt, though it wanted but little, as you see, of sending me where I could never again see the prettiest maid in three counties. Well, that shot angered me, and I made at him. But he was the better mounted, and leapt his horse over the hedge, and so away over the fields, while I pounded heavily after on my tired beast.   When I gave over, the coach was far and my nag well-nigh foundered.   But one thing I learned of him."

" Ay," cried Prue eagerly, " and that was—— "

" That he was no true man, but a devilish priest of Rome."

" O Mr. Kidd," says Prue, " how you will ever be frighting a poor girl!   How knew you that ? "

" As he leapt the hedge," said Kidd, " being a

bad horseman, he was near losing his seat.   Arrived
the other side, he saved himself by clutching at the
sorrel's mane, and in that had almost lost both hat
and his red wig but for clutching at those in turn.
But as the wig shifted I saw his own hair, dark and
short, and a little round place atop, bald and shaven.
A priest he is, and Sir Michael loves not such cattle
on his land.   So indeed, dear Mistress Prudence, I
must find and tell him what is doing.   Will you not
grant me but one more ?   My news was worth
it.''

Whatever it were he asked, I do suppose he
shortly obtained it, for very soon I heard upon the
stones the hoofs of his departing horse.   Hoping
that Prudence would follow him round the back of
the house to see him join the little troop at exercise, I thought this was the moment for pressing on
to the stables.   So, wisely tucking my sword again
under my arm, I made a run for it, which took me
round the corner and fairly into the arms of Prudence, whom I clutched firm and close in my own to
save us both a fall.   At first her fright to be so
suddenly seized in the arms, as she thought, of
some ruffling gallant was luckily too great to let a
sound escape her; and when I loosed my hold and
clapped my hand upon her mouth, it began slowly
to dawn upon the terror-struck eyes raised to mine
in mute appeal that 't was none but I; whereupon,

being released, she fell to laughing most con-
sumedly, pointing at me the while a most derisive
finger, till I could not but think all was not well
with my unaccustomed attire, and shrank together
and cringed from her in fashion most unmanlike.

And, when she could for laughing, " Oh, dear
Mistress Phil ! " she cried, " whatever your plan in
this pretty masquerade, none will take you for a
man if you do stand so."

Which did but add anger to my desire of carrying
through my plan; so that, drawing my body most
martially erect, and seizing her by the shoulder with
my left hand, I raised the other as if to cuff her,
and threatened as much if she did not hold her
peace and immediately lend me her aid.   And this
did mightily sober the girl, who, seeing me so terrible, ran out at my bidding to the stable, returning
quickly with the news that there was not a man
about the place, all being gone to see the drilling.
Very bravely I then swaggered across the yard and
in among the horses that were left.   And there
Prudence followed, panting with excitement and,
as soon appeared, not without admiration of my
assumption of manhood.

" Oh, but indeed I ask your pardon, dear Mistress
Phil," she cried, " for so laughing at the figure you
made.   If you but carry it thus none who does not
know you for Mistress Philippa Drayton will know

you are not a man.   Do but let me set your beautiful hair more in fashion of the great wigs Mr. Kidd
tells me are worn by the gentlemen, even on horse-
back and in armor.''   And with a great coarse stable   ·
comb she pulled and twisted till she had my hair,
which for the first time I was glad grew not so long
as thick, to hang evenly round the shoulders behind, and over them in front in two heavy curling
masses.

" And now for a horse," I said, when this was
done.   It took no long time to see that my choice
lay between Meg, that I have already told of, and
Roan Charley, a gelding of no great size but great
beauty of proportion.   He was grandson of that
Barbary sire my father had purchased so dear to
enrich his stock.   Roan Charley had to the full the
spirit and much of the fleetness of the Drayton
barb, with more bone and greater power in the
hinder part; whence it came, I suppose, that he
was the best leaper I ever sat, while his grandsire
would not, or could not, clear so much as a fallen
tree-trunk.   He was generally accounted difficult
and contrary in handling, but he and I were seldom
long in coming at an understanding.

Now for the work I had been watching all morning from my window I had certainly preferred Old
Meg, as we had come to call the mare, more from
her sure and trusty manners than her years.   But,

9

for the odd and elfish look of her, my vanity bade
me pass her by and clap my father's best saddle on
Charley.   At first he gave me some trouble in this,
thinking, said Prue, some strange gallant was about
stealing him.   When he fidgeted a little with his
heels Prue screamed, and would not come near to
help.   The saddle was heavy and the sword mightily
in my way, and each time I would have flung the
first on Roan Charley's back, round would go his
hindquarters, and, as I followed, the sword would
again come between my legs and stop me, while he
eyed me with teeth gleaming and ears laid back.
At last I was fain to set down the saddle and caress
him with voice and hand, making love to him till
he knew me again, and, indeed, well-nigh said as
much.   After that, saddling and bridling were soon
done, and Charley led into the yard, where, Prue
being with much difficulty and in terror of her life
persuaded to take him by the head, I was soon upon
his back.

   Now here, as once or twice before, I must tell of
things that I did not know till after they were done.
For even though it seem somewhat to break the
thread of narrative to leave me running Roan
Charley in the park to use him to my handling and
my knees to my father's saddle, while I tell of
events, some far, and others close at hand but beyond my knowledge, yet I hold it ever more easy

for the reader to take his history, public or private, in order of occurrence, and so to hold in his hand all the threads that must knot together at that point for whose sake the story is told. For in life all is so large and complicate as to seem, in the little eye of man, confused and purposeless; and great part, I think, of our joy and interest in living it is found in the unexpected nature of its events. But in those pictures of life furnished us by drama, history, painting, or romance our pleasure is altogether of another kind. Here the artificer, choosing out of the multitudinous mesh threads such only as lead to his particular nodule of the mighty tangle, concerns himself and us with the convergence and final meeting of these; so that, if he but tell and we read aright, we see step by step the working of his little providence. And here our pleasure is not in astonishment, but in truth and sequence reasonably set forth. " This thing is coming," we say; or " That could have fallen no otherwise "; and we read on, and sometimes, perhaps, perceive some glimmer of the order lying in the greater skein. But all this Mr. Telgrove would call plagiarizing; and it comes, indeed, in the first instance, from his head. If he read it ever, he will confess me a better listener than he is wont to think.

CHAPTER IX

CAPTAIN ROYSTON'S troop was of that portion of the army which, after the pomp of entry into Exeter, had been quartered at Honiton. There, waiting at an equal distance from his own home and the city of Exeter, and unable to get so much as an hour's leave of absence, he fretted not a little at his situation, seeing that the further advance might be undertaken at any moment, and he be carried on the martial tide past both those havens his soul was longing after (but it was one in especial, if what he now saith must be believed). Upon the afternoon of that same Sunday whereon Dr. Burnet preached in the cathedral Captain Royston was surprised by a summons to report himself without delay before His Highness at headquarters. The order was brought by M. de Rondiniacque, a young Huguenot gentleman who had been transferred from a lieutenancy in Ginkel's Regiment to the personal staff of the Prince, on account not only of the charm of his manners and the quickness of his parts, but also, it seems, for the esteem in which his family was held by the veteran Count Schomberg, who, with hundreds of other French gentlemen of high birth and the proscribed religion, had left his country and attached himself to His Highness of Orange. M. de Rondiniacque and Captain Royston had long been fast friends, and both were glad of the ride together, and of such conversation as could be had in fifteen miles of wet and mud, travelled with the hard riding M. de Rondiniacque's orders enjoined. Arrived at the Deanery about seven o'clock of the evening, they were summoned at once to His Highness's presence, where they found beside the Prince none but Mr. William Bentinck.

In regard to the conversation that here took place, I am the better able to give some account of it that I have two narrations to draw upon—Captain Royston's, namely, and M. de Rondiniacque's.

As they entered the room, His Highness, seated at the table, was uttering the last words of a conversation, apparently of some earnestness, with Mr. Bentinck, of which, however, the only words that reached their ears were these: " No, William, no! Where I must trust so much I will trust all. The lad is true, and my interests are his."

These words, spoken in the French language, which the Prince used always with greater fluency and a nearer approach to exactness than the English, showed to Captain Royston with some clearness not only that the talk had been of him, but

also that Mr. Bentinck's words, which he had not
heard, had been in the nature of a warning. Knowing well that this faithful friend and servant of His
Highness had never looked on him with the same
favor shown him by the Prince, Captain Royston
was as little surprised by the slight he guessed as
troubled by the antipathy he knew. And he, being
too proud of nature to seek its reason, I was moved
one day many months after, and in happier times, to
enquire it myself of Mr. Bentinck, who very freely
and kindly told me that they had been in Holland
no little troubled with an inroad of gallows-birds
and broken men seeking asylum under the cloak of
persecution suffered for opinions political or religious. Hearing some talk of a man slain in anger,
he had rashly (as he said to me he now perceived)
classed Mr. Royston with these, and had on two
occasions declared himself opposed to his advancement; all which, I can well see, had in it the
makings of a very pretty quarrel but for the
haughty indifference of Captain Royston, leading
him, as it would often do, to contemn and eschew
explanation in his own behalf.

The Prince now turned sharply to Captain Royston, and at once informed him that he was chosen
for a service of great secrecy. " And I believe,
sir," said His Highness, " that I have chosen well.
For I know you, Captain Royston, to be a brave

man, a bold horseman, and acquainted with this countryside, and believe you a gentleman of honor."

His Highness here pausing as one that asks a question, Captain Royston said very simply that the last head of His Highness's opinion was as true as the two former, as he would know if he saw fit to use him in a matter of delicacy.

On which the Prince continued: "I do not doubt, Captain Royston, that something at least of the difficulty of my position in this disturbed country has been long clear to you. Victory in a pitched field over a proud and unconquered people, to whom I come as a friend invited, will hurt my cause no less than defeat. It is not every man that will act as this old Sir Michael Drayton, who, his mind once determined, is eager to take risk among the first." And here, perceiving the pleasure in Captain Royston's countenance to hear his old friend thus singled out for praise, His Highness enquired did he know that gentleman, and, being answered eagerly that he did, cast upon Mr. Bentinck a little glance of triumph, as a man looks who says, "I told you so." Then, "You have friends of the best, Captain," he continued. "And as it is not given to all to act with the courage of your friend, while there is scarce one but wishes me success in some measure, 't is a plain duty laid upon me to use all means to draw them to me, and so

secure a peaceful issue.   I have this night received
a letter from one high in King James's favor, en-
nobled by his master, and holding in his army high
rank, while he also exercises through his wife much
influence upon our sister, the Princess Anne; and
so, indirectly, upon her uncles, my Lords Clarendon
and Rochester, her cousin-german, Viscount Corn-
bury—and—and—is it possible," he added, with
an odd smile, " that I forget her husband, Prince
George of Denmark ?   Now, in this letter," said
His Highness, tapping upon the table with a paper
he held folded in his hand, " in which there is
much of his attachment to the Protestant religion,
but more between the lines, as I read it, of the high
price he would have for a firm continuance in that
faith, this noble officer proposes coming to terms
with us.   We shall doubtless have him sooner or
later, but sooner is my purpose, for the sake of his
following.   He has left the royal army, now sta-
tioned at Salisbury, and while his escort in two
divisions, each of which supposes my Lord C——
to be with the other, is on the way to the capital,
he himself with one companion has by this," said the
Prince, glancing at the clock, " with forced riding,
reached the town of Sherborne, where, under the
style of ' Captain Jennings,' he will lie this night at
' The King's Head.'   How far, Captain Royston, is
this town of Sherborne from our present position ? "

For a little time Captain Royston pondered, and
then replied that the distance was something over
fifty miles.

"And how long," asked His Highness, "would
it take you to ride to Sherborne by night, Captain
Royston?"

"The roads are very bad, and heavy with the
rain, Your Highness," said Captain Royston; "but
with a fresh horse from here, a remount from the
stables of my troop at Honiton, and a third that I
shall doubtless find at my own house of Royston, I
will do it in ten hours.   If the clouds should break,
the moon might help me to better it by an hour."

"And how far is this house of yours, Captain?"
asked the Prince.

"Royston Chase and the hamlet of Royston,
Your Highness," he answered, "lie midway between Chard and Crewkerne: as the crow flies, some
three and thirty miles from Exeter, and half as
much, or thereabout, from Sherborne."

"Is it at present inhabited?" says His Highness.

"By my mother and a few old servants," said
Royston.

"Is the lady of your mind in politics?" continued His Highness; and being answered that she
was, he then asked Captain Royston to do him the
honor to be his host on the following day.   "I shall
go to Chard with Count Schomberg and a troop of

cavalry," he said, " to inspect the outposts that lie
there, and ostensibly to take notice of the country
for purpose of strategy. About two hours after
noon we shall arrive and ask hospitality of madam
your mother — it may be for the night. Meantime
you, Captain Royston, will have conducted Colonel
my Lord C——, with all secrecy and discretion, and
by hidden paths and byways when possible, to
your house, where we can privily accomplish that
personal meeting he so much desires, and contrive,
I doubt not, to fix the price of his treachery. Mr.
Bentinck, sir, considers that I err to trust you so far
with my secret purposes. But I intend employing
an English gentleman in a service as much to the
advantage of his country as of myself, and I would
not have him think it is my habit to deal with
traitors. While, like yourself, Captain, I vastly
prefer the open field to the dark ways of intrigue,
yet, in this case, though I am, as the world knows,
no Jesuit, I hold the great end in view to justify
the means we are to employ. And, when all is
said, the private motives of his lordship are no more
concern of ours than—than—" he said, pausing
with a smile, " than his Protestantism. He is a
good soldier, and, if I am any judge, bids fair to be
a great one; so I would have him an instrument on
the right side."

His Highness then gave to Captain Royston a

pass under his own seal, very comprehensive in its
terms, laying also before him a like paper sent by
Lord C——, bearing the signature, " James R."
M. de Rondiniacque has since told me of the lofty
manner in which dear Ned would have declined this
last.   But His Highness insisted with some sharpness, saying: " You will take no escort, Captain,
and these scruples are petty.   And," he added
more kindly, " let us hope that its use, if needed,
will prove, after all, in the interest of His Majesty,
my uncle.   It shall not be our fault, sir, if it do not."
 Now since the attempt of one Gerrard and others
upon the life of the Prince, Mr. Bentinck had endeavored with a subtlety of precaution truly wonderful to protect his friend and master from such vile
and hidden enemies.   For, however strongly the
instigator might be suspected, the instigation was
never proved, and the instruments had control of
agencies to the full as cunning and secret as any
that Mr. Bentinck, with all his servants and cor-
respondents, could bring to bear.   Before Captain
Royston, therefore, had gotten himself to horse,
this gentleman took occasion to draw him apart,
and, laying aside for the moment his wonted un-
graciousness of demeanor, warned him privately
and kindly that, many bad men being about, and the
neighborhood of so large a force offering much opportunity of disguise and concealment to the evilly

disposed, it was before all to be desired that no word of His Highness's purposed visit to Royston Chase should go abroad. Captain Royston very civilly thanked him, saying that he was of a like opinion; that not even to that distinguished gentleman to whom his mission was would he impart the name of his destination; but only to madam his mother, should he have the fortune to speak with her that night while changing his horse, would he tell so much as should ensure His Highness a fitting reception.

I am not to give a particular narrative of that tedious, rapid, and cautious ride, for the most part in the dark, from Exeter to Sherborne, but only to touch upon such incidents therein as may serve to throw a little light upon the events that ensued,— events of which the result came so near the tragical that even now a shuddering will accompany their memory.

At the door of the Deanery a fresh and powerful horse awaited him. He was as far as Honiton accompanied upon his road by M. de Rondiniacque, who was entrusted with an order to the colonel of the Swedish Cavalry. As they rode from the Close, his companion pointed out to Captain Royston a fellow that stood at the corner with his back to the wall.

" 'T is the same we saw at the ale-house, half-way from Honiton," said M. de Rondiniacque. He

then turned his horse and enquired of the sentry
that paced the Close a little higher up, did he know
that short, stout, and red-haired fellow, or anything
of his business; to which the soldier answered that
he was something in the way of a sutler, or perhaps
a dealer on commission in supplies, to the various
messes. And, while M. de Rondiniacque was thus
out of ear-shot conferring with the musketeer, the
man at the corner betrayed to the eyes of Captain
Royston some perturbation of countenance. As
the friends continued their road to the left from the
mouth of the Close, Captain Royston, turning in
the saddle, perceived this loiterer, whom he suspected for a spy, to be already making off swiftly
in a contrary direction.

The tedium of the first ten miles was well be-
guiled by the gaiety of M. de Rondiniacque, and
marked by no incident but the sudden passing at
full speed of a fine horse mounted by a bold but, as
appeared in the brief glance, an ill-seated and in-
experienced horseman. A sudden gleam of the
moon shining upon this figure as it disappeared
round a corner of the road a little in advance of
the two officers, M. de Rondiniacque observed that
he believed 't was the same fellow with the red
head they had already twice that evening encountered. A little later Captain Royston took note
that, whoever the reckless rider was, he had either

checked his pace or much increased the distance between them, since the sound of his flight was no longer heard.   And so for the time the matter passed out of their heads.

The last five miles of the road to Honiton, being in fair condition, were accomplished at a good pace, checked only by an accident of a very trifling sort. Captain Royston, ever a man of great knowledge and consideration in horseflesh, his beast having stumbled and partly fallen among some loose stones in a dark part of the way, dismounted to examine what injury the animal had taken.   Waiting beside him, M. de Rondiniacque continued, in tones audible enough, their conversation, which had reference to the Prince's intended visit to Royston, the words he used chancing to indicate both time and place.   Before remounting, Captain Royston observed that the disposition of the stones of considerable size which had caused the mishap appeared rather of design than accident, and as he bade his friend hold his peace the ears of both could clearly distinguish a rustling among the bushes that here divided the sunken road from the adjoining fields.

I have been thus particular over the early portion of Captain Royston's midnight ride because it afterwards appeared they had been spied upon to some purpose.

Arrived at Honiton, and learning that the badness of the road that leads through the hamlet of
Royston was through the long wetness of the
weather grown extreme, he resolved upon taking
another, with the chance of a remount at the house
of a gentleman well known to him, who lived at a
point fitly dividing the remnant of his journey.   So
he sat him down while his best charger was a-
saddling to write a brief letter to my Lady Mary, in
which he did but cautiously inform her that his
" honored master " would visit her on the morrow
with a good company in attendance, and signed
himself her " obedient E. R." This letter entrusted for conveyance to Royston Chase by the
first light to a trooper of great fidelity, Captain
Royston set out on his way to Sherborne by a road
somewhat longer, indeed, than he had purposed
using, but promising greater expedition and security
at this hour and season.   Reaching " The King's
Head " at Sherborne about six of the morning (it
being that same Monday upon which the exercising
of Sir Michael's little squadron of horse did begin),
he was at once introduced to " Captain Jennings "
in his chamber, who, having dressed and eaten, was
soon mounted, so that, riding with the light, and
freshly horsed, but with some expense of time for
caution and the using of byways, they were safely
housed at Royston Manor an hour before noon.

Nor is it wonderful that poor Ned, having ridden at least eighty miles upon five horses, with no sleep in thirty hours, and scarce a mouthful of food for fourteen, after noting with regret that there was not one among the servants whose face he knew, did fall asleep upon his bed in all his travel-fouled clothes. Awaking, like a true soldier, an hour before His Highness and the escort should arrive, and asking of the servants why he had not seen his mother, he received from a very civil fellow, who seemed above the rest, a letter written by my Lady Mary in characters much shaken with some emotion, wherein it was set forth that, rather than compromise her loyalty in receiving His Highness, she had left the house free to her son, but herself, with the two old servants that were left of those he knew, had fled to the King's camp at Salisbury. Although vastly put about by this ill news, and, as he thought, great discourtesy of his mother, he put the best face upon the matter, that he might in no manner seem to belittle her in her dependents' eyes, and set about preparation of hospitality. Lady Mary was ever a notable housekeeper, and it was no long matter to load tables and dress beds, the less that it seemed much had been already begun before her unkind departure.

CHAPTER X

WITH all this we have yet come no further than the noontime of the Monday; but I have yet one more thread to gather up before I come again to my proper part in this tale.

That stranger, the sight of whose back so frighted me, foolishly clad in boy's garments, that I dared not risk encounter with the gaze of his eyes, was, though, alas! I knew it not, my brother Philip. When I did pass through the great hall on my way to the stables, he had just come to an end of some talk with Simon Emmet, who was then gone to fetch Sir Michael.

From his errand Simon hoped little good, fearing of the ills that might arise from Philip's return at this conjuncture, most of all the perturbation of spirit into which it was like to cast his master. So much, indeed, he said, with such plainness as his old and unbroken affection for my brother would allow. There is no little reason to suppose that, even more than the lad's father, Simon Emmet had been grieved by Philip's adoption of his mother's religion. For Philip, upon his arrival and encounter with the old man, was no sooner recognized than he was asked if it were indeed true that he was become a priest: and when Simon was assured that so it was, he counselled a speedy departure, since no good would come, Sir Michael being minded as he was, of their meeting.   Being told, with that gentle severity which did use to sit very nobly upon my brother, that he must inform his master with no more ado, he yet in going must turn at the door to deliver a parting bolt through the man he loved at the creed he abhorred.

"Now, I bethink me, Master Philip," says Simon, "there is, when all is said, some good come of your heresy." And when Philip said gently that he hoped indeed it was so, but saw not how he meant it, Simon gave answer that, old man and sick though he was, Sir Michael upon that dire news had gotten a mind to live, and had lived ever since, in the firm intent that, as long as he might prevent, a Papist should never rule at Drayton.

"But, Simon," says Philip, with a sadness political rather than religious, "there was surely a time when my dear father had preferred a Papist in his house to a Dutch Calvinist on the throne."

"Ay, Master Phil," says Simon, with an old man's chuckle of much cunning, "but that was before the throne had tried a Papist," and so left him.

And I do suppose it was while I listened unseen

to little Prue's willing news from her lover on the
flags of the stable-yard that my two nearest kin
were threshing out, in the great hall behind me, a
question that can never be settled.   There was no
quarrel between them, but little that was common
to their two minds.   And that day the little seemed
altogether naught.   Yet in temper the two men
were as like as unlike in thought.

Now Philip's change of faith had but strength-
ened, and in a manner embittered, the old Cavalier
devotion to the house of Stuart.   Being commissioned by that great religious society of which he
was a member, and whose power is as far-reaching
as its means are often hidden and subtile, to travel
from London through the southern and western
parts of England, exhorting, persuading, and com-
manding the Catholic gentry to remain constant in
the royal cause, he had, at the end of two months
so spent, at last arrived among us.   He now told
his father that he held it within the spirit of his
commission, if not of its letter, to use upon him,
did he waver in that political faith of which his life
hitherto was so noble an exhibition, the same arguments and modes of appeal he was daily employing
upon those of the true faith.

" You lack, however, in dealing with me, my son,
one weapon—and that your strongest,'' said his
father.

" And that, sir ? " said Philip.

" The appeal to religious authority, my boy.
And yet I scarce see by what means you do bring
it in use; for I hear that His Holiness is ever at war
of one kind or another with King Lewis, and favors
rather the cause of that alliance of the Empire with
the Protestant Princes, of which His young Highness of Orange is the soul and spirit. I warrant,
lad," said the old man, with some grimness of
humor, " you find the Pope but an unhandy weapon
in your schemes and plots."

" I obey orders, sir, but do not deal in plots,"
the son replied, with a pride that matched the
father's.

" Art not a Jesuit ? " asked Sir Michael.

And Philip answering, proudly and yet with much
humility, that he was, Sir Michael would have
known of him what he did when the bidding of the
Society of Jesus ran counter to His Holiness's
policy, or enjoined action inconvenient with the
honor of a gentleman. But Philip, avoiding the
former question, was yet stung into reply on
the second, saying boldly that the spiritual de-
scendants of Loyola were much belied, and had no
traffic in the plotting of underhand schemes.

To this his father, with much warmth, but with
a greater kindness than had yet appeared in his
address, replied: " Truly, I think they do not—

through such as thou, my son. Believe your old
father, lad; your superiors are men of a boundless
statecraft and a subtile, and well know their tools.
Who that has knowledge uses an axe to do the office
of a file ? But files they have, and augers even
down to the finest gimlet; and these also work
among us."

"Be that as it may, sir," answered Philip, " my
mission is honest and open. I come to conjure you
to hold faith with the cause in which you have so
nobly spent your blood, your sons, your land, and
your gold."

"There is nothing left me but my daughter and
the ragged edge of life, Philip," said the old man,
with a great sadness. "And these, too, would I
spend, as I thought, God knows, to spend all that
is gone,— for the good, I mean, of England. But
not as you would lay them out, Philip; not on
James, his harlots, priests, and bastards. The King
is the slave of priests as his brother was of women;
and, Gad 's my life! the late King was more English in 's tastes. Women may harm the king, but
your priest in power is death to the kingdom. I
have learned one thing, son Philip, in my nine and
seventy years: that a man's king is much, but his
country more. But it is enough. Let us leave the
matter, or, God forgive me, I shall end by lauding
the man I have most hated — the one Englishman

since I drew breath that was feared and honored by Pope, Emperor, and Kings.   And since ?   We have been laughed to scorn of the Spaniard, spat upon by the Hollander, and paid—God's blood! ay, paid by a filthy Frenchman!"

" You have called a man traitor for less words than these, sir," said his son, mightily amazed.

" Traitor!" quoth Sir Michael, with a great bitterness.   " We are all traitors now.   It is the curse of God upon a wicked and adulterous generation. There is no man among us but some will say of him, ' There goeth a traitor,' whether to his king, his country, or his God."

Then Philip: " If I must choose, it shall be to all before my God."

" Ay," said Sir Michael; " but in my plain English way of thought, Sir Priest, no man betrays his country but is traitor to his God."

And so they made an end, and Philip mounted his horse and rode away.   And all that day I knew not that my brother had stood in reach of my arms. These things and the little more I have here to tell of Philip I learned after from his own lips.   Riding sad and thoughtful from the house he did meet, at the turn of the avenue where it opens upon the road, a short, fat man, with red hair that matched ill with his dark and oily skin.   His horse, though good, seemed but now painfully to recover from hard running. The fellow's countenance being not unknown to him, Philip was the less surprised to be addressed by name as brother, and asked had he forgotten the speaker. And when he was at length remembered for one Francis, that was in the time of Philip's novitiate a lay brother in no good odor of repute, he told with some boastfulness how he had received priest's orders and the conduct of a great mission, concerning which he was loftily mysterious, saying only it was a great work for the subduing the heathen; to compel a blind and unquestioning assistance in which he had powers granted him, he said, over any member of the Society he should encounter. At present, he added, he was to be known and addressed only as Mr. James Marston of the city of Oxford. He then commanded Philip's attendance upon him, and, on his demurring, showed him such writings as convinced my dear brother, rightly or wrongly, that he had no choice but to obey. Which he did, riding with him sadly enough, and wondering, as he has told me, whether he were not soon about to give the lie to that proud speech wherein he told his father that he, no more than the Society of Jesus, did deal in plots. I will here say that grave doubt has since been cast upon the authenticity of the alleged commission of Brother Francis. Philip has ever held that he was deceived by the man; that the papers were either forged, or used to ends far other than their purpose.

Mr. William Bentinck, whose great knowledge of hidden affairs as well as his lack of bias in favor of that Society entitles his opinion to a greater value, thought it to be a case in which one had been employed that might, in event of failure, throw the fault upon a body of men as accustomed to be blamed as to do good. However it may be, we shall never certainly know the truth of the matter, since the destruction of the papers and other accidents have put it quite beyond the power of any man to enquire further with hope of success. One thing at least is certain: that Philip was as ignorant as innocent of the purpose to which he was led.

And so I find myself in the saddle, taming Roan Charley in the park, where I have, in a manner of speaking, patiently awaited my reader through the tedious course of two chapters.

CHAPTER XI

WITH my horse reduced to some show of order, but yet champing fretfully at his bit and throwing back his head in such manner as but for my quick avoidance had endangered the soundness of my own, I cantered gaily to that part where the exercising was, with head erect and a firm hold upon the great war-saddle that seemed no longer too vast to grip between the knees. There I perceived that Simon Emmet was at great pains to get the words of command and their significance not only into the heads of his troopers but also into that of Christopher Kidd, who there was sweating visibly in attempt at once to control a fresh horse he had gotten, and to repeat after Simon words of whose meaning he had less knowledge than the men that, for lack of a better, he was to command. At once and without a word I fell into line, and, after a few mistakes, very successfully put myself and Roan Charley through the simple evolution in progress. At first Simon did not mark me, being the more busied that the dulness of Kidd was much increased by his amazement at the sight of me.

But when at length Simon saw the direction of his awkward pupil's regard, he as quickly perceived his new recruit.

Giving the command to halt in his great voice of an old sergeant of horse, he walked up to me, saying, with a rough petulance: " How now, young gentleman ? What have you to do among these ?" Then, at the laugh with which I answered him, he drew near and understood. And mightily put about he was, and would have me at once return to the house.

But, " Tush, Simon!" I said, smiling on him in the fashion I had used from a child when I would have my way rather than his, " do I not do it all fit and properly ? You are not to know who I am, but a young gentleman that would exercise with you."

" You must leave the ranks," said Simon, gruff but wavering.

" So I will indeed," I answered, " if Mr. Kidd will but take my place."

And this Christopher, ever ready for Prue's sake to pleasure me, very readily did, without more said; whereupon I took his place, and, before Simon had well lowered his brows of amazement, I was giving out in the greatest voice I could compass all the words of command I had spent my morning in learning from my window. The troop, falling in with the jest, acquitted themselves so well that

Simon did not interfere; and I had halted them at
length with intent to coax old Emmet to fetch my
father, that he might see how good a man I was,
when from round the corner where lay the front of
the house there came a great and growing confusion
of sound: the wheels of a coach, the hoofs of many
horses, and a mixed murmur of voices. And then
the great voice of my father rang out, at the sound
of which all was hushed; wheels stopped, horses
stood, and men held their breath. Bidding Simon
keep his men as they were, I cantered round the
southeast corner of the house, and, checking my
horse, stood for some minutes unmarked in the confusion, to observe a scene not a little curious.

The coach was my Lady Mary's, easily recognized
in our parts for the newness of its fashion. By its
side stood our friend and neighbor, Sir Giles Blundell, that instant dismounted, and opening the door
that my lady might descend. Behind him were
two young gentlemen, one of whom held Sir Giles's
horse by the bridle. My lady, of a pallor very
death-like, and stumbling as she stepped down
from the coach so that she was like to have fallen
but for the ready support of his hands, said a few
words to Sir Giles, but all in a voice so low from
weakness of fatigue and the faintness of terror as no
word of it to reach my ears. His answer, however,
was given clearly enough. And as he spoke my

father, till now delayed in his descent of the steps by the lameness of his leg, drew near and stood beside my lady, leaning upon his stick.

"Indeed, dear madam," said Sir Giles, "I will do no such thing. I and my friends here are vastly pleased we were in the way to rescue you from such evil hands; 't was a small service we are proud to have rendered to so good a friend and neighbor. But to ride further to Royston Chase on the mere chance of some danger to His Highness of Orange, that has an army to protect him, is but to mix ourselves with a game we are well resolved to watch at a safe distance."

"Ah, Giles," says Sir Michael, who had known him from a boy, "your father had been of one part or the other. What, in God's name, is coming to England, when Englishmen are found that cannot even take a side?" Whereupon more words to little purpose ensued, Sir Giles and the two other gentlemen at length departing as they had come, after replying with much forbearance to some heated and scornful animadversions of my father upon the lukewarmness of their conduct.

Gratitude for what these gentlemen had done in her behalf and the need of recovering her spirits from the great perturbation into which they had been thrown by the events of the morning kept my lady silent until their departure was accomplished,

when she turned to Sir Michael with a great be-
seeching in her countenance, saying: " Surely you
will help me, my old friend." On which he gave
her assurance he would do all he might, but told
her he was yet ignorant what was her trouble and
need. And it is great wonder to me that all the
time she was telling and he hearing her story neither
did observe me sitting there on my horse, and but
partly hidden from their eyes by the branches of a
tree. But her eagerness was well equalled by his
interest; and there was a great bustling of our
hostlers and her two servants about the coach. For
one of the horses had fallen when brought to a
stand, and lay, it seemed, at the point of death,
two more being in a very bad case.

In brief, the tale she told him, of which I heard
near every word, was this: that one had come at six
o'clock of that morning with a letter from her son,
announcing a visit, as she interpreted its terms,
from His Highness of Orange; that by nine she was
well advanced with her preparation for his fit reception, when all was thrown into confusion by the
sudden arrival and enforced entry of a strange and
ill-assorted body of men, acting, with a silent obedience truly wonderful to see in so unlikely a comradeship, under the orders of a little fat man with a
dark face and red hair. This fellow, after he had
compelled her with the threat of death and a pistol

at her head to write that letter to her son which I
have already mentioned, did force her, with her
maid and one man-servant, into the coach which
the other was to drive, a ruffian of decent mien
being seated beside him with a loaded pistol to
quicken his obedience and despatch.   One other, in
like manner persuasive, was in the coach, while
Red-head and a fourth with a led horse rode beside.
This party, in the endeavor to reach Salisbury, but
much delayed by the devices of my lady's coach-
man, after escaping the pursuit of Farmer Kidd,
had fallen the more easily before the gallant assault
of Sir Giles Blundell and his friends that they were
weakened by the absence of their leader; he having,
as I believe (though this came not in Lady Mary's
narrative), lost his way in drawing off Christopher's
attack, and, being minded from the first to return
before the end to Royston Chase, and falling in
with my brother Philip, was glad enough to enforce
his attendance as a guide, if not also to vent an old
spleen by making of him an unwilling accomplice
in his wicked purpose.

Of the three villains left with the coach, one was
slain in the rescue and the other two escaped on
their horses.

My lady ended her tale by telling her fear that
the life of His Highness was aimed at, and imploring
Sir Michael with tears that he should at once send

his men (for Simon had by this brought his troops in very fair order round into the drive) for the warning and defence of His Highness; adding most piteously that her fear was no less for the honor of her son and his father's house than for the life of the Prince.

" Ay, madam," says my father; " but since there is none to lead them, and they are like a flock of sheep lacking a shepherd, they must wait the time of writing a letter."

" Write ! write ! " cried her ladyship, wringing her hands, " write! while even now it is perhaps too late! "

" I would I had one left of them all," said Sir Michael, with a groan; " or anybody with a head-piece on a sound body. You see what I am, and Simon is well-nigh a cripple these three years."

And with that I cantered up to them; and, bringing suddenly my horse to a stand, and saluting very finely, *more militari*—" I will go, sir," I cried.

" Who 's here ? " cries my father, and " Mercy on us! " says my lady, like any milkmaid, in one breath with him.

" Who but your son Philip ? " I answered, laughing gaily, and, I think, blushing a little, as well indeed I might. " And your son Philip is the best horseman in the country; your son Philip bestrides the best nag in three; and your son Philip knows the crow's-road to Royston, while it is of common knowledge that he has a very pretty head-piece on his shoulders."

My father being past speaking for amazement, my lady breaks in with: " Thou 'rt a brave girl, but why this masquerade, dear child ? "

" To convince Sir Michael Drayton," I pertly replied, " that there is some use even in daughters, when they can hold a sword and sit in a war-saddle of Prince Rupert's time."

Sir Michael here made to seize my bridle, but Roan Charley had caught excitement from my voice, and a little slacking of his rein with a pressure of the knee at once put him at the distance of three great bounds from any detaining hand.

" Come back, Philippa! " cries my father.

" Not so, dear sir," said I, turning in the saddle, " for I shall go, an you will allow it."

" The roads and fields are not safe for thee, child," said he, " with so many bad men about, and an army close to hand, else were I willing enough."

" Then let these men follow me," I cried. " Simon will tell you, dear sir, that I can give and take the word of command. Christopher has no wit to handle them. Send the six best mounted, and let them come up with me if they can, and I

will give Roan Charley to him that reaches Royston
neck and neck with me.''

And if they answered me again I heard it not,
for Charley was away, taking in his stride the fence
of the paddock that lies behind the stable; and although that way did mean a leap-out at a point
where the fence was high, with the ground falling
sharply on the other side, we did the second jump
as well as we had done the first, and so gained three
hundred yards on the pursuing troop, whom I
already heard pounding after me with many a
hearty cry and much rattling of harness.

11

CHAPTER XII

TWO years after it happened my husband and I did ride over the same course of my crow's flight from Drayton Manor to Royston Chase. And it was matter of some surprise to me, and of more to Ned, ambling in cold blood over the fields and viewing the leaps that I and Roan Charley did that day take in company, that I had not only the courage for such feats but also the fortune to come through it all without misadventure.

I must indeed suppose that I did myself choose my path and guide in it the gallant little horse; but, were I to trust merely to the memory of feeling, I should believe that I sat in the saddle like one in a dream, while Charley, with the inward knowledge of some homing pigeon, galloped straight for the place where lay all my hopes and fears. 'T was but twice that I had any sight of my escort —first, turning in my seat as Charley reached the level of the meadow-land below the hill that falls away from the home paddock, I beheld them, close massed in a body, rounding the bend of the fence away to the right above me, and just about

commencing the descent; and once again, after the
roan had leaped into, and well-nigh miraculously
scrambled out of, an ugly and broken gully that lies
near half-way between Royston and my father's
house. For as Charley heaved his body with a tearing, scratching, and clinging most wondrous cat-like
upon the safe ground of the further bank, I looked
back once more and spied them bearing off to the left
for lower ground and easier passage; but by this they
were a straggling rout covering much ground, so
hardly already had the pace and distance with the
differing weight of riders told upon the various mettle
of the horses. Indeed, the next two miles did tell
not a little even upon Charley, being a rising stretch
of ploughed land in condition very grievous for his
smallness of hoof; but coming thereafter to grass, he
was mightily refreshed, and cleared two fences and
a little bank of earth with bushes atop in his old
gay and light-hearted manner.

And after this we were not long in coming to the
road, which being in good condition for the season
and weather that it was we made the remaining
miles at a very pretty pace.

Now the front of the house at Royston Chase
stands but a little back from the road, behind great
gates of wrought iron, hung upon mighty pillars of
carved stone. These stood wide as I galloped up,
but the way was barred by two soldiers, of mien

immovable as the brazen gates of Gaza. By their
black cloaks of fur I knew them to be of that Swedish Regiment of Horse in which Captain Royston
held His Highness's commission. They were, however, dismounted for sentry duty—an office for which
I could but think them ill chosen when I perceived
that not one word of the English language did they
understand, and would neither let me pass through
the archway into the inner court of the house, nor, .
when I had come to the purpose of moving further
down the road and leaping both hedge and ditch
into the orchard, would they let me depart. For
one of them did lay a great hand on Charley's
bridle, saying something to his fellow in a manner
easy of comprehension, though the words were to
me without meaning. And I truly believe that I
was in that moment very near to discovery of my
sex. For answer to his jest I struck the fellow
across the face with my loose gauntlet, at the same
time with great quickness using both spur and rein,
so that Roan Charley in a single movement reared
himself almost upright and swerved aside. This,
coming right upon the blow he had received, caused
the trooper to loose my rein; which before the
other could seize we were away at the best pace we
could make.

Now, some three hundred yards down the road
seemed the lowest part of the bank and hedge en-

closing the little field that here divides the beautiful
orchard of Royston Chase from the highroad.   But
even at this point, I thought, the leap was hard for
a horse that had already done so much; wherefore
I had determined to pass on to that little cross lane
that leads from the road to the gate at the lower end
of the orchard.   But even as I was so resolving I
heard behind me the cries and hoofs of mounted
pursuers, and in front, coming from the very lane I
had purposed using, a patrol of three men of this
same Swedish regiment.   And so jump we must, or
altogether fail, it seemed, in that for which we had
ridden so far and so fast.   Charley, too, seemed to
understand, and for a few strides we both steadied
ourselves, taking deep breaths of air and watching
the hedge for a thin spot.   And I have always
thought 't was Charley that found it—a spot where
the growth of bramble on the bank's top was so
scarce as to let the narrow edge of the earth mound
be clearly seen.   But whether the will were mine or
his, the doing of the matter was Charley's alone, and
very well, for a tired horse, was it done.   Knowing
he could not with sureness clear both ditch and bank
in a single spring, and feeling that his mistress did
leave the manner of this last and most difficult passage of his hard run wholly to his clever legs and
wiser head, my little horse, as if he had been twice
the age he was, most soberly took his leap from the

roadside, and landed with his four hoofs bunched
cat-like in a cluster on the summit of the bank in that
place where I have said the growth of brush and
bramble was thin.   Here, for the space of two
heart-beats, he poised himself, in which time he
judged so well both his own flagging powers and the
wider and unexpected ditch on the further side, that
he was able with a second leap to land us safely and
gently beyond it on the rain-softened earth of the
ploughed field.

Now, even in the brief moment when Charley
swayed on the top of the bank and gathered himself
for that second spring, I had time (so swiftly works
the mind in the tension of danger to be forestalled)
to note two things: that my pursuers on their heavy
chargers had balked the leap; and that in the
orchard, across the little ploughed field and beyond
the low fence, were many people, walking to and
fro among the fruit trees; and I knew from their
carriage, from the sheen of armor, and the gay colors
of the various habits, that they were no common
soldiers; and as Charley foundered wearily but with
great courage through the heavy plough my heart
was high with the thought that fortune had brought
me the straight road to my end.   And then we
reached the fence, which proved higher than I had
thought; yet did my brave nag pass that too, very
cleverly bursting with his knees the highest rail,

which he was too tired to overtop, and though he took the grass among the trees beyond with a little stumble, it was his first and last mistake, from which quickly recovering, and, as it seemed, well aware that his work was done, he stood like an image of stone, with forelegs stretched in front and nose near down to his knees.

And then I thought the whole world did heave and turn and swim before my eyes, and all that I saw through the mist of its convulsion was two long, shadowy arms reaching from opposite quarters for Roan Charley's bridle; all I thought, that little was the need to hold a horse that had turned to stone; all I heard, the sound of a voice far off, that said: " The Prince of Orange; there is a plot; look to his safety; search the house, the grounds, or they will slay him." And then slowly the earth settled again to its place, the mist began to clear, and I knew the voice for my own. And I saw, as one that wakes from a dream, that he who held my bridle on the near side was Captain Edward Royston, and straightway I was within a little of so addressing him, but bethought me in time, and, looking round, asked where was the master of the house.

Upon which he replied: " I am Captain Royston; what is to do ? "

" Sir," I said, very solemnly (yet, for all the gravity of the case, I was at pains to keep back a

smile when I so addressed him, and saw that he
knew me not), " Sir, His Highness is in danger.
Madam your mother has been by force taken from
home, but is now in safety; the servants that you
find in your house are evil men, and of the plot."

Then he that held my horse on the off side, whom
I afterwards knew for that great person that for discretion I shall still call " Captain Jennings," took
his hand from the bridle.

" The lad speaks truth," he said; " a word with
you, Captain." With that he drew Ned aside, and
while they spoke together (" Captain Jennings "
telling, I think, how he feared unjust suspicion of
his own connivance if aught befell His Highness) I
marked that six Swedish troopers did approach,
threading their way through the trees from the gate
in the lane that I have above mentioned. Also,
between them and me, but nearer by no little distance to where I still sat upon Charley's back, I saw
a man stand leaning against the wall of the granary
that stands in the orchard, and thus hidden from
the advancing soldiers that were still, as I supposed,
in pursuit of poor me. And this man, whether
from description or from something high and noble
in the aquiline countenance of him, I knew at once
for William, Prince of Orange. Now, even as I
gazed in idleness of wonder on the man I held
greatest in the world (for did not Edward Royston

serve him with reverence and ardor ?), I saw that a
little door in the granary, on His Highness's left,
was slowly, slowly moving back upon its hinges,
and a moment later I had one glimpse of a fat face
and a red head peering from the narrow slit of that
opening. I thought of Farmer Kidd's tale, and
again of Madam Royston's, and straightway drew
my sword and clapped heels to my horse. Roan
Charley, for all his fatigue, responded very gallantly,
and in three of his long bounds we had been beside
the Prince, but for a fellow, long, lean, and black-
coated, that drew a pistol from under his breast,
which he fired in my face in the same moment
as he leapt at Charley's head, whereby he undid
himself, for, as the horse reared in terror, I, in as
much, struck spurs in his sides, and Charley leaping
forward, we rode clean over our assailant, whom I
struck at wildly with my sword as he fell. Charley
must have found foothold upon some part of his
body, for I remember still with a thrill of sickness
the softness under foot.

Hereafter my recollection of the *mêlée* that ensued
has little clearness; all was noise and confusion, the
band of conspirators having burst out from their
hiding in the granary in desperate effort to achieve
their wicked end even in that eleventh hour and
very moment of discovery. And even then they
might have found success but for Roan Charley and

his rider, which is to me ever a joy to remember;
for, though I recall little and confusedly what befell
around me, I know that after the fall beneath
Charley's hoofs of that rascal (the same that Ned
had supposed a very civil servant of his mother), we
reached at once the door in the wall of the granary;
but not in time to prevent the sortie of three men
with sword and pistol in hand (the rest, I believe,
came forth by a door on the other side). With
two of these His Highness was very speedily and
coolly engaged, while the third was aiming a clean
downward cut at his head with a great sword whose
gleam seems yet burned in upon my eyes as I write
and remember. And then, in some manner, Charley
and I were upon him, and my blade received the
stroke meant for His Highness's unprotected head.
And after that I thought something did break (as
indeed it did, being the blade of my brother Rupert's
sword). I heard the shouts and the running feet of
friends closing round, and then all was darkness and
nothing.

The next I knew was a burning in mouth and
throat, and awoke to find myself swallowing some
liquid, very foul and ill-savored, held to my lips
by a gentleman I did not know. I afterwards
learned the liquor was Dutch, and called *schnapps*,
the man none other than the great Count Schomberg, late Marshal of France, and once high in favor

of His Majesty King Lewis; but now chief in command under His Highness of Orange, having abandoned the highest of military honors and the favor of the greatest King upon earth for the cause of religion.

So, opening my eyes and looking round, when I had done with coughing over that vile liquor, I saw not only that a numerous company stood around, but also that here and there upon the grass among the trees lay several men, in strange and twisted attitudes such as I had never before seen ; and something told me that these were dead; and I knew that I was upon a little field of battle, and straightway was like again to have swooned, when one behind me said in the French language and kindly tones, but in manner of speech more guttural than men of that nation do mostly use: " Poor lad! 'T is like enough this is his first sight of blood."

Which words, calling to my mind how I was habited, and the whole memory therewith of the part I played, did somehow stiffen my courage and arouse my spirit, so that I said, with what of hardihood I could bring into the words: " Indeed, I ask your pardon, gentlemen all. 'T was the fatigue, I do suppose, of riding fifteen miles at such a pace, and to the back of that my great fear for the life and welfare of His Highness of Orange. I pray you, tell me," I continued, looking round among the company, " whether His Highness be unhurt ?''

And then one came from behind me, and spoke to me in that same voice that had but now pitied me in the French idiom for my first sight of blood-shedding. And when I saw him I knew him for the great Prince I had ridden to defend. This time, however, he spoke in English, using that language certainly with little ease and frequent errors, which yet I shall make no essay to reproduce in this my narrative, lest I should thereby bring something of ridicule into an address ever princely and dignified, and, on this occasion at least, full of grace and courtesy. Much, I know, has been said and written of the harshness of his manner, the bitterness of his tongue, and even of a certain Dutch boorishness in behavior, of all which I saw nothing at our first meeting.

Three months later, when our troubles were well past, Mr. William Bentinck did tell me one afternoon that we walked in St. James's Park, how to this great but somewhat phlegmatic nature the excitement of danger was a kind of stimulant necessary to the bringing forward the lighter and most pleasing qualities of his character; that he had never seen him gayer, more kindly, nor lighter of heart and countenance than in the press of a losing fight, himself dismounted and fighting hand to hand

with an advancing enemy, merrily jesting the while
his left hand wielded with deadly effect the sword
that his right arm was too sore hurt to hold.   And
I do suppose it was to this quality in him that I
owed the sweet and noble charm of his first reception of me.

" Young gentleman," said His Highness, stretching out to me his hand, " it seems that I owe my
health and perhaps my life to your timely presence
and your sword."   And I, here falling upon one
knee to receive and kiss his hand, perceived that in
my right I still held the hilt of Rupert's toledo, with
the three inches of blade that remained to it.   "And
I hope," continued His Highness, as I let it fall
upon the grass, " that the sword has taken all the
hurt to itself."

" I thank Your Highness," I answered, as I rose,
" I have taken indeed no hurt at all, and should ask
your pardon for so unsoldierly swooning in your
presence.   But indeed 't is the first time I have
seen sword drawn in anger, and I had ridden near
fifteen miles at extreme speed to warn Your Highness of the plot that was toward."

" And from this good fellow I hear not only of
that great and rapid riding, but that you come from
my friend, Sir Michael Drayton," said the Prince,
indicating with his glance Christopher Kidd, who
stood by, loosing the girths of his steaming horse—

the only one of my company that had yet overtaken his leader. " Are you then Sir Michael's son ?—or, perhaps, his grandson ? "

" Neither the one nor the other, sir," I said, glad that he did so form his question; " but I do use to live at Drayton Manor, and Sir Michael is my nearest of kin that lives." And I was glad that Captain Royston was beyond ear-shot, being busy among the prisoners taken, whom very shortly he left in the hands of their guards, and approached the Prince, saluting as he came.

" There are five slain upon the ground, Your Highness," he said, " and seven taken in the act, of whom six bore arms; one of these is even now, I suppose, at the point of death, and one other, I think, has made good his escape, he being the thirteenth, which makes, as far as we are informed, the full tale."

" See that no more slip through your fingers, Captain Royston," replied His Highness, with something of severity; adding more freely that he was indebted to them all for prompt and vigorous defence of his person; then, perceiving that Captain Royston lingered with further matter in his mind, he asked him what it was.

" With Your Highness's permission I would speak briefly as Edward Royston of Royston, rather than as one holding Your Highness's

commission," he said; and, the Prince nodding as-
sent, he went on to express in words very simple and
well chosen, the dismay he had felt, and the extreme regret and shame he had suffered, that so
wicked an attempt on His Highness's life had been
made on his land and under the very walls of his
father's house.

Now when the Prince had noted the honesty of
his handsome and open countenance, and perceived
the simple candor of his address, his heart — by no
means the easiest, as I was soon to know, of such
access—was a little touched; for, with much benignity, laying a hand on Ned's shoulder, he said
very kindly that his satisfaction with the officer was
only equalled by his obligation to the host; in proof
whereof he then expressed his purpose to entrust to
Captain Royston's keeping for the coming night the
persons of himself and the seven prisoners.   His
conference with "Captain Jennings" being but
commenced, he purposed after dinner to continue
in conversation with that gentleman until a conclusion should be reached; to send him on his way with
two troopers as far as Sherborne that same evening;
and to return himself to Exeter the following morning, going somewhat out of his way, did nothing
intervene to forbid, in order to paying a visit to the
venerable Sir Michael Drayton, to whom, said His
Highness, he felt himself in much obligation.

At this point he was interrupted by a very dreadful groan from the wounded prisoner, and—" I fear, Captain," he said, " there is one of our prisoners will soon be in stronger keeping than even your fine house and great loyalty can give him. Let us see if anything may be done to lighten his pain." Whereupon His Highness drew near the dying man, who had been moved a little apart from his fellows.

Captain Royston and Mr. William Bentinck, who, with displeasure clearly marked upon his countenance, had followed the Prince's words to his host, joined him by the side of the dying man, of whom my view, as I stood modestly behind, was plainer than I could wish. Indeed it was a dreadful sight that I take no pleasure to recall. His Highness, bending down very tenderly, wiped the bloody foam from the tortured lips; the wandering eyes fixed themselves upon the face of the man they had watched to slay, and then: " The priest — the priest!" said the dying man.

" Poor fool!" muttered Count Schomberg in French; " he fondly hopes a priest might yet bring him to heaven."

" The priest—the priest!" repeated the sufferer, but more faintly.

" A priest may at least smooth his passage from earth," said the Prince, very pitifully, when one

stepped out from among the prisoners, saying: " I
am a priest. If he needs the comfort of the
Church——"

But the dying man interrupted his words. With
a last effort he raised himself a little, and said in a
stronger voice, but broken with gasping sobs: " It
was the priest—it was he that brought me here—
brought me to this. God's curse upon him!"
And so he died.

But I marked that his eye had not fallen upon him
that offered the comforts of religion. This man
was tall and dark, of a countenance marked by great
nobility, and expressive of a great sorrow, of which
I could not readily determine whether the cause
were constant or occasional, so suitable did it appear to the lines of a face at once ascetic and
severe. There was that in his eyes, dark and deep
set, moreover, that drew my gaze in a manner I
could by no means account for—which is indeed
little wonderful, seeing the man was my mother's
son and my father's, and I knew it not. To myself
I had just said that the man was not wicked, and
but suffered for his evil company, when the Prince
addressed him in tones very different from those I
had hitherto heard him use: " You keep ill company, Sir Priest," he said.

There was a little pause ere the priest replied,
while the two men gazed, each unyielding, in the

other's eyes.   Then: " That I am not of the company you find me in," said the priest, " is less strange than to find a Prince of Your Highness's descent and marriage alliance consorting with rebels and traitors.   In good sooth, I took less pleasure in these misguided and hapless wretches," he went on, speaking with a scornful kind of pity, " than it appears Your Highness does make shift to find in his uncle's rebel subjects.   But I will tell Your Highness, more for the satisfaction of my carnal sense of honor than in hope or wish to obtain credence of him, that I had no part or lot in this attempt at wicked murder.   Your friends," he added, waving his hand in indication of the officers standing by, " will doubtless tell you that I neither struck blow nor carried weapon.   For myself I will add that I knew not the purpose of their gathering."

" I do not believe you," said the Prince.

" I do not expect belief," said the priest, unruffled in his calm.

His Highness turned from him in a disgust I thought very discourteous, and at once directed Captain Royston to see them all under lock and key.   And so the prisoners were hurried off to the house, and I stood wondering had I ever before set eyes on this naughty priest, when the Prince approached me, saying, as if nothing had interrupted our conversation: " I am sorry you have broke

your sword, my pretty lad." And as he spoke
there gathered around us some half-dozen of the
officers and gentlemen that were there — Count
Schomberg, to wit, and Mr. Bentinck, with him
that we addressed as "Captain Jennings," and one
that I was soon to know as M. de Rondiniacque,
and some others. "But that loss," His Highness
continued, "is easier repaired than the cleaving
asunder of my poor brain-pan had been, which was
like enough to come about, gentlemen, I take it,
but for the lad here and his horse and sword."

"It is very true, Your Highness," said M. de
Rondiniacque; then addressing me, he observed,
courteously enough, but with something of raillery
in his tone, that, if the guard I had used was not
altogether of the schools, it had yet saved His
Highness's life as surely as could the interference
of a *maître d'escrime*.

"You are a good Protestant, M. de Rondiniacque," said the Prince, "and therefore, I make sure,
read your Bible well and often." And at this the
little company laughed as at an excellent jest.
"You will no doubt have observed in the course of
that reading that the pebble and the sling of the
son of Jesse were sufficient to the overthrow of a
most mighty man of war, even as this youth's sword
came between my person and death, while the *maître
d'escrime* was not in the way."

His Highness here turned again to me, detaching at the same time his own sword from his side. He then drew it from its sheath, and, laying that upon the grass, wiped the blade very carefully with his handkerchief. And I do think the significance of that action would have made me well-nigh faint with sickness, with that poor fellow that had died in cursing some priest lying so near and so still, had not His Highness straightway handed me the hilt of the weapon that slew him.

"I prithee, good lad, take this in place of that which is broken," he said.

And then I forgot the dead man, and grew first hot and then cold for the great kindness shown to me. I dropped upon my knee, and—"I humbly thank you, sire," I said, "for so great an honor."

He reached out his hand to raise me.

"Kneel not to me, boy," he said; "nor call me sire. I am no king. But I hope you will keep the sword. 'T is a good blade."

"'T is the same," said Mr. Bentinck, "that His Highness did use at the siege of Maestricht, the day he received the musket-ball in his arm."

"You speak truth, friend William," replied the Prince. "That was an unlucky siege. I hope the sword will not bring you my ill-fortune, young gentleman; for I am at times an unlucky soldier. But, indeed, it is Count Schomberg here must bear the blame of Maestricht."

"Did he run, sir ?" I asked with simple curiosity, as I gazed in wonder at the famous veteran.

"Ay, that he did," said the Prince, with a smile of much amusement, and also with something, I thought, of bitterness in the little lines about his lips; "for he was on the other side and ran after me. King Lewis has done me one good turn. His breach of faith with the Huguenots has made us friends. Is it not so, Count ?" With which words he stretched a hand to the late Marshal of France; and then, turning again to me, he raised and gave me the scabbard of the sword, saying as he did so: "If you ever need good office of me, lad, bring me that sword as pledge of the boon you would have, even as we read in the romances was the custom of the princes of olden time. I have said it is a good blade, and I will buy it back with anything that lies in my power."

"Your Highness makes too much of my poor service," I said, as I thrust the sword in its sheath. "I did but what lay on me as a duty."

"I could wish all men did so much," he answered. "Will you have a commission in my army ?"

"Commission !" said Mr. William Bentinck, with

a kind of grunting laughter. " Commission! Why,
't is only a boy ! "

" I am no boy, sir," I replied. " But, indeed I
doubt I am not man enough."

" Ah, well," said His Highness, " there is time
enough. Princes, my good lad, are of all men the
most exacting. Where we have encountered one
act of good service we have ever an eye to receive
more."

But here an orderly officer approaching from the
house cut short this interview, no little to my satisfaction, although standing apart I could not but hear
his report, which he said he had been bidden by
Captain Royston to deliver to His Highness. It
seems that, upon the noise of the fighting in the
orchard coming to the ears of the troopers that were
off duty and dining in the great kitchen of the
house, they had turned out helter-skelter and run to
our assistance, thus leaving for some minutes house
and stable unprotected. When all was over, and
the men settled again to duty and leisure, it was
found that one horse was gone from the stable,
another man's cloak, and the helmet of a third; the
conclusion being, in short, that the escaped con-
spirator had passed that way, and was the thief.
Which matters did afterwards prove not only true,
but of much import to the fortunes of Drayton and
Royston.

And thereafter came Captain Royston himself from the house to bid His Highness and following to dinner. To which His Highness bidding me with the rest, we left the orchard, and through the gardens drew near to the house.

CHAPTER XIII

I WAS now soon to find that it may be easier to assume a part than to throw it off. At His Highness's invitation I was no little dismayed, having at the moment but one desire — to get me home, I mean, without delay. At thought of the feminine armor of a petticoat I was filled with a courage greater than any I had yet appeared to show. So armed, I felt I could even, without overmuch blushing, confess the sex of Sir Michael Drayton's messenger. But this greatness of heart did at once forsake me, falling away into my great boots, as it seemed, at first thought of standing up in them and their kindred garments to say, before all these soldiers, or any one of them, " I am a woman ! "

Seeking, then, for some means of evasion, I laid my hand, on our being come near to the house, upon the arm of M. de Rondiniacque, thinking his frank and laughing countenance to offer sure promise of a kindly nature. On his then pausing to observe me, I did draw him a little to one side, asking if it were possible and convenient to him to make my excuse to His Highness, seeing I was much set on returning immediately home.

He clapped a hand upon my shoulder, and looking down upon me very kindly, with yet a comical glitter of mirth in his eye,—"Why, my brave boy," said he, "I would very willingly do you a service, whether for your brave deed or your pretty manners. But, if you will take an old soldier's counsel," and at this word he twirled his small and very black mustachios mighty fiercely, "you will not risk offending so great a man as William, Prince of Orange-Nassau, in so strongly rising a tide of your fortune. *Mon Dieu!*" he cried, laughing and looking in my face too close and keenly for my comfort, "if the lad is not shy and timorous as any girl!" And with that he thrust his arm through mine, and, "If you will ever bear that commission His Highness named," he said, "you must learn to sit at meat with soldiers without blushing. Come, let us go in and contrive that we sit together. I doubt not that and a bumper or two will give you courage!"

After which I dared say no more, but, as he would have haled me by force into the dining-hall, I begged him stay a moment while I spoke with Christopher Kidd, to whom calling as he hung forlorn and hesitating on our rear, I begged him to ride out and pick up as many as might be of our

straggling troop, and to send them one and all back
to Drayton with news that all was well.   Some
signs of mirth appearing upon Christopher's face,
which in that predicament of mine I found very
foolish and inconvenient, I continued in harder
tones and with words of command in place of forms
of request: " Though you are but a soldier of a day,
Kidd, I believe you know very well under whose
command Sir Michael Drayton's small body of horse
left home.   Find of them such as you may within
the space of two hours, and see that they carry out
my orders.   At the end of that time you will report
here to the officer of the guard, and await my
further pleasure to escort me on my return.   I dine
with His Highness."

Though little used to command, I was not unaccustomed to be obeyed, and Christopher, closing
his mouth on his foolish grin with a jerk, saluted
and marched off to the orchard and his horse with
promptitude worthy of a veteran.

" Well spoken, little soldier ! " cried M. de Rondiniacque.   " These raw levies are the devil, and
thrive on a diet of brimstone.   'T is true they need
curses for the most part, but, *mort de ma vie !* we
have not all such eyes as you to flash lightning on
our recruits."

" He did begin his drill no earlier than this morning," said I, with assumption of much carelessness;

for the anger that had, I believe, stayed Kidd from calling me madam, had left me so trembling that I feared M. de Rondiniacque holding me by the arm should perceive it. He but said, however, I should make an officer one day, whatever became of Kidd, and hurried me into the dining-hall. As we entered, the Prince was about taking his seat, and in the slight bustle of the rest following his example, M. de Rondiniacque and I slipped into two vacant seats at the lower end of the table.

On His Highness's right was seated " Captain Jennings," on his left Count Schomberg. Captain Royston also and Mr. Bentinck were at that end of the table, while I found myself, to my great discomfort, surrounded by junior officers of various nations, and, for the most part, younger even than my friend, M. de Rondiniacque. With at first great intent of courtesy, they hurried me from one embarrassment to another. Now they would have me drink deep; then, by way, I do suppose, of enlivening my spirits, they plied me with polyglottic histories of amorous adventure, growing by steady degrees ever less pleasing; till at length, finding me grow shorter in reply and shrinking closer, as it were, into my shell, they abandoned the attempt to include me in their talk, and chattered among themselves as I wish, rather than believe, was not their custom. Much, I thank Heaven, from the babel

of the many tongues, I missed; yet did I perforce
hear more than enough.

After sitting no great while at meat, His Highness, to my great satisfaction, retired, requesting
the attendance of " Captain Jennings " alone, and
making Captain Royston, as their host, occupy at
the head of the table the seat he was leaving.

More than once before the Prince's withdrawing,
I had found Ned's eyes fixed upon me, with the
gaze of one that in vain pursues a memory intangi-
ble.   Now, although it had mightily pleased me to
bewilder the man in baffling his pursuit had we been
alone together, I yet, in that company I was in,
found his enquiring regard not a little disconcerting;
and, soon perceiving that his changed position at
the table increased the frequency of the attack, I
made shift to summon sufficient courage to ask his
permission, on some plea of fatigue and indisposi-
tion, to retire.   Which request he very courteously
granted, begging, however, that I would not leave
Royston before he should find time and opportunity
to speak with me.

And so I found my way to the one chamber in
the house that I knew; madam's withdrawing-room,
to wit, which I had twice entered when Ned had
taken me, a little maid, to see his mother; a large
room, whose casement, broad, low, and heavily
mullioned, looked out with a very noble aspect

across copse and meadow, where the land fell away
to the southward beyond the stream whose rocky
channel had been one of the defences of the house
in former days.   And, as I stood idly gazing from
the window, and drumming upon the panes with
idle fingers, and wondering when Farmer Kidd
would return, I remembered how in the old days
Ned had told me of some wondrous means of escape
that there was from that old house, which he would
one day, if I should grow wise enough, reveal to
me.   And I wished that I had learned it then, that
I might use it now, and so be quit at once of
Prince, breeches, and a false position.

The landscape fading into the early darkness of
late autumn, I stretched myself, half sitting and
half lying, on the settle near the fire that burned
fitfully on the great hearth of the chamber; and
here soon forgot the passing of time in a doze induced, as I suppose, by the warmth of the fire, and
the fatigue of my ride and the subsequent excitements.   From this slumber I was aroused, how
long after my falling into it I know not, by the
entrance of a trooper, doing duty as servant, and
bearing two heavy and branched silver candle-
sticks, filled with lighted candles.   I was yet rubbing my eyes to clear my head of sleep and dreams,
and striving to sit upright, when I caught my right
spur on my left boot, and straightway remembered

who I was, and how little like it I appeared. And then, close on the heels of the soldier with the candles, comes to me M. de Rondiniacque.

" Aha, my toy soldier! " he cried, as his eye lighted on me, " so 't is here you have been hiding. And sleeping, I see. Well, you may sleep on, if you will, for His Highness bids me bring you his most urgent request that you will here stay the night, in order to accompany him in the morning on his intended visit to your kinsman, Sir Michael —something—— " .

" Sir Michael Drayton," I replied. " I do suppose, sir," I went on, " that the Prince's urgent request differs little from a command ? "

" Faith, you suppose well, young gentleman," said M. de Rondiniacque. " And therefore I made bold to send your man, when he returned from fulfilling your order, back to the place you named. Captain Royston has already much ado to feed and bed us all."

" And did Kidd obey your orders against mine ? " I asked, rather that, saying something, I might cover my dismay than in any anxiety of discipline.

" Having seen us together, I think he made little distinction, my little bashaw," said M. de Rondiniacque, laughing. " I threatened him, moreover, with your displeasure, if he delayed. And now I must to His Highness."

And with that he left me, thinking very sadly I
had enough of being a man.   Had there been a
woman in the house, I had gone to her, and told
her my story.   But to none of all these men did I
dare to breathe my true name and state; unless,
indeed, it had been to Captain Royston.   And I
murmured over to myself that title, which did ring
so strange, and yet so proudly, in my ear.   It went
stiffly, too, upon the tongue that was once used to
say: " Hither, Ned; not so, Ned; nay, Ned; but I
will have it so."   Well, Ned,. I thought, was ever
tender with me, and I might, indeed, at a pinch,
make shift to tell him my name and troubles; but—
and then in my mind there lifted up his head a little
devil of mischief, and I vowed I would not so tell
him till I should be enforced; but, having taken a
vagary to be a man, I would hold fast to my purpose, that I might from behind this mask see more
of the man and to what he was grown from the boy
that had been my playmate and childhood's lover.
I was fain not a little, moreover, certainly, to discover with what complexion of memory he retained
the thought of little Philippa Drayton.   And I
thought it was mightily in favor of my plan that,
although on that great night of his escape from
Kirke's men, we had spoken together and our hands
had met, yet since I was a little maid he had never
looked upon my countenance.

At last I heard his step in the gallery without, and, for all its weight and its jingle of sabre and spur, I had known that footfall among many, even had I not known him in the house.

Captain Royston came into the chamber, followed by him that had but now fetched candles, but bearing this time an armful of wood and a blazing pine-knot. To draw my old friend's gaze, I heaved a great sigh, and gazed sadly in the fire, and knew, though I scarce saw, his eyes to turn on me. He crossed the room to the further corner, where I could well mark him without any show of particular regard, and threw wide a small door disclosing the foot of a narrow and winding stair.

" Go up," said he to the soldier, " to the room above; kindle a good fire upon the hearth; light the candles, and when the fire is well burning, return hither and stand sentry over this door till His Highness come."

And as the man ascended the stair, Captain Royston closed the door behind him, and turned to me, who kept my gaze fast on the fire.

" 'T was a heavy sigh you heaved as I entered, young friend," he said, in a most gentle voice.

" Yes, faith," I answered, " it was heavy." And again I sighed.

He then asked me what it was did make me sad,

and I replied I did not use to be from home, and
was mighty lonesome.

"Nay, lad," he cried cheerily, laying a hand of
comfort on my shoulder, "'t is but till the morrow.
You have to-day borne yourself like a man; be not
now homesick like a very maid.   There is company
enough.   Why didst leave the table?"

"I was near falling with fatigue, sir," I answered; "and—and—and, in truth, I liked not the
talk at the table where I sat."

"Poor lad!" said he, gently patting the shoulder
where his hand did lie, and thereafter drawing the
hand away; "poor lad! Would you grow to be a
man? Harden your ears—your ears, mark me, not
your heart."   And I said nothing to him, but to
myself that I feared both would need it ere long.

And then there came to us M. de Rondiniacque
in search of Captain Royston, crying jovially:
"Aha! have I found you, truant Master Host? His
Highness did but now ask for you, and wonders
somewhat, I think, at your long absence."

To which Royston replied: "I warrant His Highness knows that a host without hostess or servants
is no little put to it to house, feed, and bed so many
guests. I will go to him, and make my excuse."
He then turned to me, saying: "Prithee, gentle
friend, be of better comfort. It is not to His
Highness alone that your great service has been

13

rendered, and I would not have you cheerless. Godemar, hold the lad in talk a while. All this is strange to him, and he is overborne with fatigue." He then took some steps toward the door, but again turned to my side, and—" Speak your best English, Godemar," said he, " and your modest jests, if you have them. None of your ribald tales,—'t is a home-bred youth." Upon which, with a kindly nod to me, and a slap on the shoulder of a weight more suited to my garments than my sex, Captain Royston left the room.

M. de Rondiniacque looked upon me with a merry twinkle in his eye.

"*Ma foi !* " he said, " M. le Capitaine lays heavy commands upon me. Must I even do as he says ? "

" It were best," I answered, with some severity, and never turning my eyes from the fire. ·

" I see not wherefore," said he; " I would gladly cheer you, lad, and he would take all the merriment from our jesting."

" Indeed," I replied, " I had rather never laugh again than hear more such talk as did pass for wit around us at dinner."

He flung himself with a movement of much petulance into a chair on the other side of the hearth, and—" My faith ! " he cried, " 't is even as they did tell me: a sorry land and a sad ! A country, *mort de ma vie !* where one must shift with beer for wine, mists for sunshine, and hags and hoydens for women."

" Alack!" I cried, being vastly amused; " have the women also displeased your lordship?"

" Gadso!" answered M. de Rondiniacque, " they have, and mightily. *Mon Dieu!* in all the days since we set foot ashore I have not seen one I would stand to observe a second time. I begin to see it is easy to be a Puritan in such a land."

And when I did not answer him, he peered curiously across the flickering twilight into my face. Anon he rose and came to me, with one hand seizing me by the arm, and raising my chin, not over gently, with the other—" *Ma foi!*" he said, laughing, " with laces and furbelows, and those great eyes, wouldst make a better thyself than any lass of them all."

So I began to tremble for my secret, and saw no way out but in anger; knowing, indeed, so little of the ways of men, that I was ignorant of running a greater danger in that attempt to avoid the less.

I straightway sprang to my feet, flinging off his hands, crying to him to let me be, or ill would follow, and laying hand upon and half drawing my sword.

" What, pepper-box!" cried M. de Rondini-acque, " what, will you quarrel for nothing? Nay," he went on, with a great laugh, " do but

see it ruffle! Come, boy, take your hand from
your sword, or I will take the sword from you."

By this, between his tone of contempt and my
own fear that I made but a sorry figure, I was
trembling with anger no longer simulated; when,
on my making wholly to disengage my sword, the
Frenchman did pounce upon me with the swiftness
of a hawk, catching my wrists, one in each of his
hands, in a grasp that seemed of iron. I would
have wrenched them free, but found each struggle
to that end did bruise and pinch my poor flesh
worse than the last. Being very near the point of
tears, while yet in my heart raging with anger, I
called aloud on Captain Royston, who, to my good
fortune, did enter the room even as I called.

" Heyday!" he cried, " what 's the matter ? Do
not hurt the boy, Godemar," he went on, when
drawing near he saw how I struggled to free my
hands.

M. de Rondiniacque laughed again as he let me
go. " The little fool hurts himself with striving,"
he said. " Had I not held him, he had run me
through with the pretty sword the Prince did give
him. *Mon Dieu !* he is anxious to flesh it."

" How is this, Master ——? " says Captain Royston, mighty sternly, till checked for lack of a name
to give me,—" on my life, I know not how you are
called."

Now this was a question I had no wish to answer without some previous consideration; so, knowing I could scarce keep out of my voice the sound of tears, the pain of whose coming was now some minutes clutching at my throat, I resolved to use them as cover to my disregarding his enquiry. " He has hurt my hands," I said, with a little sob, rubbing my wrists the while in the manner of a spoiled and petulant child.

" What, baby!" he cried; " I give you a friend to cheer you with his good heart and ready wit, and you must needs fall a-wrangling with him; and then, because he would curb your childish passion, must you weep like a very boy unbreeched ? "

" I do not weep," I said; yet could I not check the next sob and some few tears that fell for the pain I had had.

" No more, lad, no more, for shame!" he answered. " There was a bold spirit in you not many hours ago. Be a man now, for the love of Heaven."

" With all my heart I would," said I, " if I did know the way of it; to the end that I might make him smart," I added, wagging my head in the direction of M. de Rondiniacque.

" Learn to take a jest as 't is meant," said Captain Royston, " and you may some day grow to it."

" I am as God did make me," I replied pettishly.

" It is rank heresy to cast the blame in that quarter," said M. de Rondiniacque.

At which Captain Royston laughed a little, but gently bade him hold his peace, saying: " The boy is in my care, and we cannot make a man of him before the morrow."

And now the entry of the Prince most happily put an end to the discussion of my shortcoming as a man. His Highness was attended by " Captain Jennings," Count Schomberg, and Mr. Bentinck, with a few other gentlemen. And as the doors were flung wide for them the trooper that had been about preparing the chamber above descended the little stair, closed the door behind him, and stood on guard immovable before it, with drawn sword.

The Prince appeared in the best of humors; of which the reason was very soon made plain.

" Captain Royston," said His Highness, coming over to the fire, " we are come to a happy end of our conferring, and ' Captain Jennings,' being pressed for time, must at once take himself again to the road. His escort is provided, and he would bid you farewell. It should indeed be to us all a melancholy parting, for 't is little to be hoped any man here will again encounter *Captain Jennings*."

When the laugh due to the jest of a prince had risen and died away, " Captain Jennings " held out his hand to his host, and said: " ' Jennings ' owes you much, Captain Royston, though you are like, as His Highness well says, never to meet him again, yet in your ear will I tell you that he has a kinsman that is his very double and his best friend. I have reason for saying that this gentleman will in the happier days to come pass by no occasion of furthering the interest of so stanch a companion, and so generous a host, as Captain Edward Royston.''

To which courteous speech honest Ned replied with some words of his duty to His Highness of Orange; and I knew well by a certain stiffness of his manner, which was still clearly marked as he wished him a safe and pleasant journey, that the favor of '' Captain Jennings '' was not such as he wished to earn.

That gentleman, after some other farewells of much grace and kindness, passed on to me where I stood apart, and with a very gracious smile on his noble countenance thanked me for the service I had done him. On my asking what that might be, he was at some pains to explain, in a voice meant for me alone, that but for my timely warning and protection to His Highness, that plot might well have had a very different and terrible ending; in the blame of which fatal conclusion he himself, from the peculiarity of his position, would almost certainly have become implicated. '' I hope, therefore,'' he said, '' that we shall meet again when I have thrown

aside this *nom de guerre* to which I have only a sort
of left-handed right by marriage and necessity.''
And then first I guessed who he was. '' But,'' he
went on, '' if I do seem to need a fresh introduction,
young gentleman, when that day comes, I beg you
will attribute my lack of memory to politic reasons.''

By which, thinking him little likely to encounter
and less to recognize me, I was vastly amused.

'' I am ready to wager, my lord,'' I said, laughing
a little, '' that the fault will be neither yours nor the
nation's, should you pass me by.''

He looked at me for a moment with a glance so
keen that I found it hard to support; then, bidding
me farewell, very shortly took leave of the Prince
and departed on his journey to Salisbury.

As the door closed upon him, His Highness
crossed the chamber and tapped Captain Royston
on the shoulder.

'' You act with little wisdom, Captain,'' he said,
with a merry laugh, '' in the moment when the
Protestant religion has triumphed over all else, to
receive with coldness an offer of favor from him
that is one day to be the first soldier in Europe.''

'' I trust, Your Highness,'' said Royston, with
something of pride in his tone, '' that I have not
yet lost the favor of him that is.''

'' I see we shall have a courtier in you yet, Captain,'' said His Highness. '' The day has been long,

and I must needs ask my good host the way to my chamber. Sleep is a fickle mistress to me, and she must be wooed in season, or she will have none of me."

"Since the terrible danger Your Highness has this day escaped in my house but by the goodness of God and this young gentleman's courage," said Captain Royston, "I am resolved to beg Your Highness's acceptance rather of its most secure than its most luxurious chamber. At the head of this stair," he went on, making the sentry stand aside as he threw open the door, "is a room neither very large nor finely furnished. If Your Highness will, however, deign to make use of it, he will find the bed good and the chamber warm. It has no other approach, and with Your Highness's consent I will myself watch here during the night, while Lieutenant de Rondiniacque takes my place as officer of the watch, which has been doubled, and commands every approach."

"I thank you for your care of my safety, Captain Royston," said the Prince. "If the bed be as good as the supper, we will ask none better between this and London. But I believe you are over-cautious."

On Captain Royston's explaining that the honor of his house was involved in His Highness's safety within it, all his dispositions were very kindly and

freely accepted. Not long after which His Highness, with some kind words to me on the service I
had done him, and of his purposed visit on the
morrow to Drayton, retired to the chamber already
mentioned, being lighted by Captain Royston, and
attended by Mr. Bentinck for some discussion of
matters of state.

Whereafter I very soon found myself again alone,
the rest departing in charge of M. de Rondiniacque,
commissioned by our host to show each gentleman
where he should lie. I say I was alone; for the
sentry at the door of the stair to the Prince's chamber counted little as company, which I was fain to
seek in the dancing of the flames upon the hearth
and in my own thoughts. These were not uneasy,
for I knew that Ned must return as he had gone,
and that a word to him would be my protection
if aught inconvenient should arise; nor were they
long, for he soon returned.

CHAPTER XIV

THE high back of the settle where I sat being between us, Captain Royston upon his return did not perceive me until, having dismissed the sentry and set his candlestick upon a table, he drew near the fire to warm himself; then, his eyes falling upon me—" Heyday, lad!" he cried, " I did think you abed and asleep by this. I scarce know how I came to forget you. Let me see — where should you lie to-night ? The house is mighty full, and I would not put you with—— "

" Let me share your watch here an hour, Captain," I said. " I am very wakeful, and it will be company for us both."

" Will you do so ? " he asked with some eagerness, and once more glancing at me with that same look, at once curious and shy, that I had before noted. " Indeed I shall be glad of your company, were it only to help me keep open eyes." And with that he flung himself wearily into a seat over against me, hitching round his belt so that his sword lay between the long legs that, to rest them the better, he stretched full before him. " I was in the saddle all last night," he went on, " and indeed it seems a week since I was in a bed. So here let us sit, you and I, with the fate of England in our hands,"—at which he pointed to the door of the Prince's stairway. " Hast recovered of the spleen?"

I answered him that I was recovered.

" How came he to anger you ? " he then asked me.

" Why, sir," I replied, " he did give bad names to all things in England; and then he fell foul of the women—and—and I do not like him."

" De Rondiniacque," said Captain Royston, " is a good comrade and a brave soldier; and, faith, I did think all women were fair to him. He will fall in love and again fall out thrice in a day. But no woman is long fair in his eyes when his fortune has been ill. There was a lass in Flanders—" and here he broke into a laugh, and I into a yawn of subterfuge, in hope to put him off his tale. For I feared, unjustly enough, more talk of that kind that I had comprehended but sufficiently to dislike. Whereat he asked if he wearied me, and I answered that he did not so, but that I would know if he were of a like complexion with M. de Rondiniacque in matters of women and love.

" Nay, indeed, lad," he answered, laughing again; " De Rondiniacque and I are little akin in

such matters. I have, as he would say, the slower
temper—perhaps the more constant."

"Constant!" said I; and as I said the word I
could feel the little tremor in my laughter which I
hoped his ear would not detect. "Constant to what
—to whom ? Ah, there is doubtless some lady that
looks out over the endless canals and ugly windmills
of flat Holland for your return, Captain Royston."

"Nay, nay," he answered, "there is no broad
Dutch face wet with tears of my causing." And
then the mirth died out of his voice, as with a very
tender hesitancy he continued: "But there is, or
there was, a little maid — a child — but, plague on
me! what do I babble of ? And what does so
young a lad as you know of these things ?"

"H'm-m-m!" said I, as one that could, if he
would but speak, lay claim to knowledge enough
and to spare.

"What, what !" he cried, mocking me. "Is
your heart even as tender as your years ? Does the
baby think he knows what love is ?"

"On my conscience, yes," I answered; "but I
may know and never feel it, I do suppose."

"What an outlandish boy it is!" said Ned,
laughing; and, more gravely, "when you love, lad,
and would have your lady look upon you, be as
when you served us so well this day, and not the
child that is disordered by the chance word of a

jolly soldier. I have heard tell that women do love one that is a man, be his vows, even as De Rondiniacque's, never so brittle."

" Perhaps they do," I answered; and wondered, sickly a little in my heart, how it would fare with me if his were so. " But," I continued, " if men's vows are so light, what of that little maid ? "

And my gallant Captain seemed to retire, as it were, again into his shell, saying he would speak of her no more, and that indeed he knew not wherefore he had called her to mind. Whereto I said that maybe I could tell him.

" 'T is little likely," said he, smiling as one that suffers the gambols of a merry child, even to the peril of a wound but half healed.

" But tell you I can," I persisted; " you spoke of her, not because she did come to your mind, but because she is never out of it. Is it not so ? "

Again he looked at me with that glance of enquiry.

" Indeed, I think it is so," he replied; " but how you should know it, Master ——, by my life, here have I had all manner of converse with you, even to the telling things that have not passed my lips this three years, and yet I know not your name. Prithee, tell it me."

" My name is Drayton," I said.

" Is it even so ? " cried Ned. " It is strange. Where do you live ? "

" From here some five leagues on the great road,
Salisbury way," I answered.

" At Drayton Manor, is it ? " he asked with great
eagerness.

" At Drayton Manor," I replied.

" But old Sir Michael," says Ned, " had no son
of your youth."

" Nay," said I, " I am no son of Sir Michael.
But he is my nearest of kin, and in his house do I
live this many a day."

" Ah, so! I have heard," said Royston mus-
ingly, " of other branches of the family. But, if
Drayton be your home, you can tell me of—of the
child, your cousin; of Mistress Philippa Drayton, I
mean, Sir Michael's daughter."

" Aha! the little maid! At last we come at his
little maid! " I cried, clapping my hands together in
a manner that suited but ill, as I suppose, with my
boots and spurs.

But he, like the man he was, being much occupied
in attempt to conceal the secret he was about re-
vealing, did not mark me, but sternly stiffened his
face and made straight his back, and replied: " I
said not it was she. But I would have her news.
Is she well, and is she now at Drayton ? "

" Gad 's my life! " I answered, feeling very blus-
terous and naughty as I used my father's favorite
oath, " it is so. She is well, and she is at Drayton.

I would she were not. She does keep her heart
safe for me, the baggage! Troth, I have little mind
to her — a bouncing, overgrown country wench, of
ill manners, loud tongue, and shrewish speech.
Pah!'' Whereat I twisted my mouth into a grimace very disgustful, and I saw the light of anger
come into his eye.

'' You shall not so speak of that lady,'' he said,
in a tone that was not loud, yet had in it that which
made one part of me shake with fear, while the rest
of the woman was singing a little inward song of
thanksgiving. Whereof it is like enough he saw in
my face some sign, for he went on more gently to
say he knew it was not so; that I but railed at her
in mischief; that I mocked at him because, with
something womanish that is in a half-grown boy, I
had divined the secret of his love. '' My heart,''
he said, rising from his seat with eyes that looked
afar, as if none was by him, '' has never left her
keeping since she did ride upon my shoulder, but
her little hands ever hold me fast, even as they did
use to cling and grip me by the hair.'' With that
he passed his hand over his head, as if he still did
feel the clutching baby fingers. Then he came back
to me. '' You see, sir, I let you know at what it is
you mock. Yet if you own the words were but
spoken in jest, I will pass the matter by.''

And then I knew that I had been playing with

fire, and made all haste to quench it, owning with
averted face that I had indeed but spoken out of
mischief to anger him, and saying that the girl was
well enough.   It was, I suppose, from pride that he
took no note of this grudging opinion, yet it did not
control his curiosity.

" And does she keep me in mind ? " he asked, as
he sank again into his seat.

" 'T is like enough," I answered, as if I cared
little for the matter.   " I have heard her name you."

" In what terms ? " said he; " I pray you, tell
me what she said."

" Indeed, I do forget," I replied, mischief rising
once more in my heart.   " And I will wager there
have been times when you have forgot the minx as
readily as I would, if you would but let me, Captain."

" A fig for your wager! ". said Royston lightly.
" Why, I have never, since I was out of England,
entered a new town but I have bought some toy or
jewel for her."   And I saw his hand steal to the
breast of his coat, and, guessing that there was a
pocket beneath, I began at once to be mighty
curious to know what was in it, and to think my
masquerade had lasted near long enough when it
kept me from my rights.

" Do you carry them ? " I asked, striving to keep
all eagerness out of my manner.

" Nay, nay," he answered; and, had he been another man, I had thought his smile and the short and hesitating laugh that followed it well-nigh foolish: " Nay, 't is but a pair of the new kid-leather gloves that they do use in France." And here he drew a small packet from the pocket I had divined, and added, with much tenderness: " They did make me think of her pretty hands, and I could no more put them away from me."

· And, as he regarded the packet and gently smoothed the wrapper, I snatched it from his hand, and—" Let me see," I said, and proceeded to unfold it.

" Gently, gently!" cried Ned; " they must not be so handled."

" Ay, they would fit me well," said I, measuring one against my left hand. " And our hands are near of a size. Will you give them to me in her stead, sir ? "

" That will I not, young Avarice," he answered, recovering the gloves with a snatch that took me by surprise. " My lady's gloves, indeed! what next, monkey ? Do you think, because you have a small fist and handle a glove like a great girl, that you will get all you ask ? "

" Well," said I, pouting and growing reckless in my delight of the game I played, " well, I shall have them of her in the end."

" No more, jackanapes," he answered angrily,
and I scarce know how I should have fared had not
the door at the foot of the Prince's stair at that
moment opened to admit Mr. William Bentinck.

" His Highness is retired, Captain Royston," he
said. " He renews his thanks to you."

To which Captain Royston replied that he wished
the fare deserved them better, and enquired whether
Mr. Bentinck knew the way to his chamber.

" I do," he replied. " I wish you a good-night,
Captain Royston. It were well," he added, with a
dark and significant glance, " that no further alarm
befell—in *your* house, Captain."

" I am so much of your mind, sir," said Royston,
" that I have asked and obtained His Highness's
consent here to watch the night through myself. I
wish you good rest." Mr. Bentinck turned again
as he reached the door, saying that His Highness
had enquired of him where the prisoners had been
lodged that were taken after the affair in the
orchard.

" They lie under lock and guard in the strong-
room above," said Royston; " all but the priest,
who is in the chamber that adjoins it on the left,
for greater safety. I did not think it well to leave
his clever head to work among them." And here
M. de Rondiniacque, looking into the room as he
went his rounds, very readily undertook, at Captain

Royston's desire, to conduct Mr. Bentinck, that he might with his own eyes, as Captain Royston said, see how these prisoners were disposed. They being departed on this business, Captain Royston stood gazing moodily into the fire. It seemed he had quite forgotten me; and, since it did not fall with my wishes to be left out of his thoughts, I plucked him timidly by the sleeve, and asked if I had angered him with my freakishness.

" No, lad, no," he answered, still gazing into the fire. " I know not indeed why I told you as much, unless it be that the Drayton face of you did bring to mind old days, and made me think my thoughts aloud. I know my poor secret is safe with a Drayton." And then he turned and looked hard in my face.

And under his gaze I trembled, and had much ado not to throw my arms about his neck and cry " Ned " to him. And yet I dared not, for shame of my clothes, and so, to change the color of his thought, I said: " That man does eye you with mistrust, Captain."

" He is no friend to me," said Ned, " nor ever has been. But His Highness has no more faithful servant and friend than William Bentinck. He had of late warning from France that the Prince's life was sought after, and that a certain priest should lead the assassins. To-day the attack is made, a

priest is taken, and all in my house, and I one of
the few that knew His Highness should come to
this place. I can scarce wonder if he look on me
with suspicion, and would see himself how we guard
the dogs above there in the strong-room."

And then Mr. Bentinck and M. de Rondiniacque
returned. The first was pleased to approve all he
had seen, but pointed out that the prison of the
priest was the chamber to the right of the strong-
room, and not on its left, as Captain Royston had
said. M. de Rondiniacque here explained that the
prisoner had at his order been transferred from the
room to the other, on the report of the sentry that
two bars in the window of the priest's first lodging
were rotten and might easily be burst.

" It will serve as well, nay, better," said Captain
Royston, still dreamily gazing into the fire. And
Mr. Bentinck, expressing himself satisfied that all
was well, departed to his chamber in company of
M. de Rondiniacque.

Now as these matters had for me little of interest,
and as my fatigue was great, I had been growing
very weary and full of sleep; so it came that when
these gentlemen left us I signified my pleasure
thereat with a great yawn of weariness and a long
sigh of satisfaction.

" Poor lad! " cried Ned, with such tenderness as
he was wont to use to the child that had so loved

and hectored him, " poor lad, you are faint for
sleep. I will see where we may put you."

" It is not sleep, Captain," I said, stifling a
second yawn. " But I take little interest in prisoners, and I am, oh! so thirsty."

" 'T is the long ride, and your dinner was
naught," he answered. " Keep your eyes open,
and watch a while here in my place, and I will bring
you food and wine. I pray you, do not close your
eyes."

And as he neared the door, I saw him start as hit
by a thought forgotten, and—"The chamber on the
right," he murmured. " How came I to forget ?
But he will never find the panel, even though he
were a Jesuit." And so, with yet another warning
that I should watch well and not sleep, he went out
into the gallery. And I sat by the fire, wondering
what those strange words should mean. Open indeed I did keep my eyes, but I believe my mind
was not very far from dreams at the moment when
a thing happened so like to a trick of sleeping fancy
that it awoke me quite. I thought that I saw, in
that dim light (for one great candlestick was above
with His Highness of Orange, the other below in
the hand of Captain Royston), a great piece of the
stone wall that made the far side of the wide and
lofty hearth slowly to draw back and recede from
my eyes, as a door that is opened stealthily from

behind.   I sat erect and rubbed my eyes, and still did it draw away from me, and made a noise of rusted grinding as it went.   And a nameless horror crept over my body till it reached and seemed to stiffen the roots of my hair.   I would have cried aloud as I sat and expected something to come whence the door of stone had gone; but before I could find voice there came from the gap in the wall the darkly clad figure of a man, who stepped from the hearth, and stood looking down upon me.   His face I could not clearly perceive, for the fire was behind him, but the sound of his voice I thought I had once already heard.

CHAPTER XV

"HUSH!" he said gently, thinking me, I suppose, as indeed I was, at the point of calling aloud on the guard. "I am unarmed, and would not hurt you if I could. What is your name?" And his voice, for all that it was young and sweet, sounded like my father's, for which there was reason enough, as I was soon to know.

"My name is Drayton," I answered simply.

"And the other?" he asked.

"Phil—Philip," I answered; and then I leapt to my feet as one waking from a dream, saying, as I did so, "though, sooth, I know not why I tell you." With my moving he so changed his position that the glow of the fire fell upon his face, and I knew him for the priest that had been taken in the orchard.

"Nor I," he said sternly, "for it is false. I am Philip Drayton."

"What, what!" I cried, in much amazement. "And is Sir Michael your father?"

"Sir Michael is my father," he replied.

"And mine also," said I, very joyfully, with yet

no thought of the terrible meaning of his presence. " I took but little from my name. Lay the falsehood on my clothes. Brother Philip, I am Philippa."

He seemed less pleased with the encounter than dismayed by my attire.

" My sister!" he said; "my sister in this guise!"

" Nay, trust me," I said merrily, " none knows me for a maid."

And then he seemed to remember something, and, laying both hands on my shoulders, he held me off from him so that the light of the fire fell upon my face.

" My little sister!" said he. " I saw you, then, in the orchard. And was it you that saved the life of the Stadtholder of Holland ?"

" So they say," I replied, doubtfully, wondering at the joy I saw upon his countenance.

" I am glad of it," he said, " right glad of it, indeed." And with that he heaved a great sigh of relief.

" Glad!" I cried. "Glad, you say! How can that be, when you yourself were one of those that would have slain him ?"

" With them indeed I was," he said; " but I had no part in the planning that foul plot, and took none in its attempted execution. Had I even known the wickedness that was toward, I would

not have obeyed what I deemed of all earthly commands the most terrible. By the happiest stroke
of chance they did move my lodging to the chamber where is the sliding panel that gives upon the
stair by which I have now reached you. Old Mr.
Nathaniel Royston did show it me when I was but
a little lad and you unborn. But he brought me no
further than this chamber. I do remember," my
brother continued, with a note in his voice that
seemed to mark the man's sadness to recall a merry
childhood, " I do remember that he said, with his
kindly chuckle, he must not show the rest of the
secret to one that like enough would some day prove
a Jesuit in disguise. Though he spoke in jest, he
was a good prophet. And now, child," he said,
with rapid change to a manner more urgent, " you
must show me what he would not."

" If you mean the secret way from the house,"
said I, " I do not know it; nor I would not show it
if I did. I am here on guard duty till Captain
Royston return."

" Sister," said Philip, speaking with voice and
words so solemn that heart and ear were enchained
till he came to an end,—" Sister, King James and
his cause are dear to me. Holy Mother Church
and her cause are yet more dear. But dearest of all
(God forgive me!), dearest of all to me now, little
sister Phil, is our dear father's honor and the honor

of his house.   It is no shame to him or to the
Drayton name that I should work or fight for King
James; none if I should spend my life to bring the
dear land back to the true faith.   But what one of
us will hold up his head again if the name must be
made foul, and stink in the nostrils of men, for a
base plot of treachery and assassination ?   Therefore, child of my father, for the name's sake, let
me go."

With that he made to pass me and reach the door
into the gallery, but I stepped between and took
him by the arms.

"Do not move," I said; "not one step, lest I
call on the guard."   And he stood like a statue of
stone, while for a few moments, stretched by the
gravity and tension of my thought into the seeming
of hours, I was silent, and then: "Philip," I said,
"if you are innocent of this wicked thing, why are
you in England ?"   And in a few words he told me
of the mission on which he was come.   Then said
I: "Will you now give it up — this mission — and
return at once into France, if I let you go ?"   And,
seeing that he shook his head, "Come," I said;
"be quick.   It is that or naught.   Swear it, and
you may go for me.   The Captain will be upon us
soon, and then it will be too late."

"Yes," he answered.

"It is an oath—a Drayton's oath ?" I asked.

" It is," said Philip.

" Then go, in God's name!" I cried. " Though, faith, I know not the secret passage, and I do not see how otherwise you should pass all the guards."

" I can but try," he answered; and again would have moved to the door, but in that moment I heard a footfall; and, being more sure from whom it came than whence, I bade Philip keep still, and ran as light as my heavy boots would allow to the door, drew it a little back, and peered into the passage. Mightily eased in mind by what I saw, which was little enough, being but the back of the sentry disappearing round the corner of the gallery, I softly pushed-to the door, whispering ere I turned: " Quick! quick! Go now. 'T is your one chance. Thank God it was not Captain Royston; and the sentry is for the moment out of hearing."

And uttering the last words I turned to find myself face to face with the man for whose absence I had just given thanks to God. He was looking at me over the table where he had just set down his candlestick beside the meat and wine he had fetched for me. And of all the terrible things of that night, none, I think, did send to my heart a pang so sharp as the sight of that flagon of wine and wooden platter of cold venison; verily, for a moment I felt, with his reproachful eye upon me, that I was indeed that base thing he could not choose but think me.

" Thank Him not too soon, thou devil's whelp! "
he said.

Philip yet stood where I had left him.   To him I
went quickly and whispered: " Go, while you may.
I will engage him.   He will not hurt me, for, if
needs must, I will tell him who I am."   Then,
going over to Captain Royston with strut and swag-
ger much belying the trembling that was within
me: " Sir," I said, laying hand to my sword, " you
give me an ill name."

" Less ill than your deeds," he answered with
great bitterness.   " I went but to get you meat and
drink, and, returning, thought of that secret way
from the room above.   I stepped over the sleeping
sentry, unbolted the door and closed it softly behind
me, only to find the bird flown.   As I drew back
the panel he had closed behind him and followed
him down the stair, greatly fearing some mischance
from his evasion, naught I imagined was so bad as
the finding you together planning his escape.   Was
it for this I did cherish you, little viper ? "

To all which, though his words did cut me to the
heart, I but replied that I was no reptile, and that
therefore he lied, hoping by such naughty words to
provoke him to quarrel with me, while Philip was
about escaping, purposing thereafter to tell him the
truth, when that was accomplished for which I
would not have him even in his own conscience held

responsible.   Me they could not very heavily pun-
ish, since from His Highness of Orange I took no
pay, nor had sworn to him any oath.   Nor was I
altogether hopeless of persuading Ned to conceal
his knowledge of what it would then be too late to
prevent.

"Let me pass, boy," he cried, "or I will whip
you soundly with my belt."   But when he would
have put me aside, as I stood between them, I held
him fast to the utmost of my strength.   Finding I
would still cling to him, he put his hand to the
buckle of his belt.

"Whip, then," I said, "for the man shall go
free."   And, though my flesh did most propheti-
cally shudder beneath the imminent stripes, I
thought that here was no bad way of gaining time
for Philip, when I should come to weep, in Philippa's proper person, for the pain of that whipping.
But he flung me off, muttering a plague on the
Drayton countenance of me, and that the priest
would make off if he did not seize him.

"He shall!" I cried, half drawing my sword.
"What!   Art afraid to draw on a lesser than thy
hulking self ? "

"False and ingrate though you are, I would not
hurt you," he said; "and I will not call upon the
guard; but I will have him again secure in his
chamber, and so shield you, little devil, from all

punishment but what I will myself administer when all is done.''

And as he advanced upon me and would have seized me, I lifted my cloak that was on the back of the settle and flung it over his head, where, for a brief space, despite his struggles, I held it. And while his eyes were thus blinded for a moment, Philip, swift and silent, slipped past us and through the door of the stair to the Prince's chamber. Royston, however, soon flung me off and tore the cloak from his head. And I saw at length great anger in his face, and with a last essay at strategy did leap to the door that gives upon the gallery, as if indeed I defended Philip's retreat; and there, with drawn sword and taunting words, I defied him. And then he came, and our swords met. And finding, as well I had known I should find, that he was too strong for me, I was, after a pass or two, at the point of calling him by the old name and of telling mine, when he did something that had formed no part of the teaching he had given me with the foils, so that I found myself speedily at his mercy, and felt the sharp, cold prick of steel low down upon my neck. And then I thought my end was indeed come, and I tried to murmur: '' Spare me, dear Ned,'' but could not.

Now all these things — from Ned's return to my foolish fainting at the first blood — that have in the telling taken so long did happen so quickly that perhaps seconds rather than minutes were their proper measure. And my enemy has since told me that what I have called my swooning seemed but the closing for a few moments of my eyes. But, however that may be, I do think it endured suffi- ciently for his great concern. For when I opened them I knew not at all where I should be until the white solicitude of his face bending close over brought me very soon to the consciousness of the strong and tender arms that held me. So, seeing I was come to myself, he led me towards the hearth, and set me in a chair. And then I began to feel a little smarting and a warmth of trickling blood. Taking my handkerchief, I thrust it beneath waist- coat and shirt, and pressed it upon the spot that did so smart, whence withdrawing it and seeing the blood upon it, I shuddered.

" Nay, nay," said Ned, while the lines of anxiety upon his face belied the little laugh he forced from his lips, " fret not for a little blood. I thrust not hard. Wherefore did you anger me, monkey ? Come," he added, laying his hand to the breast of my shirt and fingering the buttons with that awk- wardness that a man has ever for garments that are not his, " I will heal it."

" No," I said, pulling away his hands, " you must not."

" But I would see the hurt, lad," he said. " I
know not why, but I am sorry I have hurt you.
God knows, I have killed men and thought little of
it, but this scratch to a child does mightily vex
me." And again he would have loosed the buttons.
" Come, open your shirt," he said.

" I say I will not. I am not the lad you think
me, sir."

But even then he did not understand, but took
my two hands in one of his, so great and strong
that mine might scarce writhe themselves about
within it, while he set himself to do what I would
not for all his asking. And so it was that I came
to the last line of my defences. " Let be, dear
Ned," I murmured, in that tone of pleading I had
ever in the old days used when his will did offer to
prove the stronger. " Let be, dear; 't is—'t is thy
little maid, Phil," I said, and dropped my eyes
before him, and let my prisoned hands lie still.

He stared upon me in an astonishment of wonder
that discovered the white all round his eyes, and at
first he would not believe.

" Nay, nay," he said, " it is not so!" And I
lifted my eyes and so looked into his that he could
no longer doubt.

" Verily, Ned, it is I. And I had told the sooner,"
I said, " but that — but that — " and, my words
then failing, I again dropped my gaze before his.

15

" Phil! " he cried.   " Is it even my little friend
Phil ? ' But,' you say—but what ? ''

" But that I would not tell you—and could not—
was ashamed, Ned, and did mightily desire to know
had you forgot me.''   And here, laying my folded
handkerchief to my wound inside my shirt, and
fastening all close above it, I did see his face so
lose color at thought of the hurt he had given me,
that I laid my hand upon his, saying: " Be not
vexed, sweet Ned, 't is but a scratch.''

" I am right glad of it, Phil,'' he answered, " if it
be so.   But indeed you should not run about in
this guise.   How came you to be so dressed ? ''

" That story must wait,'' I replied merrily.
" But 't is the first time, Ned, and shall be the last.''

" And if you must needs be a man,'' he went on,
" but for a day, you should cleave like a man to
one side, and not be so greedy of strife as to draw
sword on both.   There will be trouble over this
priest when he is taken, as he will be, by the guard
without.''

" Listen, Ned,'' said I.   " That priest is my
brother.''

" What! '' he cried.   " Surely it is not Philip! ''

" Philip it is,'' said I, " and no other, though I
did not know him until he told me even now in this
room.   And also he did tell me, Ned, that he had
no part in the assault upon His Highness.''

" So much," said Ned, " is true. I marked
him."

" He told me, moreover," I continued, " that
the business that brought him to England was fair
and honest, though it was for King James.   There
was another priest did force or trick him into com-
panying with the murderers.   Ned, dear Ned, I did
mean letting him go for our father's sake and our
name."   And here I found no power, and perhaps
little will, to restrain the catch of a sob in my throat.
" Men   must   not say ' spy,' ' plotmonger,' ' assassin,' when they say Drayton, Ned.   You do
forgive me ? "

" Right gladly," he answered, and seemed to
muse for a little.   And then, " 'T is well," he said,
" that I did not wake the sentry that lay sleeping
at his door."

" Why did you not ? " I asked.

" Because," he replied, " though I thought all
was safe, I would not have it known that I had left
my post."   With that he went softly to the door of
the gallery and listened.   " It is strange," he said,
when he was come again to my side, " that I hear
no sound of his capture.   Yet he could not pass the
sentry at the stair-head."

" He did not go that way," said I.

" But it was to defend that door," he retorted,
" that you drew on me."

" Ay, dear Ned," I answered, " but that was to deceive you."

" But why, cunning one," he said, " did you not at once tell me all ? "

" I feared you would be mighty stern," I answered; " also, I was loath to tell you who I was. Moreover, Ned, I did think it best for you to have neither knowledge nor share in his escape, if I might procure it without your aid. I was afraid for you."

" And yet not afraid of your life ? " he asked.

" Nay, that too. But I thought," I replied ruefully, " that I had enough cunning of fence to keep you off for a while; for I did often use to hold my own with the foils against you. In extremity I was to cry: ' 'T is I, Ned! kill me not!' But you were so fierce and strong." Whereat he laughed a little, sheathing his own sword and handing me mine.

" These are not foils," he said. " But, if your brother went not by the gallery, where then ? Is he returned to the chamber above ? " And he pointed to the gaping mouth of the secret stair.

And right upon his words Philip entered the chamber from the Prince's stairway, and, closing the door behind him: " I am here, Royston," he said.

Royston heard, and, turning, grasped him by the hand. " Ah! so it was there you did hide, old friend," he said. " Faith, they did spoil a good

man of his hands when they made you priest."
And then I saw Ned's eyes travel to the door just
closed; and he dropped Philip's hand, and his face
blanched.   "In the name of God!" he cried,
" what did you up there ? Say that you were not
in the Prince's chamber!"   And for the first time
and the last I saw Edward Royston shaken by a
passion of fear.

" It is from his chamber that I come," said Philip,
speaking and bearing himself with great serenity.

Poor Ned caught his breath with a sound sharp
and hissing.   " Then, as there is a God above us,"
he whispered, " if any harm has happened, I will
slay you and the maid your sister, though I do love
her, only before I kill myself."

" Go," said the priest, pointing to the stair,
" look on your Prince as he sleeps."

" Yes, I will go," replied Ned, flushing a little
with hope born of Philip's calm.   " But I will not
leave you free."

I caught his great horseman's pistol from the
table where Ned had laid it after escorting His
Highness to his chamber.

" Go up, Ned," said I; and to Philip, as I pointed
to a chair, " Sit there, brother." And to Ned
again: " If he but rise from his chair before you
return, I will shoot him, as surely as you shall kill
me after him. Is it primed ?" I asked, for the

pistol was of the pattern then coming into use, dis-
charged by means of a falling flint. And he, taking
it from my hand, and raising the dog, and peering
into the pan for the priming, I added: " But he
will not move, for he has done no wrong."

He put the weapon in my hand. " You will not
fail me ? " he asked, with a countenance very awful
to see. For answer I looked once in his face. He
turned and went swiftly through the little door and
up the stair.

Philip, as I think, knew it was no vain threat that
I had made. But I, believing his conscience clean,
had little doubt of a willing captive.

The time passed unbroken with a word; hours it
could not be, but whether minutes or seconds I do
not know. And somewhere in the heart of my
confidence there throbbed a little pricking pain of
doubt. For, brother as he was, to me the man was
yet a stranger. What if he were of those with
whom all means are held lawful to the cherished
end ? Had not I, but an ignorant girl, done for
one end what I had held base indeed for another ?
And for answer I clung to the stock of my weapon,
and swore he should die if His Highness had suffered.
For not only Drayton, but Royston honor also lay
in the hollow of my hand. But I swore, too, that I
would not long survive him; and, if Ned would do it,
even death would not be wholly without sweetness.

At last a step was on the stair, and my eyes went again to the little door. And, when I saw his returning face, I laughed aloud.

" You may well laugh, Mistress Philippa," he said, sheathing the sword that had not, I suppose, left his hand since it had leapt from the scabbard on his first doubt of Philip, " for I was indeed a fool to doubt him." Then, turning to Philip: " I did you wrong, Drayton," he said; " the blame must lie on the evil company we did find you in."

" I should myself, I fear, doubt any man in such case," answered Philip.

With that they fell to considering what should be done. Philip was at first for returning to his chamber above. But Ned had already taken his resolution. Sir Michael, he said, should not, in the sweet evening of a life of honor, see his house come to shame. " You cannot, I do suppose," he continued, " bring proof or witness of your innocence in the matter ? "

" He that alone could clear me," replied my brother, " is escaped. Moreover, I do not think he bears me any good-will."

" Then you must go," declared Royston, in accents very positive.

And I could not find it in me, for all the risk to him, to say him nay. So without more ado Ned went to the hearth, where, by means I did not till long after understand, he very quickly closed the opening in the wall whence Philip had entered. He next caused to appear, on the opposite side of the fire, a passage that was the counterpart of the first. He then returned to the table, and, pouring out wine from the flagon he had brought for me: " Drink," he said to Philip, " and listen.   There is little time to spare, for the officer of the watch will soon go again upon his round. You found but half the secret.   There," he said, pointing to the grim aperture in the wall of the hearth, of which the dancing light of the flames served but to mark the deeper gloom, " there is the other half.   Descend these stairs and follow the gallery. You cannot miss the way.   It will take you out among the rocks below the bridge.   Thence follow the stream until you are come to the old mill, whence you may with ease reach the highroad."

" From the mill," answered Philip, " I shall know my way.   God bless you, Royston!   It is for the old man's sake."

He grasped Ned's hand, laid his own upon my head as if in benediction, and would have left us.

" There is one word more to say," said Royston; and Philip turned on the edge of the hearth to hear it.   " I cannot let you go," continued the man who would not take the smallest risk of harming his master even in the moment when he was going

open-eyed into the danger of branding as a traitor,
" I cannot let you go to do further hurt, how honest
and open soever, to the cause I serve."

" As I gave it to my sister but now," answered
Philip, " you have my promise to do nothing for the
King, nor against him of Orange, until I have set
foot in France."

" It will serve," replied Ned.   " But — " he
added, and then paused, as if with a hesitation of
delicacy.

" What ?   Another doubt ? " cried Philip, with a
laugh.

" They say — with what truth I do not know,"
continued Ned, —" but said it is, that those of your
order have strange quirks and quibbles to ease the
conscience of oaths and other matters."

" Ah ! " said Philip.   " On what, then, or by
what, shall I swear to you ? "

" Swear me no oath," answered Royston.
" Give me your hand and your word as a gentleman of England to abide by the spirit of your
promise."

So Philip gave him his hand and a straight look
in the eyes.

" You have it, lad," he said, in convincing accents of simple truth, and so left us, disappearing
into the dark chasm of the wall.

Now Ned had but just closed behind his retreat

the door of stone (by that means which I now know, but will not here set down; for who can tell if political trouble be even yet forever at an end in England ?) when there came a hand upon the door. Ned dropped into a seat, muttering: " But just in time!" while I, feigning sleep, stretched myself in my corner of the settle.

" Is all well, Captain ?" asked the cheery voice of M. de Rondiniacque, as he entered from the gallery.

" All is well, Lieutenant," replied Royston, with a very fine assumption of carelessness. And then the officer of the watch drew near, looking down upon me, as I suppose (for my eyes were fast closed), with curiosity.

" *Ma foi !* " he cried, " the peevish youth leaves you not, Captain. He is mighty pale in the face for one that sleeps."

" He is little used, I think, to fatigue," replied Ned. " Is all well without, Lieutenant ? "

" *Mon capitaine,*" said De Rondiniacque, " not a mouse stirs." And so saluted and retired as he had come.

When the sound of his feet had died away, " Thank Heaven ! " I whispered, " the danger is past ! "

" For your brother, yes," Ned answered softly. " For us it is to come."

" Nay, indeed, I hope not so," said I. " And for him, how shall I thank you, Captain Royston ? "

" Dear child," he said, with a flash of eagerness lighting his eyes, " do not call me captain. Were I not like ere long to be a man disgraced, I could ask you for thanks, but—— "

And I, who had ever wholly trusted him and desired nothing so much as that he should ask in payment what had long been his, made no parley with modesty, but at once replied: " Nay, but ask, dear Ned; do but ask. You will never in my eyes be disgraced."

But when he began to reply that it was a great thing he would ask, of which the granting would bear the balance well down on the other side, Dame Fate played the careful *dueña* to the poor maid that thought herself in hands safe enough without any such protection.

I mean that before Ned was well launched in that tale of what he would have of me, the door at the winding stair's foot did again open; and, of all the many times these divers doors had in the last few hours moved upon their hinges, this was the worst opening; for, wrapped in a great black cloak thrown hurriedly around him, there came His Highness of Orange. And, but that I knew none other could then come that road, I do not think I should have

known him for the man that had of late bid me so
kindly good-night.   For over his face was a cloud
of anger very awful to see.

We sprang to our feet, and Captain Royston
saluted.   Passing this military courtesy unacknowl-
edged, the Prince at once addressed him in a voice
so harsh and with a manner so cruel (as it seemed
to me) that I fell into a great fear and assurance
that he had by some means discovered both too
much and too little; and my heart seemed to melt
to water within me, so that I despaired of ever setting my lover right in the eyes of his Prince.

" You watch well over my slumbers, Captain,"
was indeed all he said; but voice and countenance
were more than words, and I felt as I have said.

" It has been my endeavor, Your Highness," answered Royston, with much dignity, and a face the
color of ashes.

" A good watch: a mighty careful and anxious
watch, Captain!" the Prince continued.   " I do not
always sleep, Captain Royston, when my eyes seem
closed, and I truly believe your care lacked little of
prolonging my rest to the awful Day of Judgment."

" I do not understand Your Highness's words,"
said Royston.

The Prince crossed the room to the outer door, and,
with his hand upon it: " I shall presently explain
them," he said, and so went out into the gallery.

" Ned," I cried, so soon as he was gone, " I will
tell him all ! "

" That you shall not," he replied.

" How much does he know ? " I asked, trembling
as I spoke.

" I cannot tell," answered Ned. " But to tell
him all in this mood will but harm you and yours;
perhaps lead to Philip's capture, and yet do me no
service. He will never pass over this one thing,
— that I did let your brother go. And he will
know that soon enough, telling or none."

And here the door opening again, we were perforce silent. I could hear His Highness's last few
words to the sentry, spoken in a tongue I took to
be Dutch, because I did not understand it, but,
among them occurring the names Schomberg, Ben-
tinck, De Rondiniacque, I guessed he had summoned those gentlemen to attend him. Then His
Highness returned into the chamber, and for a
while we stood silent, regarding one another as
the footsteps of the sentry died away down the
gallery.

At last Royston would have spoken. " Your
Highness— " he began.

But the Prince interrupted him. " Be silent," he
said, " and wait."

So in silence we waited, but how long I do not
know. At length came M. de Rondiniacque, to be

soon followed by Count Schomberg and Mr. Bentinck. These two had, it appeared, resumed their
clothes in haste, and concealed the disorder of their
attire each in long horse-cloaks, even as His Highness had done. And in these three stern figures of
Prince, soldier, and statesman, close wrapped to the
chin in dark and twisted folds of cloth, there was, I
thought, an awful likeness to the bench of judges
that sat in Hades.

When the last had entered, the Prince thus addressed the three: " It seems, gentlemen, that in
the master of this house I have an enemy."

At which point Mr. Bentinck, without at all staying the flow of the Prince's words, ejaculated a deep
and guttural " Ah! " as one finding but what he
had looked for.

" I therefore purpose, gentlemen, to question
Captain Royston in your presence, and thereafter
to take your censures in the matter of bringing him
to fitting military trial for treason."

" I am no traitor to Your Highness, nor to any
man," cried Royston, with blunt indignation.

"That we shall soon see, I believe,"said His Highness. " Did you not appoint yourself this night, with
my consent, the innermost guard of my person ? "

" I did," answered Royston.

" Then where is the prisoner; he that called himself priest ? " asked the Prince, turning on him a

gaze that called to my mind tales I had read of the
Inquisitors of Spain, so piercing and ruthless was it.

" He is escaped! " replied poor Ned.

" By your aid ? " asked the Inquisitor.

" By my aid," replied the accused.

" He was here in converse with you ? "

" He was."

" By what means did he avoid the guard ? "

" That," said Royston, " I will not tell." And
his eyes flashed, and his head, never humbled, rose
yet more erect; and I knew he was glad he could
now use boldness where he saw he was to expect
no mercy. And, of the three men that were listening to these questions and answers, one said:
" Oh! " another " Ah! " while the third drew in
his breath with a sound of hissing.

" I see, gentlemen," said William, " that you
mark him." Then, to Royston: " To what end did
you aid his flight ? Will you at least tell me that ? "

" Nor that neither," said he boldly, yet without
insolence.

" The priest," said His Highness, " did enter my
chamber while he thought I slept."

" 'T is like enough that he did," replied Royston.

" And afterwards you also," said the Prince,
" with naked sword."

" I did," said Royston, " but to no end but to
be assured of Your Highness's safety."

Now when Captain Royston had first declared the escape of the priest, I had marked M. de Rondiniacque step for a moment into the gallery, whence he soon returned.   It appears that he had in that moment's absence despatched one of the three soldiers that were on duty without the door to the room on the floor above, whence that escape had been effected.   This man now rapping upon the door, M. de Rondiniacque opened to him, heard his report, and returned to his place beside Marshal Schomberg.   His Highness observing these movements, and enquiring what was to do, M. de Rondiniacque replied that it was even as Captain Royston had said, the priest's door being unfastened and his chamber empty.

His Highness acknowledged the news with a brief gesture, and continued: " Do I then, gentlemen, greatly err to suppose that this house has been a snare to us ?   Do not the events of this night give a dreadful significance to those of the afternoon ? "

" It is plainly so," said Count Schomberg.

" Your Highness," growled Mr. Bentinck, " knows well my opinion, from the warnings I have already given him."

As it appeared now M. de Rondiniacque's turn to add his voice to this concert of his superiors, while yet no sound came from him, the Prince turned upon him a keen glance of enquiry.

"I must agree, Monseigneur," he said, with a very lively distress appearing in his countenance, "unless, indeed, there be some reason behind it all, which Captain Royston may now disclose. I have always found him a gentleman of the nicest honor," he continued, gathering courage, "and I observe that there is against him no proof but what his own word has afforded. None saw the unfastening of the door, none saw the man's escape: it were more after the fashion of the vulgar traitor to deny all, and to ascribe his appearance in Your Highness's chamber—" and here the good Frenchman checked his speech.

"To what, sir?" demanded the Prince, the gloom of anger growing, I thought, yet deeper upon his face.

"To the disordered fancy of an uneasy sleeper," replied De Rondiniacque fearlessly.

"Your advocacy carries you too far, Lieutenant," said His Highness, in tones that I feared must at once silence our only friend.

"Your Highness will pardon me if I point out that I make no defence for Captain Royston," insisted De Rondiniacque, stepping a little forward with a graceful ease and a frank glance in His Highness's face that I think had taken by storm any woman's heart less strongly garrisoned than the only one in reach. "I but point out the traitor's refuge, of which he has made no use. If I err in saying as much, I will beg Your Highness to remember that the accused gentleman has been my friend and comrade.'' With which words he saluted and retired to his former position. And I think that what he had said and the way he bore himself were not wholly without effect upon the Prince: for he turned to Captain Royston, and asked him, with some slight approach to gentleness, had he any explanation to offer.

'' I can but assure Your Highness,'' said Captain Royston, '' that throughout I have done nothing adverse to Your Highness's great cause, nor to his person, nor to the honor and faith I do hold them in.''

'' And is this all ? '' asked William.

'' Before these gentlemen, sir,'' he replied, '' it is all. But I hold the true fulness of the matter ever ready for your private ear.''

'' My private ear, sir,'' answered the Prince, '' is like to be much abused if I give my closet for every traitor's subtile excuses.''

'' I offer none,'' said Royston, with the rigid pride of despair.

'' And none,'' said His Highness, '' save in this company, will I hear. Keep your tale, sir, for to-morrow's court-martial. You are under arrest. Your sword, Captain Royston. Lieutenant de

Rondiniacque, see to it that this one at least do not escape." And then, as poor Ned slowly drew his sword, and tendered the hilt to the Prince, His Highness, waving it aside, signified to M. de Rondiniacque by a gesture that he should take it.

" 'T is not such," he said, " that I have need of."

Which bitter speech came near to breaking down the restraint in which the man had held himself. I saw the blood fly to his face, the half-step forward, the hands clenched by his sides; I heard the one dread word on his lips. " God—!" he gasped, and again curbed himself.

" No words of heat, sir!" said the Prince. " I did once take you for my friend. Is mine the fault that you prove an enemy ? Weigh well what defence you will make to-morrow; let me warn you that courts-martial in time of war are swift in procedure and deadly in sentence. Should such court hear from your lips no more than we have now heard, make your peace with God." And with that he would have left the room; but I, beside myself with terror, caught him by the arm, and tried to speak.

The Prince, however, shook me off, bidding me roughly not to court his notice; saying that this was not a court of justice nor of favor, but a camp; and that I was happy not to come within the purview of its jurisdiction.

But I found my tongue, and said: " Your Highness must in courtesy hear me."

On which, with little enough, he bade me speak.

" I do solemnly swear," said I, " before the God
that shall judge us all—— "

" Beware, young man," interrupted His Highness, " lest you take that awful name in vain."

" The more awful, great, and holy," I replied,
" the readier my will to take it now. And even so
I swear that Captain Royston is no traitor. What
he has done, I have done. I will tell Your Highness
all."

" Be silent," said Ned. " I do forbid it. You
harm my case."

" Nay, then," I replied, " I will not. But it is
even as I say."

The Prince looked in my face, and I thought that
his did a little soften. " I would I believed you,
boy," he said, in gentler tones. " But I do not
believe."

And with that a great hope sprang into my mind,
and — " Some day you must believe," I cried.
" But now I will ask no more than Your Highness
has already granted." And I drew forth from its
sheath the sword His Highness had given me.

" What is your meaning ? " asked the Prince
sternly, the frown coming dark again across his face.

" They say that I came between Your Highness

and great danger," I replied, with an inward prayer
for the courage and the skill of words that I so sorely
needed, " in recompense of which you have given
me this sword. According to the word that was
given with it, I now render it again," and here I
knelt before him, holding out the weapon by the
blade, the handle toward the Prince, " praying that
my friend, Edward Royston, Captain in Your Highness's Swedish Regiment of Horse, may stand in
rank, duties, and honor, as he stood before this
matter did arise. And I ask, moreover, that, when
there shall be an end of the present troubles, Your
Highness will bring him to fitting examination and
judgment, to the end that his virtue may appear to
all men."

" 'T is a request of many heads and much length,"
said the Prince, with a smile of much sarcasm.

" Indeed, it has but one head," I replied. " I
pray Your Highness to suspend his case till the
war be done. Is it granted ? "

" No," said the Prince; " it is not granted, and
it shall not be."

" And wherefore not ? " I demanded, with a boldness that does at this present vastly astonish me to
think on.

" I gave the sword, with its pledge," he replied,
" to one I thought loyal to my person and a friend
to my cause, the liberties of England. I am not,

and may never be, a king; and I have not learned,"
he said, with irony very cynical, " to grant favor to
traitors."

" But you are a great Prince," I persisted; " a
Prince, I have heard tell, that never departs from
his plighted word. This pledge I hold until it
be redeemed. Again I entreat Your Highness to
return to Captain Royston his sword."

" Give me that in your hand," he said, after a
moment's thought, which had taken him, with a
few pondering paces, to some distance from the
spot where I yet knelt. But as I rose to bring it to
him, I believe he read in my face the joy that I felt
within, for, raising his hand with a gesture that at
once checked my advance—" Nay," he said, " I
will not give him back the sword he has dishonored.
But, for my word's sake, he has his life and liberty.
Let him begone. And if he cross my path again, to
raise his hand by never so little against me or mine;
if he be found after this night ever within my lines,
he dies—as spies die, *Master* Royston," he added,
turning upon him a glance of keen contempt. Then,
after a little pause, he said, with great solemnity,
" May the life I give serve unto repentance."

In that moment I think poor Ned's heart was
very near breaking. In a voice slow and measured
from the restraint he used, he said that he would
not accept his life at such a price. His Highness,

replying that the choice did not lie with him, turned sharply to me and said: " Give me the sword."

And then the sight of the stricken man's white and ghastly face — stricken for his faith to me and my people—inspired my heart to the most audacious act of my life. I took the sword by the hilt, and, pressing hard upon it with both hands, bent down the lower part until a portion lay upon the floor. On this setting my foot with all my body's weight to back it, I wrenched the hilt over toward the point, so that the blade broke some seven inches from the end. M. de Rondiniacque, stepping forward to arrest my purpose, was too late. I waved him back with a gesture I took to be mighty full of haughtiness, and, standing firm upon the fragment, I presented the hilt to His Highness of Orange. On the snapping of the blade the Prince had started in anger; as I handed him the truncated weapon, he drew back and—" What is this ? " he cried.

" Your Highness grants no more than half my prayer," I replied. " I render half the pledge."

" The greater half," he said, and in despite of himself he smiled.

Being by that smile much emboldened, I answered: " Then I am more generous than William, Prince of Orange. For life," I said, lifting from the floor the broken point of the sword, " is less than honor. Yet, like His Highness, I keep the point that kills."

CHAPTER XVI

WHEN I try to write that part of my story that should here immediately ensue, I find the attempt at first more destructive of the feather than the nib of my pen. If I close my eyes and seek to live again in memory the hour that followed upon what I have last related, the result is always the same: I find myself awaking, as it were, from a kind of inner dream to the outward consciousness of heavily pouring rain, the rhythmic jingle of bridles, and the discordant squeaking of wet saddle under wetter boots.

For Ned and I are out in the foulest night of that foul November, and Roan Charley beneath me makes brave use of his tired limbs to come the sooner at his own stable. And then the sound of Ned's voice speaking to his horse in some manner brings back to me a few incidents of our passing from my Lady Mary's withdrawing-room to this wet and pitiless night; things which at this time of writing I do not clearly nor directly recall, but merely remember that I did then recollect; how His Highness had turned his back upon us, and departed in company of Mr. Bentinck and Count Schomberg; how Ned had sworn he would not leave his own house, saying they should hang him in the morning if they would; how M. de Rondiniacque and I had between us well-nigh forced him from the house; and how, with the Frenchman's help, I had gotten the two of us to horse; and how this good friend had, ere we left, said many things; but not one word of his could I recall.

So, having gathered out of my stupor the remnants of the nearer past, I was already again in my mind busily at work with divers plots and plannings to bring out of this dismal present a glorious and golden future. This change had been indeed brought to pass; nor was Dame Fate's change of front tedious of accomplishment; but I feel it is due to any that reads me to confess at once that the passage from evil fortune to good was the work rather of the hand of God and the goodness of men, than brought about by any skill or wit of the poor maid that would gladly have foregone all merriment here and hereafter to see once more a smile on the lips of the man she loved.

I have said that the present was dismal; to my companion, indeed, it could be no otherwise; yet to me the awful gloom of disfavor and disgrace was somewhat lightened by a little throb of joy, trembling and intermittent indeed, but growing in force, ·

and of decreasing interval, as the horses swung, splashing through rain and mud, and their riders spoke never a word. I was a woman; and I was out alone in the darkest night of our two lives with the man who to me was all men since God gave me memory; I had him to myself, to cherish, to comfort, and, if it might be, to serve; what else should I do, but, woman-like, yearn over him with bowels of compassion, and rejoice that I was the angler that should, if it pleased Heaven, fish his soul from the dark and turbid waters of despair?

At length—" Ned!" I cried, but had no answer; and again, " Ned! dear Ned!" with no better luck. So I pushed my horse over against his till our knees came together, and laid my hand on his arm. And then somehow I knew, dark as pitch though it was, that he turned his head to me.

" Though you be unhappy," I said, letting of set purpose the catch of a small sob come into my voice, " you do not need to flout your little friend. 'T is very like you think it all my fault, but all I could, since Philip left us, I have done,—all, I would say, that you would let me do."

" More!" he cried in answer; " you have done far more than I would have had you do; for I believe you did save my life. If I thank you now," he added, with great bitterness, " I do fear my words will lack the ring of truth."

" Nay," I said, as coldly as I might, in hope to engage his interest, " there is but one owes thanks for that; and it is not you."

" Who then ? " he asked, but languidly, as having little care for an answer.

" Who but the person," I replied, " in whose sole interest it was saved ? "

" You speak in riddles, lad," he said, and then at once burst into a very hearty laugh at his own mistake; at which my heart danced within me to a tune very sweet; for laughter was at least a step in the way I would have him walk.   " My wits have gone browsing like sheep," he went on.   " Life is sweet, I do suppose, and soon I shall thank you.   Even now I feel the savor of it coming back to me.   Let us push on," he said, and put spurs to his horse.

When I was once again by his side—" Ah ! " he cried, " one is a man again with a horse between his knees."

" I do not know," I replied.   " Was it for that you called me lad, Captain ? "

And so for a mile or more we talked.   There was indeed but a poor heart in what gaiety we used, but it served to lead at last to matter more important. And then I found his purpose was but to escort me in safety to my father's house, and himself pass on; whither, he would not say, and at length confessed he did not know.   And I vowed in my heart he

should go no further than Drayton, but bided my
time.   There followed, in a bad part of the way,
a little silence.   And now the rain, for some time
slackening, ceased altogether, and a little pale light
from the moon struggling through the clouds, we
drew together again.   This time it was Ned did
break the silence, and his words showed me he had
begun to review that night's work.

" That was bold juggling you did with His Highness and the sword, mistress," he said.   " Wherefore did you break it ? "

" Because I hold men should keep faith, even
princes," I answered, " and I will make him fulfil
his word, up to the hilt — I would say down to the
point, which I keep until it is earned."   And I felt
for the fragment of His Highness's sword in the
place where I had it safe hidden.   And then I drew
rein on Charley, catching at my comrade's rein with
the other hand.   " O Ned ! " I cried, " how am I
to do all this, if you will leave me ?   Take me and
your story to my father, and among us we shall find
a way."

In the pale moonlight I could see his pale face,
and on it I read the bitterness and sorrow of a conflict that he deemed finished.

" Sweet mistress," he said, " you must not tempt
me.   This thing is the fault of no man, but the
hand of fate is heavy upon me.   Since we were

children together, it is somewhere written that only
in danger and disgrace may I meet you.   I do believe that in your heart you know much that, but
for what has happened this day to part us, I would
say to you.   I will not say it, and because I will
not, I must leave you when I have brought you to
your father.   Do not urge me again.''

   '' If all the world cried out upon Philippa,'' I replied, feeling in my heart as those must feel who
take their lives in their hands to carry through some
desperate enterprise, or to die in default of success,
'' and would have her guilty of all the crimes a
woman could guiltily do, I would laugh them all to
scorn while you held me innocent and dear.''

   '' Comfort you might find in my faith,'' he said,
'' even as I find much in yours.   But you would
not company with me, nor let your name go with
mine in men's mouths; and much less would you
wed me before your name was cleared.   It is perhaps the last time we shall speak together, little
Phil, and my despair shall bring me one good thing:
because I have no hope, I will tell you now very
fully and frankly what has been in my mind to say
since my weight on a horse's back was less than is
now your own.   When I left Oxford to come into
the west in those days of Monmouth's trouble, my
tongue was ready and my heart hot to tell you my
love, and, having told, to ask yours, and with it the

sweetest wife in all England.   Now, I must tell and not ask.   I say, then, Philippa, that I love you, that I shall love you, and that I have loved you, for how long it is hard to know, but truly I believe my love began when you sat in the dust and looked to me for comfort, stretching up your little arms, tremulous and appealing.   Ah!'' he cried, '' with what an urgent and tender clinging they held me as we fled from pursuing Betty.''

'' I did then think, Ned,'' I murmured, '' that the little horse had wings, and that we fled together from Betty and all troubles forever.''

'' It was only Betty then,'' he answered, with a little laugh that hurt me to hear.

'' And it is no worse than Betty now, dear,'' I cried, '' if you will but keep me with you.   I have but just gotten you again.   Three years is very long and lonesome.   Do not leave me.''

Our horses were standing, and the moon showed me his face and the great struggle that there was in him between tenderness of love and insistence of duty.   And I saw the softness die out of his countenance, and the features grow set in resolve.

'' I forget,'' he said, drawing the reins short through his fingers.   '' Let us press on; 't is six good miles yet to Drayton.''   At which his horse broke into a canter.

But, when Charley would have followed, I drew

rein, kicked feet from stirrups, flung my right foot
over his neck, and so slipped to ground; let slip the
reins, and so sat me down forlorn by the roadside.
So far I had acted of design, to the end that Ned
should return, and I have my way to the full as the
one price of proceeding further.   But, when Roan
Charley, having twice snuffed at my crouching figure, set off whinnying in pursuit of his fellow, I
burst into tears wholly devoid of affectation, weeping for the loneliness that was my own making, and
the stubbornness of a man's will that I could not
break.   And, the soft thud of hoofs on the wet and
sandy road now seeming to die away with growing
distance, I did begin to feel that the childish weapon
I had taken in hand was indeed turned against myself.   To set the coping on my misery, there came
a great and sudden gust of wind, and with it, across
the moon, a thick storm-cloud, from which fell a
driving slant of heavy rain, shutting out at once all
sight and sound, as it were with a thick blanket of
cold and turbid wetness; so that, drenched to the
skin, I soon shivered as much from cold as from the
sobs that shook my overwrought body.   Now that
he could no longer hear my voice, I found some
dismal comfort in leaping to my feet and crying
aloud on Ned to come back; and, even as I called,
fell to running with weary and staggering feet, in
pursuit of him I believed far away, until I pitched

well-nigh headlong, not into his arms, for they were
stretched wide, holding a horse in either hand, but
upon his broad breast, where I soon laid my head;
crying, as I clutched him by the shoulders, that he
had left me too long, and frightened me.

" Why, Phil!" he answered, " I heard your nag
following, and, even when he drew abreast, it was
not at once I knew you were not in the saddle."
And here I felt his right arm move behind his back,
to pass his horse's bridle to the left hand that already held Roan Charley's. " But when he pushed
close," he continued, " and his swinging stirrup-
iron struck my boot, I turned to find the voice and
eyes I dreaded were no longer near. And then,
sweetheart, the rain was upon us, and in the darkness it was little speed I could make returning, but
must needs dismount and go gingerly, for fear of
riding over you. How came he to throw you,
Phil ?"

Perceiving that alarm had brought back all his
tenderness, for here his right arm came round my
neck in an embrace most sweet and full of protection, I cast to the winds my facile repentance for
the trick I had played him, and answered him thus,
using what remnant of dignity I could muster:
" 'T was not my good Charley that did cast me off,
Ned. But when I found you would not heed
my prayers; when I found that for some fancy of

what the world should say of us you would again
leave me alone, with, this time, perhaps, no hope of
a return; when I thought how bitter three years of
waiting have proved for a half-fledged maid, and
perceived how much worse a thing were waiting
without hope or limit for a woman grown, I dismounted and sat me down by the roadside.   For I
said I would never return to Drayton to see go out
again into the night, alone and unhappy, the man
that has saved our honor, giving to us out of the
abundance of his own."   And I waited for him,
but even yet he would not speak.   "What! will
you shame me, Ned?" I cried.   "Must I even
say more?   Then I here solemnly vow that unless
you now say to me all—ask of me all that you would
were you now as famous as Marshal Schomberg, and
as high in favor as Mr. William Bentinck, I will not
budge from this spot."   This, with voice and bearing no doubt vastly heroical, I said.   But, fearing
it yet insufficient, I added shudderingly, in a manner I have since thought most humorously batheti-
cal: " And I almost die for cold."

Now, scarce even for my children, can I set down
very particularly what followed.   But there was
much rain, and now two arms about me, and my
head lay where it is not yet tired of lying, while my
lover let flow in words the passion of his love that
had so long been pent and dammed up in his heart.

17

And I remember that when he kissed me, there came between his lips and mine a patch of mud, cast there doubtless by the feet of his horse in his flight from me; and also that we laughed together like children with no sorrow upon them, as he did try in the dark to wipe it away with his handker-chief, and how some of the soil did get in my mouth as I laughed.   So strong in memory is often a little matter of this nature that when, not two days back from the time I sit here writing, being abroad with Colonel Royston to see some sport with Sir Giles Blundell's hounds, I received full in the teeth a hoof-shaped clod of earth, I was, for all the pain and discomfort of it, translated at once from the free air and pale, sweet winter sun back to that foul and bitter night and its dear core of love, red and glowing with the fire that shall comfort and illumine us both to the end of our days.

Now, how long we stood there, how long we talked, and how long we were silent I do not know. But Dame Nature the stepmother had become Mother Nature our friend; and wind, cold, and wet were but the veil she cast kindly to wrap our sacred hour in holier secrecy.   And when again a little light showed from the moon, of course it was the woman that cried: " Why, Ned! where are the horses ? "

I will not dwell on the labor to pursue and catch

our nags. The charger, at length responding to a
cry his master used, was caught, mounted, and ridden in chase of Roan Charley. So I was again for
a while left solitary, but in a state of mind how
different! Not now did I sit forlorn with my
feet in the ditch, but tramped cheerily forward;
for I had his promise not to leave me again, but to
lay the whole matter before Sir Michael, and to
abide by his advice. For Ned, notwithstanding
the anguish of his disgrace, did in his modesty set
so low a price on the action which had procured it,
that I think it had not yet become clear to him how
wholly my very just and most noble-minded father
must be engaged to counsel all things in the interest
of Philip's savior.

It was not long before I encountered all three returning to meet me, truant Charley grown reluctant
and rebellious. And thence into Drayton village
the way seemed short indeed. Only twice did Ned
refer to his misfortune and the anger of His Highness of Orange; once, in saying it was strange a
single night should hold the greatest joy and the
greatest sorrow he had known; and again, when I
said many hard things of the Prince, he would not
hear me, saying he was not to blame; and then he
asked me did I note the last words of M. de Rondiniacque as he bade us farewell. 'T was that gentleman's opinion, it appeared, that the Prince was

in his heart not sorry to find in my importunity good occasion to avoid the scandal that must arise from a court-martial held upon an officer whose family was so well known in the neighborhood at present occupied by his army. M. de Rondiniacque had added, moreover, that he believed His Highness's anger much exacerbated by a lurking doubt as to the substantial guilt of one he had hitherto highly esteemed. All this I must have heard as one in a dream, and the narration of it now furnished me with material for the more sober thoughts that occupied the almost unbroken silence of our passage from the village of Drayton to the house.

It was now more than an hour past midnight, so that it was with no little surprise we beheld, through the ill-closed hangings of the windows, the great hall bright with candles and fire. As he lifted me, now well-nigh crippled with fatigue, from the saddle, I prayed Ned to enter quickly and engage whom he should find for a moment in talk, while I slipped quietly by to the refuge of my chamber. In the morning I had trifled with the fancy that it were better to be born a man; now I knew it was best of all to be a woman; and thus I had no mind, while I could still by some sense of lingering contact mark the places where my lover's kisses had fallen, to be seen in the garb I wore by any man or woman whatsoever. And Ned, acting most comfortably in

accordance with my desire, I was soon fast in the
haven of my room, of whose door I did that night
but once again draw the bolt; and even then I do
think it was rather from desire of the food and the
posset that she carried, than from any need of her
company, that I admitted Prudence; and of the
torrent of questions with which my ears were as-
sailed as she tenderly waited on me, I answered few
and heeded none. I would have been alone to
think of Ned, and of the change of so strange a
sweetness that I now began to discover in myself.
I was indeed in that temper of mind wherein a
maid will find even the object of her thought a
hindrance to the right management of her thinking;
and so I got very quickly to bed, feigning sleep to
escape little Prue's chatter, the while I hugged to
my breast the memories of the journey homeward;
cherishing the sweetest fragments for a perpetual
possession.

But feigning passed very soon into reality, and
the last I recall of that night is my dreamy watching
of Prudence, as she busied herself, with a bearing
of no little pique, in hanging out poor Rupert's
clothes before the great fire, and muttering dark
sayings of the folk that had secrets, and how, if that
were the way of it, she could, nay, would, keep her
own to herself.

CHAPTER XVII

IN telling how we came happily through this
trouble of Captain Royston's disgrace, I perceive that there is from this point a greater number
of those incidents in which, although they are necessary to the proper understanding of my tale, I had
myself no personal share. While, however, my
knowledge in such case is but second-hand, it is
hearsay of the best quality, drawn from divers wit-
nesses whose testimony I have found seldom divergent. I therefore purpose in my remaining chapters
(now happily few), for greater ease to the reader, to
make of what I know and what I believe a narrative
as plain and straightforward as I may, without
further reference to my sources of information,
which would but encumber those efforts at despatch
that must, if my story cannot, earn me a reader's
approbation. Colonel Royston, coming fresh and
crammed with law from the justice-room (he being
of late on their Majesties' Commission of the Peace),
tells me that hearsay is not evidence. To which I
can but reply that such as I give will be nearer the
truth than much that he hears on oath.

When Ned, covering my retreat, presented himself before my father in the dining-hall, he found
Sir Michael seated in his great chair by the hearth;
on his one side at respectful distance stood Farmer
Kidd, while on the other, and close to his father,
sat Philip.

Now Kidd, much delayed by the foundering of
his horse, had come in about midnight, bringing
the first clear news of my safety. He had found
Sir Michael in some disorder, between the pain in
his leg, much aggravated by his vigil, and anxiety
for his daughter. Poor Christopher was like to have
suffered in consequence; for Sir Michael, while filling him with food and drink, rated him soundly for
leaving me behind, and would have had him return
at once to Royston. Philip, whose name and face
had gotten him a good mount upon the road,
arriving about half an hour later than Christopher,
found him dulled with fatigue and feeding, and
halting half-way between slumber and tears. My
father's mind was soon at rest about his errant
daughter; for, when he learned that Ned Royston
had me in charge, and knew that I was Philippa, he
merely said that I could not be in safer hands, and
thereafter addressed himself at once to the consideration of Philip's story.

" And so, dear sir," said my brother, when his
tale was done, " give me a horse and money, and I

will make my way back to France, that I may keep faith with Royston, and set myself again to serve those that sent me into England.''

'' Not so, Philip,'' answered his father, '' for I will give you nothing to become once more the active enemy of the Prince of Orange. If I do clip thy claws, thou must stay with me till these troubles are done. I like not your faith; Gad 's my life! I like not your cause, for all it was once mine. But yourself I do love. For the sweet sake of your mother, son of mine, stay with me whom all have left.''

'' A Drayton, sir,'' replied Philip, '' must do his part, on what side soever it has pleased God to set him.''

'' You are right, lad,'' the old man answered; ''and therefore will I give you neither horse nor money.''

Thus it was that upon his coming amongst them Captain Royston had but to tell the dreadful sequel of Philip's escape. But, between his very cordial greeting of Ned and the hearing his story, my father, with a fine discretion, begged Kidd that he would attend to the Captain's horse, the grooms being all abed. Which Christopher very willingly hastened to do, preferring a stable and a bed of straw to the dining-hall and Sir Michael's varied cheer.

His story told, and they asking where was Philippa, Ned answered, between draughts from a great

tankard of spiced ale, that he believed I was gone
to my chamber.   On this Sir Michael himself
hobbled to the room where lay my Lady Mary,
whence he transferred Prudence from attendance on
her ladyship to the duty she vastly preferred, of
waiting upon me.   Alone with Ned, Philip at once
declared the purpose of making his way to Exeter,
and of laying before His Highness, in the act of sur-
rendering himself, the true state of the whole matter.   Sir Michael returning in the midst of Royston's
objections to what he called so useless a sacrifice,
the matter was debated among the three far into
the morning, my lover concluding that ill was best
let alone, for fear of worse; my brother, that he
had no choice in honor but to give himself up; my
father, that they were both fools, and that he himself was the person to set the matter in its true
light before His Highness of Orange.   And so they
separated for the night, which of them all being in
most need of rest it would be hard to say.

But my good father, before he slept, paid a secret
visit to the stable, there leaving orders with Kidd,
the sleepy chief of a sleepy band of agrestic warriors
(for the squadron I had led out at noon was at length
painfully gathered in and billeted in the hay-loft),
and with the chief groom of his own establishment,
that no man (adding hastily, " nor no woman neither ") should take horse from their door without

his own express command. For he feared that either Ned would escape him, and so cut this knot of his own generous making; or that Philip would effect an early start to throw himself, with little gain to us all, into the hands of his enemies. And so, after threats of the most terrible, which served at least, as the sequel shows, to keep his commands from mixing with their dreams, Sir Michael got him to his bed where, if the just indeed sleep well, he slumbered very peacefully till the unwonted hour of nine in the morning.

I do not think that poor Philip found much sleep. The choice between divergent duties, with harm to his family involved in one decision, to a brave and generous friend in the other, may well keep even the just awake. The household being much belated, he was able between six and seven of the morning to let himself out unobserved. On coming to the stable, however, he found that he could on no terms but Sir Michael's order be furnished with a horse; not even with that which had brought him to the house the night before. After some minutes of deep thought, he hastily penned a few lines on a leaf of his tablets, which he then tore out and carefully folded, begging Christopher, as he loved the honor of the house, to keep it unread and undivulged until two o'clock of the afternoon, when he should hand it to Sir Michael. But if, as he deemed by no means likely of occurrence, His Highness of Orange should before that hour honor Sir Michael with a visit, the letter must at once be delivered. With which he left the yet sleep-ridden Christopher, willing, indeed, to do his behest, but so mightily astonished at the mystery in which he found himself involved, that he failed even to mark the road of Philip's departure.

The letter, which I hold to be a notable example of my brother's forethought, I will give here rather than in its place of coming to light, for the better understanding of Philip's motive and action.

" To My Dear and Honored Father : Being re-solved to do what I may to repair the great evil I have brought upon Edward Royston, and fearing hindrance at your hands or his, I have taken myself off while you are yet sleeping. Finding, however, that you have laid a strict embargo upon the stable, I go first afoot to the Grange, where old Simcox will doubtless mount me with the best in his stable.

" I call to mind some words of Royston's, however, of His Highness of Orange intending a visit to Drayton. Now, although it is more than likely he has foregone this purpose after what ensued upon my escape, it is yet pos-sible that some compunction of his own hastiness, or return of gratitude to Philippa, may bring him to your door. From the Grange, therefore, I purpose taking the road to Exeter that runs by ' The Crow's Nest,' whence one may see the roofs of Drayton. I shall be particular not to leave that point before the stroke of noon. If, therefore, the improbable occur, and the Prince be come, or announced to come, to Drayton before that hour, I beg of you, my dear sir, to fly the old flag from the turret mast; which, if I see, I will make the best of my way back to you, knowing that you will not contrive from my plan a *ruse* to lure me home against my conscience.

"If the Prince be gone to Exeter, and I there get audience of him, remember that even the failure of my plea for Royston will not injure your own subsequent representations, but will rather by corroboration of evidence strengthen them. Your obedient son,

"P. D."

Thus it ran. The Grange, I should say, is the old Holroyd house, and Simcox, my father's bailiff for the estate.

So much for two of those that sat so late in the hall.

As for Ned, neither joy (if, as I suppose, some joy was in him) nor grief, of which he thought never through life to be rid, was to prevail against the oppression of sleep long denied. He slept as the dead sleep, till long after my father was abroad.

But for a soporific commend me to a decoction of new-found love and great fatigue of body. It was from the pleasant action of this sleeping-draught that I awoke to find my chamber bathed in the first sunshine of many dreary days. And, as I lay with eyes half opened, I felt in my bosom a gladness answering to the sunshine without. And searching in my mind for the threads of memory that should

join my life with the day that was past, and tell me
the reason why I was glad, I found that the answer
was *Love*. But a little cloud soon driving across
the sun had also its inward response in my half-
awakened spirit, and I asked myself was there then
some evil thing in this sweet world of mine?

And so I stumbled heavily upon the memory that
Ned's love had in its fulness come to me in the very
hour of disgrace. And then I awoke from a maid
floating blissfully upon the sweet sea of conscious
repose to the woman fain to pay the price of love in
deeds for her lover.

Prudence was not far, and I was not long in dress-
ing. Having, however, more food for thought than
use for my tongue, I by and by perceived that my
little handmaid was very ready to make cause of a
tiff out of my silence. This might have passed, for
I thought with a gentle word or two and a smile to
turn aside the coming storm.

Nor had I much doubt of success in this, when,
after watching my face a while in the mirror, she
exclaimed: '' Why, madam, how beautiful you appear this morning! One would think some great
good thing had befallen you yesterday, rather
than a great fatigue. You are vastly changed,
madam.''

'' Nay, Prudence, be not so fanciful,'' I cried,
marking, nevertheless, in the mirror how the color

rose in my face. "Pray, child, what difference do you find?"

"It is hard to name," she answered, "but 't is there. Your regard is large and tender. Your eyes, madam—your eyes hold some secret of joy."

Here she paused a while, turning her gaze from the mirror to my face itself. Then at length: "Why, madam, I have it," she cried; "you are in one night grown to be a woman!"

To hide my cheeks, that would soon, I knew, most furiously glow, I turned to the wardrobe to take from it the gown I proposed wearing. But when she saw that it was the finest in stuff, and latest in fashion of all my slender stock, her curiosity broke out afresh. Receiving no reply to her many questions, she watched me in dumb displeasure, while I shaped a piece of black plaister, and applied it to the little wound that Ned's sword had made on my bosom, for the gown, being cut somewhat more freely open than I mostly used, would have left the scratch uncovered from the air. All this was more than Prue could bear.

"I do perceive," she said, with pale cheeks and tilted chin, "that in some manner I have offended madam, since she no longer gives me her confidence; I fear it is no time to ask her advice in a matter that gives much distress and anxiety to one

that she was wont to hold her very faithful servant.''
Whereupon she left the chamber very quickly, giving
me no space to appease her anger.

Finishing my toilet alone, I began to wonder
what was this mighty secret with which she had
now twice threatened me; and, doubtless, nothing
but my great preoccupation of thought saved Mistress Prudence, privileged person although she was
become, from a mighty smart reprimand on our
next encountering for her petulant conduct.

That excellent dignity of bearing which I believed
myself to have endued, as well as my finest gown,
was destined to be spent (if indeed it were not altogether thrown away) upon old Emmet and a single
waiting-maid. From Simon I learned that it had
been thought well not to disturb the three gentlemen, whom he supposed still sleeping. Lady Mary,
he added, had been much shaken by her adventures
of the previous day, and found herself unable to
leave her bed. So I sat me down alone, and made
a meal of most unblushing amplitude. Since I was
a child, I may say, I had never known myself to
lack good appetite, and I now found that so far from
weakening my desire and enjoyment of my victuals,
as would seem most fitting in a young woman of
sentiment, the fatigues, emotions, and excitements
of the day before had but set a keener edge to my
relish of these, as of all other good things in what I

could but think, despite all drawbacks, was a very
engaging and gladsome world.

Now it was a custom with me to have Prudence
wait upon me at breakfast, arising, I suppose, from
a certain loneliness I did use to feel when my dear
father's ailments would keep him for days together
in his chamber. She being this morning absent,
and I asking where she was, Simon soon made it plain
that he was not pleased with his granddaughter.

" Faith, madam," he said, " I cannot tell where
she is. The little baggage grows past my holding.
She is as full of mysteries as an egg is full of meat."

" Nay, Simon," I answered, " 't is no mystery.
She spoke very boldly to me but now, and fled to
avoid correction. I make no doubt she is gone for
comfort to Christopher Kidd."

" There 's more in it, madam, than Farmer
Kidd," answered Simon, his old head shaking with
the ominous relish of him that justifies suspicion of
evil. " A loaf, a cheese, and a great piece of salted
beef are this morning missed from the larder, and,
as I live," he cried, peering into the great beer jack
that stood upon the table, " who but the hussy
should have taken more than the half of the ale that
I drew for breakfast? She did pass through the hall
on leaving your chamber, madam; Christopher and
all his men are well fed in the kitchen, and have but
to ask for what they lack."

And here I was scarce able to hold back my laughter. The picture of little Prudence, so dainty and modest, for all that something of coquetry was part of her nature, so feeding a secret lover did mightily tickle my fancy.

" Do not fret for the ale, Simon," I said gaily. " Please Heaven, it will find its way down a thirsty throat. If Prue be the thief indeed, I shall know the drinker before sunset. She is a good maid, and will not long keep a secret from a mistress that holds her in much affection and esteem." These last words were as much for the other serving-woman that was by as for Prue's censorious grandfather.

Sending word to Lady Royston that I would gladly know when her ladyship was willing I should wait upon her, I now retired to my garden, finding more company in its few remaining flowers, and in the fresh and sunny autumn air, than in a house but yet half awake. And I had within me, whether carried from the house, or gathered from the sweet odors drawn by the sun from the sodden earth, I know not, a sense that some great thing was coming; that this was but the lull before our wits and tongues should be again engaged in a conflict for love, for honor, and perhaps for life.

And I knelt on a little stone bench, warmed with the sun, and prayed to Him who did make these three best things, that wit might be keen, and

18

tongue eloquent, to set them high above doubt and question hereafter.

To me, after it might be half an hour, came Prudence, bearing in a very innocent countenance an expression of injury most Christianly endured. Madam Royston, she said, would be vastly obliged by a visit from me, but she was bidden by Captain Royston to say he had matter for my ear that was of moment, to be delivered before I should speak with madam his mother.

" And where is Captain Royston to be found ? " I asked.

" He is now taking his breakfast in the hall," answered the little minx, vastly demure.

" And why was I not informed that he was risen ? " I demanded.

" If madam gave order to that effect," she replied, " it came not to my ear."

This petty vantage of feminine fence had not long remained hers, had I not been more concerned to reach the great hall than to open a general attack in the matter of the missing beef and beer. The better part of the way to the house I ran rather than walked — that part, I mean, that is not in sight of the hall windows. Within I found Ned alone, eating his breakfast. A cloud of gloom was over his face, and, though he rose with great courtesy and alacrity to meet me, his greeting seemed rather a submission to my embrace than the clasp of an ardent lover.

It is not unlikely that in a happier hour I had taken this reception ill, but, thinking I could read his thought, I let it pass, which I was soon very glad to have done, when his words made it plain that I had not read him amiss.   For a while I pressed him with food, with questions of what rest he had taken, of his mother's health, and with other talk indifferent to the issue that yet, as I plainly saw, did lie between us.   But, do what I might, I could bring no smile to his face; I could see the man held a tight rein upon himself, for all he could not keep his eyes from taking full account of my person on this his first seeing me after so many years in the full light of day, and in my proper garb.   And there was great holiday in my heart, for I knew that I pleased him well; had I not the word both of mirror and handmaid that I was not ill to look upon ?   Moreover, those eyes of his, re-strained though they were from all expressive ad-miration, could not conceal something that I took to be a kind of hunger.

At length, finding that his discomfort was in no way diminished, I asked him, speaking mighty small and meek, what it was he wished to say to me, before I should pay my respects to my Lady Mary.

" I would pray you," he answered, " by no means at this present to make mention to my mother of—of the matter — I mean, of my disgrace with His Highness of Orange."

It was only by an effort, it seemed, that the last words could be uttered. I arose from the seat whence I had confronted him at the table, dropped him a little courtesy, and walked toward the door. But, passing behind his chair as I went, I felt my heart so filled with pity and sorrow that I knew I must either fall into a passion of tears or speak more fully and closely with him who now bore such things for me and mine. So behind him I stayed, and, casting an arm about his neck, " Ned," I whispered, " dear Ned, wilt in no manner be comforted ? "

His voice shook a little, in spite of that curbing rein, as he answered me. " Where lies the comfort that I should take, sweet Phil ? " he said.

" 'T is unkind in you, dear, to make me speak unmaidenly," I replied. " I know your woes, but is it, then, nothing that I also share them ? Am I perhaps of no account, for that my love is no new thing ? "

" Your love, Philippa," he said, in a voice that was now become very tender and solemn, " is a pearl of price so great that but yesterday it was all I asked of Heaven. But shall this jewel be set in a

filthy copper ring ? I know, sweetheart," he went
on, " that you have found me churlish this morning. But since I awoke I have one only thought in
my mind, that I did wrong last night, with my
honor thus overshadowed, to tell you of my love."

" Nay," I said, " there was no telling; and there
needed none."

" Did I not tell you— " he began.

But from over his shoulder I gently clapped hand
upon his mouth, crying : " Hush, dear Ned !
'T was this way that it befell. Listen, for all else
is what you have dreamed." And I took here the
tone and manner of one that tells to a child the
sweetest fairy-tale he knows. " Two did ride in
the night. The two had each a heart, and the heart
of one was sore hurt. Now of the other the heart
was well and safely lodged behind a little secret
door. And this door was never opened, though
there was one did know the way to it, and at his
knock it had been wont of old to move somewhat
ajar on the hinge. But in that dark night the heart
that was hurt did cry aloud, and — and that small
door did fly open, and now, Ned—— "

" Ay, sweetheart ? " he said, as I paused; and
he tried to look round at me: but I would not let
him.

" And now, Ned," I continued, " the door is
closed forever; but the heart is abroad, and hath

no home but here." And here I slipped to my knees by his side, leaning with hands tight clasped in supplication against his breast. " My lord," I said, " must even keep his promise to his handmaid, who will gladly bear all that she may share with him. But, without his presence and his love, the sun will be darkened to her eyes all the days of her life."

And so there was an end; for his arms came about me and ended all strife between us even to this moment of writing.

CHAPTER XVIII

A ND thus my father surprised us, by which accident we were not a little taken aback. My
lover, however, rose bravely to the occasion, and
very plainly and without any mincing of the matter
asked him for my hand in marriage; saying in conclusion, however, that he was aware his present state
and condition might well justify Sir Michael's re-
fusing to grant his request: "Which, sir," said he,
"I had not made until cleared of all suspicion of
treason to His Highness, but for you knowing me
innocent, and the recent avowal of my affection
being by surprise, as it were, wrung from me."

"Indeed, sir," I broke in, hoping by a little
boldness to cover my confusion the better, "there
was no surprise but this same gad-about daughter
of yours. It was through no fault of his, for none
but I did wring from Captain Royston that offer of
alliance he now seems minded to repent."

"Be silent, child," said my father; "Captain
Royston stands in need of no champion with me."
Whereat I was abashed to a blushing hotter than
before. "My lad," said Sir Michael, "I have

twofold reason to be glad.   It would go hard with
me to refuse the man who has done for my name
what you have done, even were he not the husband
I have this many a day desired for my child.   And,
if we cannot put you right with the Prince, we must
together endure.   But I hope for better things."
And with these words my father drew me to him,
and put my hand in that of Captain Royston.

There is no need to rehearse all that was said and
felt on this occasion of my betrothal.   There was
among us regard so reverent, friendship so strong,
and acquaintance so well tested of time, that the
dark shadow hanging over could not, even while it
chastened, in any way jar with nor distort the joy
of the two who saw the future each in the other's
countenance; nor of him that saw in the faces of us
both a vision of the past that was ever green and
poignant in the young heart of the old man.

And as I left them to visit Lady Mary, now too
long neglected, my father told me that I had gained
a husband such as is not had every day.

So I went to my lady's door, and there, very
proud in the thought that out of all the world Captain Royston had chosen me, I loitered a little; for
I hoped that my cheeks would presently lose something of the telltale color that still seemed to burn
in them.   And after I entered her chamber the
time for a while went so exceedingly heavily

that I think it but charity to take my reader
elsewhere.

Sir Michael and Captain Royston were now for a
space engaged in discussion of the future. But, as
they neither knew that Philip, in the obstinacy of
his opinion, had escaped them, nor that events now
in preparation should very shortly change the complexion of the whole matter, their animadversions
and reflections upon this occasion are become of
little moment.

Now my father, on his coming which did so
mightily abash me, was carrying under his arm in
its sheath the sword which, in its day and his, had
been so terrible to many a man of the Parliament's
forces. It was indeed many years that he had not
worn steel at his side; but it was ever a custom with
him, upon any occasion of state, danger, or solemnity, to fetch with him in the morning this sword
from his chamber. More than once or twice, when
I was a little maid with a conscience not seldom ill
at ease, has the sight of that honorable blade,
tucked slantwise beneath his arm as he painfully
descended the great stair of a morning, driven me
to hasty repentance and confession of yesterday's
prank or peccadillo.

My father, then proposing that they should take
the air a little, since the sun continued bravely to
shine, remarked, as he laid this sword upon his chair

by the hearth, that his companion had but an empty scabbard dangling at his sword-belt. To Sir Michael's civil offer of his own good weapon to replace that so unhappily lost, Ned replied that he thanked him, but would make shift for a while with the scabbard, having a mind to fill it again with the only blade that fitted it, if haply it might be done. And as he spoke his face was suffused with a flush of deep crimson; the only blush, my father said, that he had ever seen on the lad's goodly countenance.

And so they walked a turn in the park, amongst the trees and the deer, Sir Michael supported, until a pleasant bench was reached, by an arm that is, I have found, very good and comfortable to lean upon ; where I, having from my lady's window seen them pass, made shift after a little to join them. Ned rose to meet me, and I was glad to see the shadow driven from his face by the smile of his welcome.

" My lady is very instant and pressing that you should go to her," I said, as I seized in both mine the hand he stretched to me.

" What, what ! " says my father merrily. " Was all this bird-like haste of swooping down upon us but to drive the man again from your side ? 'T is early days, little Phil—early days ! '

" Indeed, sir," I replied, panting a little yet for

the speed I had used, " I would not have the man
leave me, and so ran to husband the minutes with
him. Nor I would not have him go to Madam
Royston, who will, without doubt, very quickly
draw from him our morning's doings."

" And wherefore should she not know them ? "
said Ned, smiling gently on me the while he still
clung to my hand, as finding comfort in the touch
of it.

" Because," said I, " we have trouble enough,
and she will surely make more when she knows.
'T is now three years past that she told me I must
look for no such greatness as to be your— " and
there my boldness had an end.

" Is it indeed as you say ? " cried poor Ned ; and
his eyes went in question from mine to Sir Michael's.

And then that little devil of mischief was in me
again.

" I vow 't is very true," I said. " Nor I do not
quarrel at that. But in this same matter she had
a promise of me, that—that—— "

" What promise was it ? " he asked, in some distress. " I do hope it was nothing foolish, nor hard
to keep."

" I had almost forgot it," I answered, lingering
over my words, " but now I do perceive I have to
the letter kept it. Yet indeed, dear Ned, it was for
some hours hard to observe that pledge, for I did

promise her that I would wait until I was asked."
And, if my jest was of more boldness than wit, the
laughter that greeted it, being compounded of love,
merriment, and confidence, lacked nothing of the
finest quality.

Conversation more sober ensuing, it appeared that
Ned, who already, before he broke his fast, had
visited her, was neither now willing to leave me,
nor, with the present load of care upon him, to submit again so soon to the searching scrutiny of his
mother's eyes a countenance that was, he well
knew, of a very treacherous honesty. For, if he
saw little need to conceal our betrothal from her,
he had no mind she should get wind of his disfavor
with His Highness of Orange. Whereupon my
father, who seemed, indeed, to preside at the feast
of our joy with a tenderness almost feminine, undertook an embassage to my Lady Mary, hoping, he
said, by discovery of the betrothal, to close her
eyes for a while to all other troubles.

He stoutly refused every offer of assistance to his
walking, saying it were best with all the pains of a
penitent to approach so awful a shrine; and so,
cheerily waving one hand and leaning with the other
upon his stick, made his way limping to the house.

It was not long after his leaving us that, although
deep in discussion of matters vastly entertaining at
least to those engaged, I heard the rapid approach

of a horse, of which, with his rider, I very soon had
a glimpse as they passed the open space between
the last trees of the avenue and the southeastern
corner of the house.

Now, while Ned spoke many things most sweet
to hear, and I, though finding my power of words
strangely contracted since my father's leaving us,
now and again made shift to answer him; and while
he was about opening that question, to this day not
with conclusion to be answered, of when first each
did begin to love the other, some part of me was all
the time with secret clamor asking who this mounted
visitor should be. What if he were from the Prince ?
And so, though I heard most of his words, and held
them all dear, I was at length in such a fever of desire to know more of what was toward within doors,
that I told Ned my presence was needed in the house,
as much in his own interest as of the visitor, and my
father that must entertain him. And I would not let
him conduct me, for I wished (though to him I said
nothing of this), in case of news, ill or good, in the
matter of his standing with His Highness, to know
it first myself; so begged him where he was to await
me a while, and left him, I doubt not, in much
amaze at the contradictions of the feminine nature.
At least it was so that I was fain to hope he explained a behavior that may well have appeared
whimsical in me; having not infrequently observed

that this is with some of our masters a means much favored to avoid the pains of understanding our vagaries even the most reasonable.

Sir Michael, being admitted to Lady Mary's presence, had come no nearer his purpose than some prefatory compliments and good wishes, when he was hastily called away to meet a gentleman that was come on urgent business from His Highness of Orange. Repairing at once to the great hall, he found before him M. de Rondiniacque, just dismounted and entered, looking with a wryness of countenance ill-concealed upon the tankard of ale held out to him by little Prue.

Perceiving his host, the French officer politely waved aside the refreshment, and bowed to Sir Michael with great reverence and all the grace of the Paris manner. Now his name, as was but natural, when it reached my father's ears, was become twisted out of all shape.

" You are welcome," says Sir Michael, returning his obeisance. " I address, I believe, M. le Lieutenant— " and there stuck.

" Jean-Marie Godemar de Rondiniacque, at your service," replied that gentleman. " My poor name, Sir Michael, has great terror for unwonted tongues! "

" 'T is then a fit companion to your sword, M. de Rondiniacque," says Sir Michael, in the older fashion of courtly compliment.

M. de Rondiniacque bowed again. " It is well if
they agree, sir," he said, " for they are my whole
estate."

" I can wish you, M. de Rondiniacque, no better," replied my father. " You come, I believe,
from His Highness of Orange."

And M. de Rondiniacque, saying that he had indeed that honor, presented a letter from the Prince,
in which it was set forth that His Highness, being
in the neighborhood, was fain to do himself the
pleasure of a visit, of necessity short, to so distinguished a soldier and gentleman, and so stanch
a supporter of that cause which the Prince had
made his own, as Sir Michael Drayton; and would
not in his coming lag far behind the bearer of the
letter.

Having read, Sir Michael was at once for calling
out his little company of armed men and putting
himself at their head, in order to meeting His Highness in the village, and escorting him to the house,
but M. de Rondiniacque very respectfully opposed
this cousre, saying that His Highness was particular
in his instructions that Sir Michael's age and infirmities should be disturbed by no pomp nor ceremony of reception.

" His Highness does me great honor," said Sir
Michael.

" His Highness is little likely to forget," replied

M. de Rondiniacque, "that, in an hour when he almost despaired of that help and countenance he was led to look for on his coming into England from gentlemen of condition, Sir Michael Drayton was the first to come forward and set a noble pattern to the rest. There are, moreover, other matters, I believe, in which the Prince holds himself your debtor, sir. But of these, being most curiously entangled with some of another sort, I am not to speak; being straitly enjoined to leave them for your meeting with His Highness."

Now these words did mightily please my father, filling him with hope by his own influence and arguments of setting all things right between Captain Royston and the Prince of Orange. So, most courteously praying M. de Rondiniacque that until His Highness's arrival he would consider the house his own, begging excuse of his absence on the ground of fit preparation to be made for the Prince, and bidding Prudence attend the gentleman's wants, he took himself off to find Philip, and with him concert a plan of action.

Alone with Prue, M. de Rondiniacque was not long in marking, according to his habit, the dainty person and pretty face of her that waited upon him. Now Prudence was never slow to observe when she had made a conquest, however slight, and soon responded to his flattery by bringing him in a flagon

something better than the ale she had observed him
to look upon so sourly.

"Perhaps, sir," says Prue, "being out of France,
you will have more thirst for good Burgundy than
for our ale."

"Pour it to me yourself, fair Hebe," cried De
Rondiniacque; and as she obeyed he smiled upon
her freely, and twisted in very gallant fashion the
little black mustachios that adorned his lip. "Nay,"
he continued: "but you must put those pretty lips
to the cup before I drink."

"Oh! la, no, sir!" cries Prue; "indeed I could
n't," and straightway sipped, making, I doubt
not, as she cried "I' fecks, 't is good!" a little
grimace of satisfaction, with lips pursed up, as
I have seen her often, like a bird uplifting his bill in
dumb thanksgiving to the clouds for water in a
thirsty land. Indeed, M. de Rondiniacque has told
me, in these days of nearer acquaintance, that things
had fallen far otherwise than they did but for the
pretty coquetry of Prudence and his own too in-
flammable temper.

If the wine was red, he remarked, her lips were
no less rich in color; which led him incontinently to
swear the wine was but the second refreshment for
his tasting; and if her coyness persuaded him to
change the order of succession, a great draught of
that generous wine of Burgundy did by no means

19

lessen his desire to taste the red velvet of her now pouting lips.

And so it was that I, nearing the door, was by a scream from my handmaid drawn with such haste into the hall that I found her in the arms of M. de Rondiniacque, whose mouth was pressed with much force and no little enjoyment to the lips he had of late compared with the wine.

At once recognizing the gallant officer for my friend of yesterday, I wished indeed that I had stayed with Ned; but in the brief time spent by Prudence in freeing herself (for she had immediately seen me), and by M. de Rondiniacque in perceiving me, and letting her free, I had called to my assistance all that dignity and state of bearing which is seldom far to seek by the woman, however young and unversed in the world, who has faith in her gown and her cause.

" Prudence! " I cried, standing half-way between them and the door, and speaking with great severity, while she, red as fire, fumbled piteously with her apron, and the gentleman sought to cover the foolishness of his face with the hand that pulled at the hair upon his upper lip; " Prudence, what means this noise and outcry ?   Who are you, sir ? "

" A poor gentleman of France, mistress," he replied, " but now arrived with word of the coming of His Highness of Orange." .

"And does that good news fetch cries for help from my serving-woman?" I demanded, bending • my brows in a frown that I would have had very awful.

"Nay, be not so moved, fair mistress," said M. de Rondiniacque, in a voice very gentle and soothing. "The outcry was for another matter, and, *foi de gentilhomme!* the fault was mine alone. It was but for—for a kiss that I did give the maid in jest."

"Such jests, good sir, are fitter for the camp," I answered, a little relaxing my sternness. Then, observing that he began with more intentness to regard me, I sent Prudence at once from the hall. When she was gone, I prayed him, with a courtesy very frigid, to let me know, ere I left him, if there were aught in which I could serve him, or provide for his comfort, ending, as I thought very artfully, with, "M. de—de—" as if I knew not his name.

"My name is De Rondiniacque," he said, smiling on me with an expression of much cunning. "I do perceive that you are at least aware of my claim to noble family. One thing, madam, there is, in which you can oblige me,—to tell me, I mean, where I have before encountered you."

"I cry you mercy, sir," I said, "for I know not what you mean." For somehow I had little mind to discuss with him the affair of last night, and was abashed, moreover, at the thought of how I had then appeared. So I spoke with a great haughtiness and disdain, and made to leave him.

But he came quickly between me and the door, and—" *Mon Dieu !* " he cried, " 't is the pretty boy of yesterday ! "

" You grow in mystery, M. de Rondiniacque," I said. " Prithee, let me pass ! "

" Nay, nay," he answered, " this loftiness shall not bugbear me, pretty one. Thou dost know thy way to a camp and out again as well as another. Faith, I did ponder wherefore those bright eyes did draw me so."

" If you continue these matters with me, sir, I must leave you," I cried, and so made attempt to pass him.

But he seized me gently by the arm. " You shall not so," he exclaimed. " Nay, do not fear I will hurt you. I do not handle a woman as I grasped that ruffling youth. How fare the pretty wrists ? "

My anger here prevailing over my prudence, I declared roundly that I would take these injuries to those that should exact account of them. Whereupon he seized me very firmly by the hand, so that I could not withdraw it.

" And tell them, too," he said, " of last night's masquerade. I will not be denied. Your secret is safe with me.   Do I not know ?   Have I not many such in keeping ?   But none, I swear, for so lovely a partner in guilt.   But it must be a bargain between us."   And as I struggled to free my hand he wound his arm about my waist, holding me with a wonderful gentleness of strength.   " Nay, do not fret," he went on, " I will not hurt you, and the bargain is soon struck.   A tender glance of your eye will pay for much, as I doubt not you have been told before.   Come, strife is folly with those that love us; and verily you are so beautiful that I love you already.   What! still stubborn ? "

" Loose me," I panted, now mad with rage and struggling.

" I vow," said he, " I am beside myself with love of you.   Oh, why so easy but one day past, and now so proud ? "

" I will call," said I, drawing breath for a loud cry.

" And not twice," said a harsh voice from the door, whither turning my eyes I beheld Edward Royston.   He had followed me as I my father, and, even as I, was arrived in a moment for M. de Rondiniacque most unhappy.   To prove this, the mere sight of his countenance was enough; I had often seen it stern, but never before so terrible.

Now, upon my entrance some few minutes before, M. de Rondiniacque had very promptly and civilly loosed his hold of little Prue; but, whether because he considered he now held a nobler prey, or because he would grant to the presence of a woman what he must refuse to the dictation of a man, certain it is that this time intrusion brought no release. With his eyes fixed upon my captor Captain Royston strode slowly up the hall till close upon us; then, pointing with his finger to M. de Rondiniacque's hand that was still about my waist: " You will need that hand for your sword, Lieutenant de Rondiniacque," he said. " Do you not take my meaning ? This, at least, is as French as it is English." And with that he struck him across the face with the glove he carried in his hand.

And then at length I was free, and quickly out of reach of my persecutor. The Frenchman stepped back, and drew slowly and with seeming reluctance; astonished no more by the blow than by this new complexion put upon the matter. I marked, moreover, with a great pain of compassion in me, how poor Ned's hand went also to his side, to find but the scabbard; and to me that watched his face the while it was plain the emptiness of that sheath did not a little exacerbate the bitterness of his spirits; so that I fell into a great fear of what he should do.

Finding, then, that he had no sword, Ned went, still with the same awful and deliberate calmness, to Sir Michael's great chair by the hearth, and brought

thence naked the sword my father had offered a
while since for his use. But, as the two men faced
each other, M. de Rondiniacque lowered his point
to the floor.

"Royston," he said with much gentleness, "I
would not hurt you."

"You had best try," replied his opponent, "for
I shall kill you else."

"I will explain the matter," said De Rondiniacque, still patient.

"You may do so," Ned replied unmoved, "afterwards—in hell."

"I do think, indeed, Ned," I here interrupted,
"he did not know me for what I am, but did mistake me for some runagate hussy."

"Then for that I will kill him!" said Ned, never
turning my way, nor taking his baleful eye from the
other's face. "If you would not see it done, go,
bid your father come to see it is no murder."

And somehow I could not altogether disobey his
word; yet I made my passage to the door as slow
as foot can go.

"And now, sir," my champion continued, "I
will show you how in England we do serve him that
affronts the daughter of his host."

"Sir Michael's daughter!" exclaimed the poor
man, so wholly careless of covering himself that
Ned's intended attack upon him was perforce again

delayed. " I knew her but for a pretty piece that
did ride the country as a lad, and that passed yesterday many hours among us. Meeting her now in
female attire, I did think—— "

" For that thought alone I will kill you!" said
Ned, and their swords crossed.

And so I fled to find my father, having for my
lover, indeed, no fear at all, but much for the
gentleman who was, when all was said, our guest,
and taken, as I thought, rather in a very luckless
error than in any wilful offence.

Now, as I passed through the lobby of entrance,
the great door stood wide to the sweet noontide air
of that shining autumn day; and I, glancing forth
to see if Sir Michael were abroad and within hail,
beheld coming up the avenue a great number of
horsemen, their steel harness gleaming in the sun
beneath the leafless trees. So I knew the Prince
was come, and hastened the more to advise my
father of all that was toward. Him I found very
soon (though my inquietude did lend great length
to the search) in the stable-yard. He was angry in
face and words, and vexed at soul, for he had just
learned that Philip was gone. He was come to the
stable to know what horse had borne his son from
the house, and it was therefore upon Christopher
Kidd that his wrath now fell. The poor fellow had
of this sort in the past twenty hours received more

than was by any means earned, and turned upon me the eager countenance of one that looks for succor.

" Dear sir," I cried to my father, " His Highness is arrived."

" What!" cried he in answer. " Why, then, was I not advised ?"

" I come to tell you," I replied. " His Highness is not yet dismounted, and with haste you may yet receive him at the door."

Now, as we spoke, Christopher had been heavily searching for something in the pocket of his breeches, which found, he hurried after us, as my father with the help of my arm made painful haste to the house.

" If the Prince be indeed come, Sir Michael," said Kidd, intercepting us at the side door of the house, " I keep my word to Master Philip, and rid myself of the plaguy thing at once." And he thrust into Sir Michael's hand a twisted and crumpled paper, and beat a rapid retreat, vanishing in the stable before my father had deciphered the last words of Philip's message.

When this was done we read it again together, and my father, after a few words of the great need there was like to be of Philip's presence among us during His Highness's visit to Drayton, despatched me in hot haste to see to the hoisting of the banner, which fluttering from the turret should bring back in the nick of time, if it pleased God, him that had, through little fault of his own, been the cause of all these troubles.

Meantime, in the hall, Ned's attack had been both skilful and bitter; so fiercely indeed did he push his opponent that M. de Rondiniacque has since taken, by his own account, no little credit to himself for the swordmanship that enabled him for a while, at least, to resist the onslaught, without, in his turn, attempting the injury of his adversary. At length, what with the fury of the attack and some carelessness on the Frenchman's part in shifting his ground, Ned had him so hemmed in and penned up in that corner of the hall that is opposite to the chief door of entrance that De Rondiniacque seemed wholly at his mercy. But, even in that passion of anger with which the despite of fortune had overwhelmed the habitual temper of his spirit, it was quite foreign to Ned's nature to take his enemy thus at an advantage. Almost in the act of delivering his point in a manner that for one in De Rondiniacque's constrained and circumscribed position would have been more than difficult to parry, he checked himself, and, retreating to the middle of the floor, cried to him to come out, for he would not willingly nail him like a stoat or weasel to the wall.

" Enough, Royston! 't is enough!" he cried, coming forward. " I did never know you bloodthirsty."

So saying, he raised his eyes and saw what Ned

from his position could not see, that within the doorway stood a small and silent group, spectators of the duel. These were His Highness of Orange and some four or five others. Dismounting, they had found no sign of hospitality but the openness of the great door, and all hesitation to enter un-announced was banished by the sound of the sword-play in the hall. The Prince stepped at once into the lobby; he then stood a moment listening to the ring of meeting blades, and to the tearing, striding hiss of their parting.

" This is no fencing bout," said he, and entered the hall.

" Bloodthirsty, forsooth! " cried Ned, in answer to De Rondiniacque's essay at peacemaking. " Bloodthirsty! I have borne enough of late to make me so, in all conscience. Look to yourself, man, for I would kill you, were you William and all his troops." And with that he fell upon him again with much fury, so that the other was beginning of necessity a more aggressive defence, when the Prince stepped between them, striking up their swords with his riding-whip.

" Since when, Mr. Royston," he said, " do you carry a sword ? And for whom ? "

But Royston, balked of his prey, and feeling the whole world in league against him, was too full of anger to show either surprise or reverence. " *Captain*

Royston," he said, with great and bitter emphasis on the military title, " has left his sword in miserly hands, Your Highness."

" How so ? " demanded William, the frown growing deeper on his face.

" Hands that grasp what they do not need," replied Ned boldly. " But *Master* Royston takes a sword where he finds it, uses it against whom he pleases, and wields it for himself."

" The fault, Monseigneur, of this broil is wholly mine," interposed M. de Rondiniacque.

" Lieutenant de Rondiniacque," replied the Prince, " I know your generous nature, and for once mistrust it. What is the occasion of the broil, as you name it ? "

With some hesitation M. de Rondiniacque answered that it was a quarrel—about a woman.

His Highness laughed drily. " I fear, Lieutenant," he said, " that to protect a man that was once your friend, you play very nobly upon our knowledge of your weakness."

" Indeed, sire," said De Rondiniacque, " it is as I say. I did wrong a lady, mistaking her for another kind."

" And did ' William and all his army ' likewise wrong this lady ? " asked the Prince.

" Indeed, no, Your Highness," replied De Rondiniacque.

" Then I must believe, Lieutenant," the Prince continued, " that it is for no kiss to a pretty girl, but for holding my commission, that you were even now in danger of your life. We have it from his own lips that he had as lief kill me as you." Then, as the generous fellow would again have spoken in endeavor to put the matter in a better aspect, " No more, sir," said His Highness; " stand aside." He then proceeded to address Captain Royston.

" Sir," he said, " I spared your life of late. But I did warn you that if found again in our neighborhood, or raising hand against us, were it never so little, you were like to get such treatment as we give to spies." And, turning to the officers and gentlemen that had entered the hall in his company, he added: " How think you, gentlemen ? "

To this question Mr. Bentinck contented himself with replying that His Highness had indeed promised as much, and that it was for him to judge whether his conditions had been infringed; Count Schomberg, who was still of the party, said, speaking in the French language, that an example would not come amiss at this juncture, for he believed these raw English levies were proving not a little turbulent and likely to give trouble. The rest, much, I think, to their honor, kept silence, having perhaps the greatest difficulty in believing the matters alleged against Captain Royston, that his confession of the night before came to them but at second-hand.

There is little doubt in my mind that the silence of these two younger gentlemen, taking sides, as it seemed to do, with the small doubt or hesitation that still lurked in the Prince's mind, added for the moment fuel to his anger. He bade the junior of them go to the escort, and send in a file of men; this gentleman, as he went, encountering Sir Michael in the doorway, after one glance in his face, stood back, giving way to him with a natural and involuntary respect. For M. de Rondiniacque has told me that my father entered the hall with that pure and noble dignity of bearing to which age, infirmity, and even lameness can but add distinction.

"Your Highness is welcome," he said, at once singling out and approaching his chief guest. "I regret my failure to welcome his arrival, and could wish I had better entertainment to give."

"I am wholly of your mind, Sir Michael Drayton," replied the Prince. "I like it so little that I take my leave of you." And with that he turned his back upon his host, addressing some words in a low voice to Mr. Bentinck.

The insult was plain, and, although he was in a measure prepared for trouble by the few words he had heard before he entered the hall, such an attack upon himself was wholly beyond Sir Michael's

expectation.   He was, however, a man to resent discourtesy most readily from the highest source.

" I will ask Your Highness," said he, in a voice
very clear and steady, " how we have incurred his
displeasure."   Then the old man drew himself to
his full height, and his voice recovered for a space
some of the fuller and rounder tones of earlier days.
" Ay, but it is," he said very solemnly, " a matter
very weighty.   Since Your Highness has so spoken,
and within my walls, I may ask the reason of it."

The Prince turned upon him with a great suddenness.   " Then know, sir," he answered, almost
fiercely, " that I was yesterday received under pretence of loyalty and friendship into the house of an
English gentleman that has served me beyond the
seas.   But the house, sir, was a trap, and I the rat
for whom the bait was set."   At this point it was
that two troopers, preceded by the young officer,
entered the hall.   His Highness regarded them for
a moment, and then continued to Sir Michael his
explanation, which rapidly unfolded itself as a
charge   against   more   than   Edward   Royston.
" Well, Sir Michael, I spared that man's life,
moved to clemency, I believe, in chief by the per-
suasion of a young fellow that did bring me warning
of my danger.   For this treacherous host, I dismissed him my service, and, if proof that I then
erred was lacking last night, it is not far to seek this

morning. For I now find the man here, with my
messenger to you at his sword's point, and threats
against me and mine mingling with his sword-play.
How shall I know this is not yet another hotbed
of false friends ? In truth, I do believe it such.
Therefore, I say again, sir, I do not like my entertainment."

" Your Highness is much abused," said Sir
Michael, mighty calmly.

" Indeed," replied the Prince, with a harsh and
unkindly laugh, " I do believe I am."

" For this is a matter," continued my father,
loftily passing over the twisting of his word, " of
which I do know the rights."

" 'T is like enough, sir," said the Prince. " But
I do not look to hear them from you." Then,
turning to the two troopers, he bade them arrest Captain Royston, saying to them and the officer that he
should hold them responsible for the prisoner's person till Exeter was reached. Now, Ned had stood
all this while with my father's sword still naked in
. his hand, the point resting upon the floor.

" Take his sword," said His Highness.

And poor Ned, by this caring little what he did,
flung the borrowed weapon on the ground.

" The sword is mine ! " said Sir Michael.

" I ask your pardon, Sir Michael," cried Ned,
and stooped to raise it, saying, as he reverently

presented the hilt to its owner: " I did use it for your daughter, sir."

For which Sir Michael thanked him very civilly, and then addressed the future King of England in words that I think he has not to this day forgot.

" William, Prince of Orange," he said, " this sword had been raised against King Charles the Martyr himself in defence of the friend beneath my roof. But now my hand can barely fetch it from the sheath. Yet is my tongue not rusted, and the old man's voice must be heard." And then, as a silence fell heavy upon the room, he added, " Ay, and heard it shall be."

The Prince turned his aquiline gaze upon him, but the man who had met and endured unflinching the eyes of the Lord Protector Cromwell was no whit abashed. I have heard old men say that thirty years ago my father's glance could be terrible as his sword; and even now there were moments when from the dimmed azure of that deep-set eye the mist of its many years was lifted, and the color grew cerulean round the keen and glowing spark that lit up, it seemed, not only the orb, but the whole countenance of the man, while it pierced the heart of the wicked, and not seldom affected even the innocent with a great fear. The Prince, like the brave man he ever was, met the old man's eye with courage.

20

" Be brief, sir," said he, " and I will hear you."
And although it was at this moment that without
we heard the clamorous arrival of a despatch-rider
who shortly after entered, with bloody spurs and
bespattered to the eyes with mud, and presented a
sealed packet to Mr. Bentinck, yet, throughout the
little commotion thus made, His Highness never
once turned his attention from Sir Michael.

" I do here solemnly declare," said my father,
" that Edward Royston hath done no treason to
you."

" He has refused all account of his action," replied the Prince, very coldly.

" And so doing," retorted the old man, " he
intended the sacrificing his own honor to mine."

" Said I not you were in league with him ? " cried
the Prince.

" Indeed, I am so," answered Sir Michael; " but
in no treason."

" If the truth will clear his name," said His Highness, " the truth must be said."

" And shall be, if Your Highness grant us breathing time of one short half-hour." And here Ned's
valiant advocate paused a little, waiting a reply that
came not, for this concession of time he was determined to win, if it were by any means to be gained;
having no mind to tell Philip's story without his
son's knowledge of the telling, and his presence to

bear witness, if need were, to the truth of the tale.
And all this while, from the coming of the courier,
Mr. Bentinck had perused the papers he had taken
from the packet placed in his hands.   He now raised
his head, and eyed keenly the two speakers, as one
that had not missed a word of their talk. " How
saith the great Prince," my father continued, " that
is come to set free a land enslaved ?   Thirty little
minutes on the dial's face ?   It is surely no great
boon to ask."

And Mr. Bentinck stepped up to the Prince, saying privately, but not so low as to be unheard of
all: " Grant it.   I have here news that do affect
the matter."

And so it came about that the Prince, with a
growth of courtesy forced upon him by Sir Michael's
bearing, did promise in half an hour's time to hear
his story in defence of the accused, asking very
civilly his host's permission to walk with his suite in
the garden that he spied from the windows until the
time were past.   So — the Prince and his following
walking abroad; my father despatching Simon and
others not only with refreshment for the gentlemen,
but also great tankards of ale and other good things
to the soldiers of the escort; Ned with his guard,
moreover, being quartered for this momentous half-
hour in my father's little chamber on the ground
floor; and I, like Sister Anne in the tale of Blue-

beard and his many wives, being posted on the roof of the turret, and, beneath a flag that would not at all, in the light breeze that there was, spread itself to my liking, watching with an old spy-glass to my eye for the horseman that should by his coming make us all happy again — there was left in the hall none but the luckless cause of this present phase of our troubles.   M. de Rondiniacque at least thought himself alone; and since he is of a nature very generous and candid, who so unhappy as he ?

CHAPTER XIX

M. DE RONDINIACQUE had little reason to hope for anything better than a second rebuff if he pursued the Prince to plead Royston's cause in the garden. He therefore sat him down in the hall where they had left him, to ponder miserably enough the mischief he had done. But scarce, being wont at times to speak to himself aloud, had he cried: " *Mort de ma vie!* but if poor Royston suffer for this, I will forswear all and turn monk" (wholly forgetting, as he was at times not a little used, the grave cause of his expatriation), when there ran lightly out from the shelter formed by the hanging that was before the door that leads to the kitchens, who but little Prue?

Now, it was not far from this door that Mr. Bentinck had stood while he read the letters brought by the courier, and it was at this point that Prudence now paused, and stooping, raised from the floor a sheet of thin paper, twice folded, which it soon appeared she had from her cover observed that gentleman to let fall. Holding this behind her back, she addressed M. de Rondiniacque.

" 'T is a mighty fine business, Master Foreigner,"
she said. " See how you have embroiled everything
with this love of kissing! It is like enough you
have by this means cost an honest man his life."

" 'T is all true that you say," replied he; " yet I
cannot tell how you should know it, if you have not
wilfully listened since ever your mistress sent you
from this place."

" I came between that door and its curtain," she
replied, " in the same moment that Sir Michael did
ask the Prince the reason of his churlishness. So it
was not long before I heard good Mr. Royston tell
how he did use the sword for Sir Michael's daughter.
And I were a ninnyhammer indeed, if I could not
from that tell the rest of the tale. Therefore, I say
again, that 't is all your fault, ill man that you
are ! "

" It is mine, indeed," said De Rondiniacque
sadly.

Then did Prudence pull a very long and solemn
face.

" Do you repent of your sins ? " she asked.

" Most heartily I do," he answered.

" And would you atone ? " she continued.

" Most gladly—but how ? " he asked.

" Will you leave kissing forever," she demanded
with great severity, " if I do put you in the way to
make amends ? "

" Ay, that, and more!" he cried, in reckless
penitence, " do but show me the way."

" Nay, softly," she answered. " 'T will take
three at least, and one of them a woman of a very
pretty wit, even if I be not mistaken, to undo the
mischief one witless man can work with this same
foolish kissing."

" Have done with your gibes!" said De Rondiniacque angrily. " I would not kiss you again if you
asked it." For which discourtesy Mistress Prue
deferred her revenge, thinking, as she has told me,
that it was but his sorrow and zeal of penitence
made the gentleman speak so unmannerly.

" Hark then to me," she said. " As I stood
there by the door, where I could hear all and see
not a little, after that the Prince had said they would
walk a turn in the garden, and while they were taking away poor Mr. Royston a prisoner, the sour-
faced man in black drew the Prince aside so that
they almost touched the curtain that hid me. And
there for a little space they stood, talking soft and
low. What is he—the surly one, I mean, that had
the papers ?"

" That is Mr. Bentinck," replied De Rondiniacque, with some impatience. " Well, what said
they ?"

" The Prince was minded that Sir Michael spoke
truth, but the man in black that they must use all

means to lay hands on the priest; he said, too, that in his letter was a paper with every mark of this priest's person, so as it might be his very portrait cunningly painted; and he said that he cared not a groat for Sir Michael, nor for poor Mr. Royston, so he might come at the priest. They are mightily in love with this priest, Mr. Mar-all, and I do think—— ''

'' Did you hear his description ? '' interrupted De Rondiniacque. '' Did Bentinck read it to the Prince ? ''

'' They should do that in the air, said the Prince. And as they went I saw how this Mr. *Benting*, as you call him, did search among the papers in his hands as if he had lost one of them. And 't is little wonder,'' added she, '' that he could not find it, for His Highness's great boot had it fast under heel the while they talked; and to that heel it stuck for three good strides of their passage to the other door. See the mark of his tread.'' And she showed him the paper she had found, with its impress of a muddy heel. '' And I do think,'' said Prudence, '' that it is, perhaps, by the grace of God, that same paper that tells of this priest's person.''

'' I see little good in it for us, even if it be so,'' said he; '' but let me read.'' And, leaning over her as she unfolded the paper, he put an arm round her waist. But Prue twisted sinuously from his grasp.

"Nay, Mr. Mar-all," she cried, "I will read it myself. I can read a bold hand o' write near as well as print." And then, after peering closely for a while at the crabbed, slanting, and unfamiliar characters upon the paper, she said dolefully: "Alackaday! 't is an outlandish thing, and will not be read. I vow 't is French lingo!"

M. de Rondiniacque snatched the paper from her hand.

"I will read it for you, my pretty one," he said.

"I am not that, thank Heaven!" says Prue, bridling, as he hastily scanned the writing.

"What! not pretty?" he asked, toying with her as it were by rote of habit, while eyes and mind were both upon his reading.

"That I hope I am," replied Prue, "but not yours. Your love is unlucky." Then, as she saw that she was like to get little sport while he still would read: "Can you read French, sir?" she asked.

"What else?" he answered. "Do I not speak it since I was weaned?"

"Ay, to speak it," said she; "that I can understand, being natural-like to a poor thing hearing no better from a child. But to read it — 't is wonderful indeed. Come, do it into English for me." Then, hearing a footstep without, she cried: "Have you mastered it? For I think he returns," and as

M. de Rondiniacque looked up from reading the last words, she snatched from him the paper and hid it in her bosom.

The next moment Mr. William Bentinck entered the hall, walking slowly and casting his eyes from side to side in anxious search of the floor for the very thing she had hidden. When he perceived that he was not alone, he asked with some eagerness whether by chance Lieutenant de Rondiniacque had seen him drop a paper. That gentleman replying that he had seen no paper fall, and proceeding with great appearance of innocent good nature to peer about in the same search, Mr. Bentinck turned his regard upon Prudence, who was about leaving the room.

She seemed, however, on a sudden to change her purpose, for, turning again into the hall, she approached Mr. Bentinck, and, speaking with a very fine assumption of timidity: " If it please your honor," she said, " was it a very thin paper that you mislaid, and twice folded ? "

" Yes," replied Mr. Bentinck very sharply. " Where is it ? "

" La, now," cries Prue, " where did I lay it ? I did think perhaps it was of import, and know I did put it in safety."

" Then find it," growled he so angrily that poor Prue appeared much frightened.

" Nay, sir," she pleaded very piteously, " do not so frown upon a poor maid."

She looked around a little, as in great puzzlement; then, feeling daintily beneath her stomacher, she produced the paper, crying triumphantly that she had said it was safe, and here it was. Mr. Bentinck was at once upon the paper like a hungry hawk, asking, so soon as it was safe in his hand, whether she had read what was there written. At which Prudence opened wide her blue eyes in an amazement vastly childlike.

" And how does your honor think I should read French ? " she asked.

" And how know 't was French," retorted her inquisitor, with bitter keenness, " if you did not read ? " But Prue was too strong for the great statesman.

" Mercy on us, sir," she cried, clasping her hands most prayerfully, " do not hang me! I' fecks I did try to read, and making nothing of it, did know it for French."

When Mr. Bentinck, for all reply, had tushed, pshawed, and growled a few words wholly inaudible, he turned sharply upon his heel and left them.

And when he was well away M. de Rondiniacque, forgetful alike of pious vow and petulant threat, seized Prudence in his arms and very heartily embraced her.

" By all my Huguenot ancestors! '' he cried, kissing her vigorously to punctuate his oath, '' but I do love thee, good wench.'' And 't is enough proof that she forgave him this breach of decorum that she said never a word of threat nor promise broken.

'' Was it not purely done ? '' she said, pushing him away. '' Now tell me what was writ in the paper. Pray Heaven you did read enough.''

'' All,'' replied M. de Rondiniacque. '' But, though I put much faith in you, I know not yet what is your scheme, nor for what reason, if it be of use to us, you have returned to the Dutchman his lost paper.''

'' 'T is as needful he should know what there is written as we, if it is as I guess,'' said Prue. '' And that I cannot tell until you give me its purport.''

'' Somewhat in this way it ran, then,'' rejoined M. de Rondiniacque:

'' ' Father Francis, otherwise and at present known as '' James Marston, of the City of Oxford,'' fat, short, red periwig, his own hair tonsured—— ' ''

Prue's head had so far nodded to each particular, but at this she checked her pretty chin in mid-air. '' Tonsured! '' she cried; '' and what is that ? ''

'' Shaven so,'' he replied, describing with his finger a ring upon the top of his head. '' There is much more in the paper, however.''

" You have told me enough," said Prue, much
elated.   " Come with me, and I will show you the
man."

" But this is not the man that escaped our hands
last night," said M. de Rondiniacque, thought-
fully.

" What matter, Mr. Mar-plot ?   Can you not see
it is the man they would have ?   Come."   And she
seized him by the hand and ran for the door, almost
dragging him after her.   But at that turn of the
gallery that leads to the stable-yard she paused a
moment.   " But in truth," she said, " it does hurt
me to betray the poor man."

" Betray ! " cried M. de Rondiniacque.

" To be sure," answered Prue ; " it will be nothing
else.   Since last evening have I hid him in the barn
loft.   He told me he was a poor soldier of His
Highness that was to be hanged for stealing an old
hen.   Now 't is a wicked thing indeed to steal a
hen, but since the hen was, he says, very tough
and bad eating, I think it a worse thing to hang
the poor man for it.   Moreover, I did once save my
grandfather when Kirke's men would have hanged
him, and the mere name of a rope would make me
pity a very Judas."

" But what made you think him a soldier, and
yet know him for a priest ? " asked M. de Rondiniacque, not a little puzzled.

" He has a sword and other vile things for killing," replied the tender-hearted little fool, " and
also a great cloak like those of the Prince's guard."

" I begin to smoke the man," said the Lieutenant, remembering the escape, after the affair in the
orchard at Royston, of one of the conspirators.

" But this morning, when I privily took him
food," continued Prudence, " the thing of steel,
which is for all the world like those of your men,
was no longer upon his head. For he lay sleeping,
and before I had him awake I had well marked the
little round spot atop of his head, which had not
long since certainly been shaven, having now but a
very short and stubby growth of hair upon it. And
he made me think, too, of a bad man that Farmer
Kidd did tell me of. So I thought he was perhaps
the priest your Mr. *Benting* hunts."

" 'T is very like," said M. de Rondiniacque.
" So lead me where he is, child. In any case, he is
a bad man."

" You would not have me betray a man for no
reason but his badness," said the girl piteously.

" I would have you spend your pity first upon the
good and innocent," replied M. de Rondiniacque,
with some sternness; and then added: " Moreover,
the man is a Papist."

" A Papist ! Ah ! I do forget," cried Prue.
" He must even make way for better men." And

with that she led him at once the same road that
the ale and beef had taken.   From which it is clear
that M. de Rondiniacque's dealings with her kind
had at least taught him the dexterous art of match-
ing a bad reason with a worse upon the other side.

Such, then, was my little handmaid's great secret,
which nothing, perhaps, but her pique at her mistress's reticence could have induced her so long to
maintain.

CHAPTER XX

MEANTIME, upon the turret roof I was enduring very tediously the flight of these anxious
minutes. The spot we used to call the Crow's Nest
is marked plain to the unaided eye by a gap in the
woods that cover the low ridge of hills along which
runs the road Exeter way from Holroyd Grange.
This break in the line of trees did I watch, it may
be, for no more than ten minutes; but if it be remembered that I knew not yet what was the end of
the struggle in the hall, that a thousand accidents
suggested by the active mind to the unwilling heart
might delay or prevent Philip's keeping of his
promise, and that even if his coming availed to re-
store Ned to the favor of His Highness, my brother
must himself run great risk at his enemies' hands, it
will be found little surprising that those minutes
were to me tense, full, and slow-footed as so many
hours.

At length in the gap appeared something—a horse
was it, or a cow? Certainly there was no man upon
its back. But it stopped in the open space. For
at least the fiftieth time I raised to my eye the old

spy-glass Ned had given so many years ago to his
little friend, and with its aid I could now see that it
was indeed a horse, with a man that led it by the bridle, and seemed, I thought, to be gazing toward me.
I laid down the glass, and in a passionate desire by
some means to signify to him the need there was
that he should with haste cover the three miles that
lay between us of broken country, I seized the cords
that held the flag aloft, and, loosing that which
passes through the little pulley atop from the pin
to which it was fast, I pulled first on the one and
then on the other cord in such wise that I made the
banner run down and up the mast again and again
like a flag gone mad.

And then once more through the glass I saw the
man leap upon the back of his horse, wave his hat
to my signal, and disappear behind the trees the
way he had come.

And I knew then that he would not be long; for
he had gone the way to take the shortest track to
Drayton, and Philip, though he had no love of
horses, could, like all his family, ride when he
pleased both fearlessly and well. I left the flag
flying, and descended the winding stair with heart
much lightened, to meet at its foot my father.

" He is coming, sir," I cried. " Philip is coming!
I have seen him."

And then I learned from him all that had happened below; and, hearing that Ned was arrested for his attack on M. de Rondiniacque, was for going forthwith to find him and to give him what comfort I was able. This, however, my father would not permit, but led me to his own chamber, where from the window we watched for Philip's coming. And although he made his return with a quickness truly wonderful, when the nature not only of the country he traversed, but also of the horse that carried him, come to be considered, so that we saw him close at hand before the Prince's half-hour was expired, yet the time seemed long indeed that he was coming, and the space left for conference when he was come appeared all too short. Having seen us waving signals to him as he forced his jaded nag up the grassy hill behind the house, he came at once to my father's chamber, where a few words told him how the matter stood. But when it was now time to descend and meet His Highness in the hall, the half-hour being expired, Sir Michael would by no means consent that his son should accompany him, having perhaps but little hope that his surrender might be avoided, yet keeping it, as it were, a last piece to move in the game. But it was good to stand by and hear these two men, so diverse in purpose, in honor so alike, and to feel in my heart so sweet a glow of pride in my own people. For I, with most at stake, could say no word to urge Philip's sacrificing

himself. But they were agreed that no claim nor
duty must be counted so great as that of shielding, and even, if it might be done, of restoring the
man who had held his own honor second to theirs.

And so Sir Michael went to meet the enemy,
telling me, as together we descended the stair, that
I was his second line of support, and that Philip,
waiting above, was his reserve, in case the struggle
should begin to go against him.

In the hall we found awaiting us the Prince and
Mr. Bentinck. In His Highness's countenance I
thought were signs of a humor more kindly than
my father would have had me to expect; for his aspect recalled rather the man that gave me his sword
than him that took from me the broken blade. I
had but one glance at him, however, for as Sir
Michael passed on to address the Prince, there came
over me a very hot and comfortless sense of shame,
along with a wish—vastly unreasonable—that they
should not recognize my features. So I turned
aside from my father, and rested my arm upon the
mantel, while I gazed blankly upon the glowing
logs that filled the hearth. And behind me I heard
my father tell, in phrases now judicial, now eloquent, and at times even impassioned, the tale of
those accidents and troubles which had brought, as
he said, his old friend, young Royston, into this bog
of His Highness's disfavor.

But before it was all told a hand touched me upon
the shoulder, and a dry and guttural voice with the
one word—" Mistress," made me turn and confront
Mr. Bentinck. His keen eyes seemed to search my
countenance for the answer to some doubt or question in his mind. " Pray tell me," he said at
length, " where is the latter part of His Highness's
sword ? "

" It is here, Mr. Bentinck," I answered, laying
my hand where I had concealed that pointed fragment of steel; " here, near the heart it shall surely
pierce if Edward Royston come to harm amongst
you."

" I did think," he said, " that you were that boy
that braved us all. And I believe, moreover, that
you had great part in the escape of the priest."

" I had indeed the greatest part of all," I answered, being now resolved to cast myself upon his
mercy; " for without my share the man had been
still fast in your hands. But oh, Mr. Bentinck," I
continued, " why are you his enemy ? "

" Enemy ! Whose enemy ? " cried Mr. Bentinck.
" Is it Captain Royston's you mean ? "

" Ay, his," I answered. " Oh! he told me that
you loved him not, but withal has no ill word for
you, declaring you always the most honest of His
Highness's servants."

Mr. Bentinck here seemed to muse a little. And

then —" I thank him," he said. " If he be the same, I were sorry to be his enemy."

" He is honest as the daylight! " I cried. " He has but wronged the seeming of his honor for another—and that other without fault but in appearance—as my father now makes plain to His Highness."

" Indeed, Mistress Drayton," he replied, speaking with a gentleness well-nigh tender, " I do hope he may." And with that he turned from me as if to rejoin His Highness. But I summoned all my daring to make a plea yet more fully feminine, being much emboldened thereto by the softness of his last words.

" Mr. Bentinck, Mr. Bentinck," I whispered eagerly, and he turned again. " Captain Royston and I were to be wed, if—if— " said I, and could say no more.

" Ah," said he, " if what ? "

" If you—if His Highness destroy us not utterly," I replied. " Grant us your aid, Mr. Bentinck." And into these words I put, I do suppose, much prayerfulness of face, voice, and gesture. For he looked a moment very kindly on the clasped hands and streaming eyes that begged his help.

" Do not weep, mistress," he said. " You shall have all I may give," and so turned his back upon me.

And here the Prince came a little toward me. "It is truly a tale of romance, Sir Michael," he said. "Here was I vainly seeking the serpent, and, lo! there is none but Eve." And then to me: "Come hither, Mistress Eve," he said. So I went over to him, and made before him a courtesy very deep and humble. "I do like you better thus, child," he went on, "than booted and spurred. Is this a true history that I hear?"

"So please Your Highness," I answered, "'t is true as the Gospel."

"How so?" he asked, smiling. "You have not heard it."

"But it was my father," said I, "that told it."

By which reply the Prince appeared much pleased, for, addressing himself to Mr. Bentinck: "'T is indeed a pious family," he remarked, "and such mutual faith can hardly go with treason. And, on my conscience, William," he went on, "the tale has an appearance." Then, to my father: "If all this be true, Sir Michael, you are much abused."

"How that, Your Highness?" asked the old man.

"By a son," said the Prince, "departing from the faith of his fathers."

"It is between him and his Maker," replied Sir Michael, with a touch of pride.

"And by me," continued His Highness, "departing from the courtesy incumbent upon princes. Does that stand in the same awful arbitrament, Sir Michael ?"

" If Your Highness do me right," said my father, " 't is between us two, and shall go no further."

" That is kindly said, sir," answered the Prince. " So, if this be all true — as it must be, if you have not all the art of deceiving the most naturally in the world—I must needs fling pardon broadcast, eh ?"

" I do not see what other course is open to Your Highness," said my father.

But here the Prince's face grew vastly stern: " Except to this priest," he said, " who, if he has not aimed at my life, is at least my enemy, however honorable."

" My son ?" asked Sir Michael; and my heart was sore to see the pallor of his cheek.

" Ay, sir, your son—I must have your son. Captain Royston's deed may become the man of heart, however ill it fits the office of the soldier. But your son is my open enemy. Must I lose both culprits ?"

And so a shadow fell again upon us all, and with it a solemn silence, which endured, I believe, all the time that I was absent from the hall. Certain it is that when I returned in my brother's company not one of the three looked as if he had spoken.

When Philip stood before him, the Prince for a

while eyed him with great keenness, which rejoiced me to see; for surely no man had ever words so eloquent to speak in his own defence as was my brother's pure and noble countenance.

" Do you come of your own will to see me ? " His Highness at length enquired.

" I do," said my brother.

" And wherefore ? " demanded the Prince.

" To take what blame I may from my friends," Philip answered.

" I have heard your story, sir," said the Prince. " If you would escape the fate that comes of ill company, describe to me now him that constrained you in this matter."

" I may not," replied Philip.

" Tell me, then," said His Highness, " what power he held over you."

" I must not," said Philip.

This reply seemed not a little to vex the Prince. " Must not ! " he cried.

" Nay, then," said the priest gently, " an Your Highness like it better, I will not."

" ' May not, must not, will not,' " said William, bitterly quoting his words; " by the rule of war, Sir Priest, I *may* hang you to that tree. Deny me not, for *may* can wax greater in other mouths."

" Hanging," says Philip very coolly, " is little likely to rob me of the power to hold my tongue."

Now during this strife, while I both trembled and admired, I had yet eyes to remark that Mr. Bentinck's gaze did wander to and fro between a paper he held in his hand and the countenance of this stanch brother of mine. At the time I knew not what it meant, but have since reason to believe it that same description of a priest that had been trodden by the heel of a prince, hid in a maiden's bosom, and feloniously perused by a gentleman of France. Finding in it little likeness to the man before him, he proceeded to the execution of a small but vastly cunning *ruse*, to discover if the man whose description he held in his hand were indeed the plotter of the late murderous attack upon His Highness.

" Your Highness," said he sourly, " this subtile fellow does well know that this Francis,"—and here Mr. Bentinck glanced with some ostentation at the paper that was in his hand,—" or ' Marston,' as he is here named, with his round body and red periwig, is already in our hands. This aping of constancy is but a means to keep from himself the blame of a complicity that the other confesses."

" Nay, faith!" cried Philip, with an eagerness wholly innocent, " I knew not that he was taken."

At this His Highness laughed loud and right merrily. " Cunning William!" he said, as he patted Mr. Bentinck upon the shoulder, " your

politic tricks are better than my threatenings.'' He
then addressed Philip in a voice much softened:
'' Mr. Drayton,'' he said, '' I ask your pardon for
my rough soldier ways. We have taken no such
person, but you have most innocently told us what
we much desired to know. Wherefore did you
scorn our hospitality last evening ? Was that also
of compulsion ? ''

'' Nay,'' says Philip, '' but to keep my father's
name clear of a most foul reproach. From the
bottom of my heart I am Your Highness's enemy.
I never cease to pray that all your purpose may miscarry. But you will not hang a Drayton and a cut-
throat in one noose.''

'' I vow,'' cried the Prince, '' you are all of one
mould, you Draytons.''

He seemed here to muse a while, and then begged
Mr. Bentinck to give order that Mr. Royston be
brought before him. And my heart very miserably
sank in my bosom, for I remembered how, but a
little while back, he had, in speaking of poor Ned,
used the military title, saying '' Captain,'' as if
restoration to rank and honor were already in sight.

Mr. Bentinck soon returned, and not long after
him came Ned with his guard, which, in obedience
to a sign from the Prince, halted at the door, where
they stood impassive with drawn swords.

'' Come hither, sir,'' said His Highness; and Ned

approaching, I saw that, although the passion was burnt out of him, and his face was worn and haggard, he still met with an eye unsubdued the glance of the man on whom his fate depended.

" Mr. Royston," said the Prince, " I have heard all this midnight mystery. 'T is a brave tale, which, in my thinking, clears all therein involved of wicked design. But no tale, be it never so true, clears you, Mr. Royston, from the great fault of aiding my enemy there to escape. You know what in war-time is the law of military discipline. Have you anything to say, Mr. Royston, before this matter be ended ? "

And Ned looked him straight in the eyes, and answered him with a very gentle fearlessness.

" I have little to say, Your Highness," he said; " and nothing of contention. One thing only I ask, if Your Highness mean to push the matter to extremity. Since I have never shown fear, I would die, if it please you, rather by bullet than the—the cord. Then, sire," he went on,—and this was the sole occasion upon which I did hear Captain Royston use to the Prince before his coronation the regal form of address,—"then, sire, shall I take with me no grudging to you."

Here following a little silence, I had much ado, for all my growing belief that the Prince did mean well by us all, to keep back the sobs that rose in my

throat and caught at my breathing. And then came
my lover's voice again. " I have failed in my duty.
I had just drawn on the seeming lad that was the
companion of my watch, because he would not let
me follow the priest. He crossed swords with me,
and I struck him in the neck,"—and here, I
thought, His Highness's eyes lighted curiously
upon me, and I grew warm with blushing as I
thought of the black patch of plaister upon my
bosom,—" and then I learned that it was no blood
of man that I had drawn, but the drops fell from
the soft flesh of a woman. And more I found that
fatal night—that the woman was she that I did love
well when she was but a little maid no higher than
my sword-hilt,"—and here the man's hand went to
his side, but found nothing,—" the sword, God's
truth! that I must not wear! And then I learned
why she would have the popish fellow escape. He
was her brother, and she loved him, even as both
did love the great old name. And I ? I loved the
maid, even the more that I had hurt her. And the
man swore—not by his order, nor by his heretic
bishop of Rome, but on his honorable lineage as a
gentleman of England, to do you nor yours further
hurt of any kind till his foot was set once more in
France. It was hard to see so pretty a maid weep;
harder, when the tears fell from eyes that had
already forgiven the wound. Moreover, Your

Highness, I did put faith in the man. Papist that he was, yet did he bear himself so as none could doubt his worth. I do but ask that, before I bear my punishment, the master I have ever served in a love hedged about with reverence and awe will put faith in my word that I had no will to wrong him, or to fail, as it seems fail I did, in the service that was due."

" For that I do believe you, sir," said the Prince; " yet can it not undo what is done."

While Ned was speaking, His Highness had seemed to my jealously watching eye not unmoved. He now laid his hand on Mr. Bentinck's arm, and drew that gentleman apart into the window which is nearest the door where Prue had played the eavesdropper. I had no intent to do the like, and it was more His Highness's fault than mine if he did not perceive that I stood so much nearer than the rest of the company that some words of his discourse with Mr. Bentinck were plainly audible to me. And, while their voices rose and fell in that murmured conference, the curtain that hangs before that little door was brushed aside, and M. de Rondiniacque, with his hat in his hand and a smile upon his lips at once merry, mocking, and triumphant, stood beside me.

" This is no plot, William," said the Prince, — " but a matter of one family." And there followed much that escaped my ear, until His Highness's voice rose with the words, " How think you, William ?   If we had this Francis— " and then dropped into the former murmuring.

" Had we the fat one," says Mr. Bentinck; " for this priest "—and at the word he twisted his head a little toward Philip, who stood by the hearth with Ned and my father—" this priest is too spare to make a meal of."

" Ay," said the Prince, " if we could but find this ' Marston,' and if it were made plain he had no ties here with these good people, we might well treat these late adventures with the largeness that safety can use."

And then much more from Mr. Bentinck that I did not hear, until he said that the good-will of such men as these was of much value, and ended with some words of Captain Royston's difficult dilemma of the past night.

" Look on her but once, Your Highness," said he, " and weigh the temptation."   So I knew he had kept faith with me.

But it was not to my ears alone that these last words were audible; for no sooner were they uttered than M. de Rondiniacque stepped forward some paces and, speaking in tones of much levity: " 'T is very true, Your Highness," said he, " as Mr. Bentinck has observed: the women of these parts are the very devil for the seducing a man from his duty."

The Prince turned upon him very sharply. " Peace, Lieutenant!" he said harshly; " such levity becomes neither my presence nor the occasion." He then turned his back upon the interrupter, and continued, addressing Mr. Bentinck: " But then—this Francis—we have not taken him. What then ?"

Again the dauntless and merry Frenchman interrupted; he well knew, I think, that the import of what he was to say would cover a measure of insolence, and could not resist the inclination to practise his raillery a little upon the ponderous gravity of Mr. Bentinck's statecraft. " Nay, but, Your Highness," he said gaily, " we have taken him. Had not Your Highness so sharply snubbed my ardor for his service, I was even now to remark that these fair ones do also at times render notable aid to his cause. Of late one did save Your Highness's life, and now a rustic Eve has put in my hands a morsel of Adam's flesh much coveted, if I mistake not, of Mr. William Bentinck here."

" What is he ?" cried Bentinck.

" Very fat, an it please you, Mr. Bentinck," says De Rondiniacque, laughing. Then, pushing aside the curtain, he opened the door and beckoned with his hand. His signal was answered by the entrance

of a company vastly comical to behold.   For little
Prue's prisoner was very roughly thrust into the
hall by Christopher Kidd, whose tall and burly person towered above and behind the little, fat, evil-
visaged priest, the yeoman grasping in one of his
huge hands both wrists of his captive.   They were
followed by Prudence, beaming with smiles at the
thought of the importance brought upon her by her
act of compassion.   And there came upon the bearing of Mr. Bentinck, at sight of the prisoner, a
wonderful change.   For his face flushed and his
eye gleamed; he forgot the impertinences of M. de
Rondiniacque, he passed over the lack of ceremony
evinced by this sudden intrusion, and pounced, as it
were, at once upon his prey.

From his own lips I have since heard the cause of
Mr. Bentinck's emotion.   He had for many months
endeavored to instil into his prince and master what
he held to be a fitting and wholesome dread of the
secret assassin.   He had indeed in those days and
during many years to come good reason enough for
his own fears, yet none could he contrive to arouse
in that most fearless of men that is now our most
gracious sovereign; who, after some abortive attempt upon his person, or upon the news of some
fresh and subtile plot discovered and prevented,
would jest lightly of the matter, or turn aside from
it with a few sharp words.

" As for assassins, William," he would say, " I hold it wholly beneath me to speak of them, and much more to give them serious thought."

Now, in this case, not only did Mr. Bentinck hope by means of this fat rascal to come at the source and instigation of the attempted crime, but also, through discoveries the captive should be compelled to make, to arouse in His Highness's mind a more sensible conviction of the dangers to which his care-less magnanimity so frequently exposed his person. Successful, however, as Mr. Bentinck ultimately was in proving to his own satisfaction the guilt of greater persons than the shaking wretch before him, I have never heard that His Highness was prevailed upon by this or any other means to give one serious thought to perils of this nature.

" Bring him here," cried Mr. Bentinck very sharply to Kidd, who pushed his helpless prisoner forward until the light from the window fell upon his ill-favored countenance. " H'm—h'm —h'm!" grunted Mr. Bentinck, as his eyes rose and fell be-tween his paper of description and the face of the fellow that trembled and sweated before him. " H'm! But the red periwig is wanting."

Whereupon Prue whips out that tangled wig from beneath her apron, vowing she had found it in the straw where the fellow had slept.

" 'T is enough," says Mr. Bentinck: then in a

22

voice very terrible and sudden he cried to the cul-
prit: " Your name is Francis."

" 'T is not," stammered the poor wretch, " nor
no such name." And his gaze went round the
room very despairfully till it lighted upon Philip.
" For the love of God, Mr. Philip Drayton," he
cried, " tell them how I am called."

Philip regarded him with a disgust that he tried
in vain to conceal.

" I have met you once," he said, " as James
Marston, of Oxford."

" Did I not tell you ? " said Francis, his face
lighting with hope.

And Mr. Bentinck laughed. " Truly you did,"
he replied, " and more than you purposed telling.
These trappings," he continued, turning to the
Prince, " are the same that were stolen from Your
Highness's guard in the affair of the orchard. I
think we have proof enough."

His Highness approached at once the window and
the prisoner.

" Would Your Holiness hang from that elm ? "
he asked, pointing to the great tree that stands over
against the stable. " If not, a true account of all
these matters will save the tree so foul a fruit. I
hear it is thought you abuse your masters as much
as ourselves, forging written powers beyond their
intent. You shall have some hours to make choice

between confession and the rope." And he bade
the guard that stood at the great door to take him
away. "And look to it," said His Highness to
the young officer, as he was about following after
his men and their prisoner, "that no woman come
near him." He then laughed a little at his jest,
which by the direction of his glance I took to be
aimed at myself, and, turning to M. de Rondiniacque, asked how he came to lay hands upon the
fellow.

"I owe him to Mistress Prudence here, Your
Highness," replied the Frenchman. Whereupon
the Prince would have Prudence to tell him of the
matter.

Little Prue, as she did afterwards tell me, was
"all of a twitter" betwixt pride and bashfulness,
and it was only with much blushing and stammering
that she at length found her voice.

"I' fecks, Your High and Great Mightiness, sir,"
she said at last, "I have been fatting him like a
great pullet in the loft of our barn. I did take him
for a soldier you would have hanged for thieving."

"How chanced it," said the Prince, "that you
knew our need of him ?"

Now this was for Prue a very distressful question,
and, since she would not tell the truth, nor could
readily think upon a fiction of any appearance, she
felt herself in sorry plight, which she made no

better by showing very plainly in her face the distress that she felt. Her rescue came quickly from a
source whence it was little expected. For her
piteous glance of appeal was cast in vain on M. de
Rondiniacque, who himself was not a little taken
aback by the Prince's question, and then in a very
helpless fashion she passed it on to me. And I, all
in the dark as I was, strove blindly for the means to
come to her aid, when Mr. Bentinck, with a little
laugh that was very dry and yet vastly humorous,
interfered.

" It were best, Your Highness," he said, " to
pass that point."

The Prince looked upon him for a moment, and
seemed to lay the matter aside in his mind for future
enlightening.

" Well, my pretty maid," said he to Prudence,
who now regarded Mr. Bentinck as if she would
willingly have kissed his feet, " we owe you some
return. How shall we render it ? "

" What I did, sir," says Prue, " was done for my
dear mistress there. If you will but add my debt
to her prayers, sir, I shall be overpaid."

" That is well said. Even the servants, William,"
said His Highness, turning to Mr. Bentinck, " in
this terrible family are at one with their masters.
'T is a tribe we had best have on our side." And
then he went over to the knot of men that stood

against the hearth. " Mr. Royston," he said,
" this matter shall rest as it stood yesternight, when
you left your house. You are free." And then
to Philip: " Mr. Drayton, you are an honest foe,
from a camp whence I have least reason to expect
such. Will you give me a promise to add to that
which Mr. Royston holds of you ? "

" Most willingly, Your Highness," replied Philip,
" if I may with honor."

" Then I ask you," said His Highness, " to abide
six months from this day with your good father.
After, do what and go where you will. He is
worth the time that will be so spent, sir. To ease
your conscience on the Roman side, Sir Priest, I
give you leave to effect his conversion "—and here
His Highness laughed very drily—" if you prove
able. Is it agreed ? "

" The punishment is not a hard one," answered
Philip. " I will observe your conditions. You
have my word."

" I shall always regard a Drayton's word," said
His Highness, with a very grave and sweet courtesy, " as *par excellence* the oath of honor. And
you, Mistress Drayton," he continued, " must I go
fight my enemies with a sword that cannot thrust ?
I do perceive I did you wrong, and now once more
I thank you for that you did yesterday. But my
sword does lack its point." And the Prince drew

from a scabbard that was never made for it the
shortened blade whose other part I guarded so
close.

" Ay, it lacks yet its point," I answered, " even
as Your Highness's clemency does still lack its
crowning grace.   The sword's latter half is not yet
redeemed."

" What, what! fair enemy ? " cried the Prince, in
tones of raillery.

" More fair I do hope than enemy, Your Highness," I replied.

" Well, pretty friend," he continued, seeming
not ill pleased, " wouldst have me thus armed ?
'T is true — in your ear — I purpose using English
swords against such good English fellows as come
not over to our side.   But what of these hordes of
Irish kerns, with Tyrconnel and Sarsfield at their
head ?   Surely on these we poor Dutchmen may
flesh our blades; and when the time comes, is it
with this you would have me fight ? "

Now, while the Prince did tease me with the
sight of his broken blade, and while I felt for words
to clothe the thought in me, I marked that M. de
Rondiniacque, as one taking time by the forelock
upon a signal long expected, went hurriedly out
from the hall, a circumstance that I had speedily
forgot but for its sequel.   Meantime I had inwardly
breathed a little prayer to God for the gift of a

prevailing tongue, and now drew from my bosom
that seven inches of pointed steel that I purposed
selling at so great a price.

" Your Highness," I said, " this kind of iron is
sold mighty dear. Ah, will a great Prince have a
poor maid that is his true servant wed with a man
unhappy all his days ? And yet a man so true, did
Your Highness know him as I have known him for
many, many years ? As he and I rode hither in the
smallest hours of this very day, it was a broken man
at my side—a man whose one half would rejoice for
his company, while the other part of him cried out
for his Leader, his Prince, his King. And, woman-
like, I upbraided you sore, finding in my passion of
pity no word too bitter for you, sir. But from him
there fell no word of blame, for no hard thought of
you did cross his mind. Your Highness, he tried
to serve two masters, indeed, but himself was never
one of them. If he did ill, it was for me—me that
he loved since his arms were my childhood's harbor
of refuge, his shoulder my horse that tired not.
For that part of your sword that you hold, you
gave me his life. For this part that I have kept,
where I hope all the days of my life to keep his
honor, give me his old rank in your service — and
ever, during his desert, his old favor in those eyes
that, when they will, can read so deep."

The Prince gazed at me a while, and his face grew

somehow to a softness that is seldom, I think, observed upon it.   And, as we looked upon each other, there was a little bustle at the door, made, I doubt not, by M. de Rondiniacque's return.

" Give it me, child," said William, and I handed him, without further doubt of his purpose, the remnant of his pledge.

" Why so ready, mistress ? " asked His Highness. " I have granted naught."

" Nay," I replied, " but love can read deep, even as the eyes of a prince."

" In this world, my child," he said, speaking still with that gentleness I had marked in his face, " there is no going back.   But, if Mr. Bentinck will fill us out a major's brevet for Mr. Edward Royston, will that serve to balance the uneven division of last night, sir, or madam ? "

Upon which the joy in my heart was so near to seeking its relief in tears that I had much ado to answer him.

" I do thank Your Highness," I murmured, " beyond all telling."   And then, finding a better voice, I continued: " And, if it please Your Highness, I will be always madam."

" Then must you begin soon," he answered; " to which end I shall impose a condition on this settlement."   But here the Prince checked himself, turning suddenly upon M. de Rondiniacque, by which action he was able to detect that pleasant gentleman in the act of restoring to Ned the sword taken from him the night before.

To my ear he has since declared that he had some inward premonition on his arising that morning that the matter of poor Royston's disgrace was by no means concluded; and this feeling, whether foresight or presentiment, had waxed in him so strong, that he had brought with him that weapon, as well as his own, in spite of his previous intent to leave it privily in its owner's house.

As His Highness turned from me to observe him, De Rondiniacque uttered these words: "Your sword, Major Royston," with so much of kindly triumph in voice and countenance that even the visage turned on him with enquiry so stern broke into a smile very responsive.

"How now, Lieutenant," said His Highness, "what is this?"

"When Mistress Drayton did begin to adjure Your Highness so movingly," said the Frenchman, "holding in her hand that fragment of Your Highness's sword, I made sure she would ask and obtain her price; and so, Your Highness, I went straightway to fetch it. And, knowing Your Highness has need not only of swords, but also of men that wield them as few but Major Royston can, I do trust I have done no wrong."

" 'T is well, sir," replied the Prince. " As it seems your nature to take much upon yourself, let it always, as now, be the discharge of my wishes."

At which M. de Rondiniacque appeared not a little disconcerted; but, since he has done His Highness many a notable service in these latter days, it cannot be said that the mildness of the reproof was ill-advised.

" But what was that, sweet child," the Prince now continued, addressing me anew, " of which I was to speak ? "

" I think, Your Highness," I replied, " that it was of some condition to be set upon us in regard to—to—— "

" Faith, I do remember," said he. " It is that Major Royston do wed you within the week, and thereafter join us at Salisbury. And quarters shall be found for the pair of you," he continued, " for if the steel be near the magnet it will not wander again." And so saying he laid his hand very kindly upon Ned's shoulder. And Ned Royston looked him in the face with that look that an hour agone I had given my life to bring into his face.

" My life is yours, sir," said he, with a blunt heartiness; and, taking my hand very firmly and tenderly in his, he added: " and Your Highness will now have from me two services in one."

And here Simon Emmet, who, upon a word of

his master, had been for some minutes mighty full
of a kind of bustling greatness, did give into Sir
Michael's hands that great silver drinking bowl that
no lip for over forty years had touched. And Sir
Michael held the bowl high, and gave it then into
the hands of the Prince of Orange.

"From this cup," said my father, "the last to
drink was Your Highness's grandfather, King
Charles the Martyr."

"Then in his name, and in the name of England,
I drink first of a loving-cup," cried the Prince;
which when he had done he passed the vessel to
me, and from me it went the round of every living
soul there present, leaving, I suppose, in the bottom
of the bowl but a few drops of wine to wet the lips
of Prudence, who, as luck would have it, came last
of all in the drinking; for, after she had tipped it
high to catch the last, she gazed beseechingly
around, daintily licking her lips the while, as if she
would know whether she might truly say she had
drunk that toast. His Highness, marking with the
rest her pretty gesture, could not forbear smiling.

"Ah, my pretty maid," he said, "it was you
that did bring us that fat rooster in the nick of
time. Do you then ask no reward?"

And Prue, as a woman can, asked of me in two
movements of her eyes a question. Once most in-
dicatively they went to His Highness's belt and

sword, and once, with interrogation as plain, to my
face, catching thence the answer before one man in
the room, I truly think, had fully gathered the
sense of the Prince's question.

"There is a thing, if it please Your Mightiness,"
she said, "that I would have."

"What is it, then?" said His Highness. "For
it seems I must spend this day in giving."

"The fragments, Your Honor," says Prue, "of
that same blessed sword."

And he gave her the broken pieces of the sword,
which in triumph she straightway brought to me;
and I hung them then and there above the hearth,
standing upon the table most comfortably thrust
into place by many willing hands.

And when it was done, I cried, facing them all in
my joy before I descended: "And there it shall
stay: and hereafter they shall say whose it was."

"'They,' Mistress Drayton?" cried the Prince.
"Who are 'they'? Thy children?"

And I wished heartily then for a more lowly
station. But princes will be answered, and, for all
the shame I felt, I answered the Prince of Orange.

"Yes, Your Highness," I said. "The children
of Royston and Drayton shall say — shall say that
it is—— "

"The sword of the Prince of Orange?" says His
Highness, willing to help me in my confusion.

" Not so, I hope and pray to God," I answered.
" May He grant that it then be the sword of their
King."

And this is the story of the sword that was his
that is the King. For my own, it did not end
there, nor is it ended yet.

THE END